The Secrets That We Keep

When Truth is the Only Freedom

Titus L. Johnson Sr.

5/23/2019

Between the corrosive soil of fiction and reality, a seed of truth is planted. Through the tears that flow from the hurt, pain, and shame, this truth is given life. Although challenged by the winds and storms of humiliation, and blame, its roots take hold. However, its potential, and its growth, depend on the light of forgiveness. Without this light, it will wither and die. Nonetheless, once fully grown, its properties are miraculous. For its petals are rich in remorse, and the flower itself possesses the power to heal. Be that as it may, this precious flower can only be grown within the hearts of men and women. As a result of the corrosive soil in which it is sowed, fiction and reality, the chance of cultivation has already been cut in half. For it is often times difficult, if not impossible, for truth and imagination to cross lines. If it were not for the very things in which we see and touch, first having existed in the imagination, crossing the line into reality would not be possible. However, he/she who has the belief and faith to plant such a seed makes this type of flower, possible.

Titus L. Johnson Sr.

Travel down the road of Daniel Carpenter, Michael Moore, and Richard Frost and witness how *"The Secrets That We Keep"* play out on three different levels, in the lives of three different individuals. It will not just be a road used to go back and forth, or from one place to another, but a highway leading to different destinations. The paste and momentum will quickly carry your feelings and emotions to places considered to be taboo. *The Secrets That We Keep* is a unique work of Literary Fiction that grabs hold of reality and uses it as a vehicle for truth. The reader will be carried through cobblestoned highways cemented with reality, personal experiences, and understanding. A winding road leading to places that will sometimes surprise, confuse, amaze, and annoy you. It is a road everyone is familiar with, but no one wants to travel on. Therefore, you are encouraged to hold on tight as you witness the lives of these individuals unfold; because one of them may undoubtedly become someone you know personally. When this happens, you will experience fiction turning into reality. In most cases, the journey will not be a smooth ride, for there are many bumps in the road. Some will jar your memory, while others may open forgotten wombs. Nevertheless, you will never have to worry about being alone on this journey. For you will always run across friends and family at the crossroads. If not, it could only mean one thing. The particular road that one of them took, has led directly to your own front door.

Meet Daniel Carpenter, a thirty-two year old white male who will be catapulted from being an ordinary delivery guy for a local meat company to becoming the Assistant Chief Operating Officer of one of the largest Media Technology firms on the east coast. His ability to shape numbers has given him a Bachelor's Degree in Mathematics, and a head start on his career. However, a nasty divorce has left him and his 17-year-old son living with his new girlfriend and daughter. Although Daniel appears to be happy with his new relationship, as well as his ascent up successes' slippery slope, inside he is emotionally battered and appears to be missing something he cannot seem to find. It is not until he begins to work at the local high school that he discovers exactly what that is. His insatiable desire to obtain what he has been missing will cause him to grab hold of the reins of power and begin using the tools of his position to dismantle the barriers which stand in his way. However, it is not long before he learns that power and success, when mixed with corruption and deceit, usually causes moral decay in the heart of the one who possesses it. Nevertheless, he will risk everything he has in order to keep both his relationship and his secrets, but it is only a matter of time before the two worlds collide.

Michael Moore is far from your average African American teenager. Unlike the majority of his childhood friends, the lifestyle he has chosen has caused him to fall through a couple of cracks in life. At nineteen, he is already addicted to marijuana and alcohol. As a result of this, he is now a high school dropout. Without a job, he chooses crime as a way to pay for his addictions. Simply put, Michael is a follower. His choices in life are being influenced by the friends he keep. It is more than obvious he is struggling with the decision-making process. It has become difficult for him to choose between doing what is right versus doing what his friends are doing. Michael is not a bad person at all. However, the consequences of his actions will soon lead him down one of the darkest alleys in America. A place where drugs and crime give birth to hopelessness and despair. Where morals and principles are twisted like pretzels and give birth to mischief and corruption.

Nonetheless, for Michael there is hope; and her name is Renee Williams. She will provide him with just enough affection to push back the darkness of despair, and his grip on her heart will be the only thing capable of keeping him from being lost between the cracks in which he has fallen. Yet the same love which rescues him will be the same love responsible for causing his worst nightmare.

Richard Frost is a fifty-two-year-old single white male working in an assembly plant in Albany New York. He has no children, no friends, and lives a very simple life. Most of his days are spent at the assembly plant followed by lonely evenings sitting in front of the computer eating fast foods. Richard has never been considered normal by any stretch of the word. That is, he seems to be lacking basic social skills, has an inability to express affection, and a dark side in which he struggles to keep hidden. Aside from these defects of character, Richard is very intelligent. Although he is an introvert who prefers to isolate, in his heart he knows he is quite different. It is the combination of these differences which reinforces the belief that he does not fit in. Nevertheless, this all changes when he begins dating his co-worker, Hellen McAllister. Her genuine concern and sincere affection will render him powerless. He will surrender to her parts of himself he never knew he had control of. Emotionally, she will end up taking him to places he has never been. Once there, his life will appear to be normal. The relationship which develops between Richard and Mason, Hellen's nine-year-old son, will prove to be therapeutic. The time they share together will aid in unlocking the levels of Richards differences, and help to peel back the many layers of his abnormalities.

Table of Contents

Table of Contents

CONCLUSION

Chapter 1

All the Pieces

The early morning light cascaded over the sheets as Daniel lie in bed next to Beverly looking up at the ceiling. He had been awake for a while, trying to get a hold of his thoughts, but they were racing through his mind faster than cars on a racetrack. He knew each one represented a piece to the puzzle that had now become the picture of his life. He was thirty-eight years old, divorced, with two children. His ex-wife Barbara had borne him both. As a result of their divorce, his eighteen-year-old daughter Samantha lived with her mother, and his sixteen-year-old son David, lived with him. He and David's relationship with his ex-wife and daughter, was shabby at best. Daniel knew this was a result of Barbara filling Samantha's heart with hate. Nevertheless, hate or no hate, the divorce was not his fault. Samantha and David would one day come to realize life is complicated. Sometimes the answers you get are not equivalent to the problems they are supposed to solve. At his age, he had finally come to understand what it meant when someone said, *"talk was cheap"*. In his opinion, it was because words lacked experience.

Daniel had been with his new girlfriend Beverly for nearly two years. They had finally made the decision to move in together about a year ago. When he first mentioned it to David, he complained and did everything in his power to convince him he was making a terrible mistake. It was a mistake that would not only cost them their privacy and independence but also his only son. David had threatened to go back and live with his mother before sharing a house and his father with a woman he did not know. To make matters worse she had a fifteen-year-old daughter. It had been a long road to getting him to accept the idea of living with Beverly and her fifteen-year-old daughter, Heather. To convince both David and Heather, living together as a family was not such a horrible thing, he and Beverly had to buy them into the idea. This was done by purchasing a couple of iPhones, several trips out to dinner, and the movies. After they began talking and laughing with one another, He and Beverly knew the battle had been won. Three months after mentioning it, they arrived at Beverly's house in a twenty-four-foot U-Haul. They all spent the entire weekend unpacking, switching rooms around and getting settled in.

Daniel had fallen head over heels for Beverly. She was always so alive and bubbly. She could brighten him up when nobody else could. Not to mention, their sex life was incredible. She made him feel as though his life was complete. He did not know what caused him to feel that way, but he knew it was something he got from being with Beverly. The living arrangement was also ideal. It seemed like everyone had the perfect schedule. Beverly was up and out of the house by six-thirty no later than six forty-five, Monday through Friday. David was up and out shortly thereafter, usually around seven. It was then Heather out at around seven-thirty, seven forty-five and then him sharply at eight. The finances were working out just as well. He and Beverly would split the bills right down the middle. The only separation in bills came when either David or Heather needed something. Besides that, everything was 50-50. Moving in together took a load off of their finances. They found themselves going out to dinner and to the movies more often. He had even caught Beverly looking at a new car magazine. It was not just some car magazine; it was from a Lexus dealership with her name and mailing address on it. Later that night in bed he had asked her about it. She told him, she was getting tired of the car she had. He knew what it meant because his own savings were getting hefty as well.

Living in Texas and working as a truck driver for one of the biggest meatpacking companies in the state had it's good and bad. Good, because it paid decently and the hours were always there. Bad, because regardless of how long one worked there, it was a dead-end job. Nevertheless, during the summer he would average somewhere between fifty to sixty hours a week. Having no alimony allowed him to save quite a bit. Daniel liked doing deliveries because the job never got boring. He met new people constantly. He got to drive all over town going places he had never been. The beautiful women were always a sight to see. The young ones had a way of making him wish he had a time machine. On the days when the time machine became real to him, it caused him to think. He would think about everything he would change if he were able to go back in time. The first thing he would change would be the loss of his mother. He missed her terribly. The second thing he would change would be the nonexistent relationship with his father. When he found himself traveling in his time machine, going about changing everything he could, the weight of his thoughts usually got heavy. It was always at this point he would stop his mind from going there because when his thoughts got too heavy, they turned into depression.

Today was an easy day. He had a total of ten deliveries, five of which were already done. Time was going by quickly. It was Friday and there were no deliveries on the weekends. He and Beverly would choose between going out to dinner and a movie, or staying home in bed and ordering out. The weekends always came and went super-fast. The light he was sitting in front of seemed to be taking forever. His next delivery was only two blocks up the road. It was called Westchester Meats. A guy by the name of Frank owned and operated it. As he pulled up in front of the store, he looked through the window and was able to see Frank and his daughter Connie working inside. Connie was seventeen. A very mature, quiet, and intelligent girl. She helped her father with the store quite often. Frank had managed to keep Westchester Meats alive for over thirteen years. It was nothing more than a mom and pop operation, but he brought in a lot of business.

He got out of his truck, opened the back, and began stacking boxes on the curve. Today was a scorcher. There was nothing like Texas heat, it would either burn you or tan you. Although he lived in Waco, most of his deliveries were in between Hillsboro and Temple. He stacked the boxes onto his dolly and headed for the front door. Frank had already propped it open when he recognized the truck sitting outside.

"Good morning Frank," Daniel said

"Good morning Daniel," Frank replied.

"How's business treating you?" Daniel asked.

"A little lean right now but staying afloat," Frank replied.

"We have everything you ordered," Daniel said.

"You have the select cuts?" Frank asked.

"According to the order, everything's here," Daniel confirmed.

"Great!" Frank said smiling.

"I see your favorite worker is here today," Daniel said.

"Yes, Connie is a really big help around here," Frank replied.

"What about the wife. How is she?" Daniel asked.

"As busy as a bee," Frank said with a smile on his face.

"Sign here. The box on top is your Select Cuts,"
Daniel said handing Frank his clipboard.
"Thanks a lot, buddy," Frank said.
"No problem," Daniel replied
"Well, it's been nice seeing you again," Daniel said
"Thanks. You have a great day and try to avoid
those maniacs out there driving around," Frank replied
"Will do," Daniel said.

He put the dolly back in the truck and pulled the gate closed. He jumped on interstate thirty-five and headed towards Temple. The traffic was moving steady so he would make good time. The next delivery was a new customer so he was excited about meeting them. When seventeen began merging with thirty-five the traffic started getting thick. As he began changing lanes, he heard what sounded like a grinding noise. It was the sudden impact and vibration that came from the back end of the truck that caused him to slam on his brakes. The force from the quick stop caused fluids to rush into his eyes. When he released the brakes, it felt as though the entire world has stopped. He looked out his rear-view mirror and saw a blue vehicle pulling off to the side of the road. He put on his blinker and did the same. He hoped no one was hurt, but more so, he hoped it was not his fault. He turned off the truck and jumped out onto the medium. To his disbelief, one of the persons in the car had gotten out and was now lying on the ground. He snatched his cell phone out of his pocket and dialed 911. Without realizing it he started running in the direction of the car towards the person on the ground. He could feel his heart pounding against the wall of his chest.

His body suddenly felt heavy and he could not seem to run as fast as he wanted to. He had never rescued anyone in his

16

entire life. He was scared.

Chapter 2
Wasted Time

Michael removed the last change from his drawer, counted it, and placed it on top of his dresser with the rest of the change he had placed there. So far, it added up to one dollar and thirty-seven cent. He was trying to scrape up enough change to start the day off with a beer. Waking up sober sucked, it always involved dealing with his feelings. The ones that made him feel as though he wasn't living right. The same ones which caused him to think about all the bad he had done, followed by the sound of his mother's voice saying; "*I didn't raise you to be like you are*." If he didn't have alcohol to drown the sound of his mother's voice, he'd put his headphones on and blast his music in order to escape it. Lately, he had managed to stay high enough to avoid those feelings and thoughts altogether. Right now, though, he needed to scrape up enough change to get a beer.

Today, he planned on going to West Palm Beach to hang out with his boys. It was how he spent most of his days, sitting around getting high, trying to figure out how to get more money. It was always about getting high, or maintaining the high he had. Michael lived with his mother and two sisters, and had become the black sheep of the family. The only time he came around was when he needed to eat, shower, and change clothes. His idea of getting money was either robbing a house, a person, a store, or snatching a purse. He knew what he was doing was wrong, but justified his actions by blaming his situation on being Black.

Although Michael's behavior was unacceptable, there was a part of his heart that was still good, that part belonged to Renee Williams, his girlfriend. Michael's love for her, went beyond love for himself. However, it seemed as though he only enjoyed being around her when he was either drinking or smoking. Renee did not drink or smoke. As a result of this, they constantly fought. She didn't like him being high when he was around her. Most of the time he would try to avoid fights with her by not going around her after he'd been getting high. The times he did end up around her after drinking or smoking, regardless of how much gum he chewed and tried to hide it, she could always tell. He didn't know how, but she knew when he was high. Although Michael had been with Renée for almost two years, and worshiped the ground she walked on, he still had a couple of girlfriends on the side Renee knew nothing about. The other two girls he was seeing knew how much he loved Renee. It was clear to them, he did not play when it came down to her. As a matter of fact, they could not call his cell phone. When either one of them needed to get in touch with him, they would call James, and James would relay the message to him.

Michael had two homies he was really close with out of the six he hung with. James and Rick were his best friends. His brothers from another mother, as they would say. When it was all said and done, it was usually him, James and Rick who always ended up together. Likewise, when either one of them got lucky enough to end up with some money they always made sure to look out for one other. Not only money, but girls also. His boys had called him over a couple of times when they had a T.H.O.T at the house. They used the term T.H.O.T. because it was a slang which meant: That Hoe Over There. He remembered Lolietta. She was a real T.H.O.T. She had given it up to all three of them. They still laughed about it even to this day.

Chillin was what Michael liked doing the most. Really just doing nothing but getting high. He wished he could afford enough money to buy one of the nice cars he had always seen dudes driving. In a way, he wished he was still in school working and making good money. However, going back to school seemed like a long difficult process. Not only that, none of his homies went to school either. How could he convince his homies going back to school was what they should be doing? He wished it was some kind of way. Going back to school while hanging out with his boys, it was too good to be true. Everybody with their own cars, taking their girlfriends to the movies. He found himself daydreaming like this a lot lately.

Michael was now sitting outside on James' porch waiting for him to come downstairs. James had called him an hour ago and asked him if he wanted to come over and smoke some weed. It was eight o'clock in the morning and kids were walking by going to school. He needed some money today. He had been broke for the last three days. His mother had given him two dollars, but he used it to catch the bus over to James' house. He hoped James was down to go into some business offices this morning so they could steal something. If they got lucky, they might end up with a purse, or something worth some money. He had promised Renee he would take her to the movies this weekend. It was now Friday and he was still broke. He had been dodging her calls because he didn't know what to tell her. He knew she was angry by the text messages she had been leaving him. At the moment, he didn't care about her text messages. Being broke was the only thing that mattered to him. James' room was directly over the front porch. Michael heard the door close and the sound of James' steps as he descended the stairway.

When the door opened, James was wearing an oversize white tank top, blue jeans shorts and a white pair of uptown sneakers.

"What up homie?" Michael asked.

20

"Nothing really, just chillin, I got some real good weed though," James said.

"You got any money?" Michael asked.

"I got like seven dollars, Why?" James returned the question.

"I promised to take Renee to the movies this weekend, and I'm broke. Got any ideas?" Michael asked.

"What about that house over on Pope Road, I'm quite sure ain't nobody home right now," James said.

"Wow!, I forgot about that house," Michael said.

"They got some nice stuff in there too remember?" James asked.

"You wanna go check it out?" Michael asked.

"Yeah, I wouldn't have mentioned it if I didn't. Let's smoke this blunt first though"
James said.

Living in West Palm Beach Florida always had its benefits. It was so big you could always find something to get into. If you were broke, you could hang at the marina and most likely still end up getting drunk. Most of the people coming back to shore had coolers full of beer and liquor they would share with you for a little help doing whatever they needed to be done. He remembered the time when he and James went to the marina of a Friday night. They met a guy who had sailed all the way from Europe. He was one of the coolest guys they ever ran across.

Rick had always been around to hang out with him and James, but since his girlfriend Alicia popped up pregnant three months ago, Rick barely came around anymore. Whenever he did pop up all he talked about was Alicia being pregnant. It was Michael and James' opinion, that Rick was stupid. He was only seventeen years old, and Alicia was sixteen. Alicia had been James' girlfriend first. Rich didn't care about James having been with Alisha, he said James was the past, and He and Alicia was the future.

Nevertheless, the guy who had sailed from Europe had let them on his boat. He must have had over 2 pounds of marijuana. Michael had never seen that much weed before. He told them it was legal in certain parts of Europe. He had taken them out sailing for over three hours. They never imagined sailing a boat could be such fun. It made Michael want to own one himself. The guy told them he did some kind of work for his government. Something to do with drilling in the ground and testing the soil before anyone was allowed to build something. It was something to do with the environment. He was an Environmental Something. Whatever it was, it paid him enough to be able to buy a nice boat and sail to America.

"Where's the blunt? " Michael asked.

"I been waiting on you to fire it up but you been daydreaming, " James said.

"Remember the time that guy took us out sailing? " Michael said.

"Man, I'll never forget that. That was amazing right? You ever think about owning stuff like that? " James asked.

"Yeah sometimes, But how do you get enough money to buy that stuff? " Micheal asked.

"By being an Environmental something, " James giggled.

"You ready to hit this house? " Michael asked.

"Hell yeah, you ready? " James returned the question.

They left James' porch and started walking up Broadway towards 59th Street. The house they were planning on robbing was about five blocks away. Burglarizing a house this early in the morning was not going to be easy. There were kids out going to school and people going to work. Plus, older people tended to either be on their porch or looking out their windows early in the morning. Michael really did not like robbing houses. He was always afraid someone would be home with a gun. Personally, he just did not like going into people houses. Today was an exception because he was desperate. He needed money, and that was that. Robbing a house five blocks away from James' house seemed like a good idea. Two more streets and they would be there. They had found out about the house three months ago. They were sitting on James' porch when a boy came up and asked if they knew where he could get some weed from. He and James had hooked the boy up. The boy ended up taking them to his house and smoking with them. The boy's mother and father were away on some trip. While getting high he had told them everything about when and where his parents worked. Just to be sure it was true he and James had gone to the house a few times after that. They had rung the doorbell, knocked on windows and looked around the outside of the house. No one answered any of the three times they had gone there. Today they would do the same thing, but this time around they would go through the back door.

When they finally made it to the street where the house was located, Michael looked around the neighborhood and did not see any cars parked on the street. He did notice one car parked in a driveway way up the Street from the house in which they were about to rob. This made him feel better. When he looked back around, James was already on the porch ringing the doorbell. While James rang the doorbell, Michael began walking around the house looking into the windows. He wanted to see if anyone was moving around inside the house. They needed to be sure no one was home.

Chapter 3

The Looking Glass

Richard pulled his Toyota Camry into the parking lot at work, turned the ignition off, and looked out the window. There was always a crowd standing at the gate waiting to punch in for work. The clock on the dashboard said it was 6:27 am. Richard was not comfortable being in crowds, and it was always a crowd at the gate right before the beginning of the first shift. His habit was to sit in his car and wait until it thinned out. It was a routine he lived by, and he followed it religiously. The more he sat thinking about it, the more he realized his entire life was just that, one big routine. The thought caused him to stir and created an empty feeling inside, as though he was not getting anything out of life. At fifty-five, he had not done much with his life or gone anywhere. He was still living in Albany New York, had no career, no friends, and not much to look forward to. He had never been in a relationship and usually spent most of his time sitting at home online. Not to mention, he worked in an assembly plant that offered nothing more than a promise of carpal tunnel and back problems.

The first half of the shift went by in a blur. It was now 11:45 am and Richard was sitting in the break room eating lunch. Most of the women in there considered him to be very attractive. Especially Helen, who happened to be sitting directly across from him smiling. They all knew he was single, and did not have any children. A few of them had even gone so far as to ask him out on a date. None of them ever said anything to him about it, but he knew they thought it strange for a man of his age not to have any children or be involved with someone. Although they tried to hide it, it was always on their faces. He believed the secret conversations between them were centered around one of them eventually tying him down. While talking with Helen one day, she had told him he was considered the perfect bachelor.

"So, what're your plans for this weekend?" Helen asked taking a sandwich out of a cellophane bag.

"Don't really have any," Richard answered.

"I saw a really nice movie coming out on Friday. When was the last time you went out to dinner and a movie?" Helen asked.

"I'm not sure, it's been quite a while," Richard said.

"Would you be interested in doing dinner and a movie?" Helen asked

Richard smiled before answering Helen's question. He was thinking about it. He could not imagine what it would be like going on a date with her. He knew what she wanted. He had always liked Helen, but she was probably too experienced for him, he would not know what to do. In a way, it sort of scared him. She would be all over him. The thought of it sent his heart into double time. He felt inadequate, like a little boy being pursued by a full-grown woman.

"I think I'll pass this time," Richard said.

"You make me feel like something's wrong with me Richard. I've asked you out three different times, and you always tell me the same thing. I'll tell you what, I promise I won't try and eat you, or jump your bones. I would really like to hang out with you. Nothing more, I promise," Helen said, almost begging.

"I don't know...dinner; movies, and then what?" Richard asked.

"We could go over to my place and have a couple of drinks," Helen said.

"I don't want to drink and then drive home," Richard said.

"Do you play any board games? " Helen asked.

"I've always loved Monopoly and Operation," Richard said.

"So, what about getting a game of Monopoly and playing over at my house?" Helen asked with a smile on her face.

"Helen, it's really nice of you to offer me over, and if I was dating I would take you up on the offer, but right now I'm a single guy who likes being single," Richard confessed.

"Well, I'm a single woman who's tired of being single. If you just give us a chance, I believe you would be a lot happier with a friend like me in your life. But I won't rush you, because as long as no one else has you, I know I still stand a chance," Helen said smiling.

"You know Helen, I have honestly never been in a serious relationship before. Like I don't have the faintest idea of what makes a woman tick. All the flowers and cards thing, I'm really not familiar with any of that," Richard admitted.

"Well, if you're willing to learn I can help you, but I promise you, love comes without flowers and cards. So, for now, let's take liking one other as a good start," Helen said.

"That's very nice of you Helen, maybe we'll do just a movie sometime," Richard said.

"What about spending the 4th of July together?" Helen asked.

"That's about three weeks away isn't it?" Richard asked.

"Eighteen days exactly," Helen Answered.

"Maybe we could watch the fireworks together, Have you ever seen the display at Empire State Plaza? " Richard asked.

"I don't think I have," Helen said.

"I think we can put that on our calendars," Richard said smiling.

"Sounds like a plan to me," Helen said returning Richard's smile.

"There's that familiar sound," Richard said, referring to the sound of the bell signaling the end of their lunch break.

"It goes so fast," Helen replied.

"What do they have you doing today, receivers?" Richard asked.

"No, I'm doing those little black washers," Helen answered.

Richard stood up and began collecting the remains of his lunch. There wasn't much to clean up. He had only brought a bologna and cheese sandwich, a half of row of crackers, and a juice.

"Be sure to put the 4 July on your calendar," Helen said as she got up from the table.

"It's already on there," Richard said smiling at her.

Richard was working in finishing. It was the department where all finished cable products ended up before being shipped out.   He knew the department inside and out. Assigning shipping labels for bulk shipments was his job description. It was amazing how many thousands of cable parts were shipped out each day. He walked over to the time clock and punched back in. Four more hours to go before his shift was over. He sat down at the makeshift desk and logged into the computer that ran the program for creating the labels. When the program finished loading it notified him of four pending labels due for printing. He was behind because some departments continued to run while other departments went to lunch. When he was not on lunch, he would print them as soon as they would become available.

He stood up and looked at the boxes which had arrived while he was on lunch. The color of the sticker on each box indicated what department it had come from and the type of cable part it was. Most shipping orders contained a variety of cable parts, which meant a variety of colored stickers. His job was to build the order based on what was requested. He looked at the first label and began grabbing boxes. He stacked the boxes onto a wooden pallet so it could be wrapped with plastic once he completed the order. Some orders would have close to twenty boxes per pallet. Most orders would average between twelve and fifteen boxes. He grabbed two of the boxes with the green stickers and stacked them on top of the other boxes he had placed on the pallet. He needed four more blue stickered boxes to complete the order. He hated the blue- stickered boxes. They were the heaviest. At this point, it did not matter. He would have to hurry up and catch up with the labels because more would be coming. He grabbed the plastic wrap and began wrapping the completed order. When he had finished, he walked back over to the computer grabbed the mouse and clicked on print.

It took him about two hours to catch up. As he grabbed the

plastic wrap, he looked up at the clock. It was 2:37 pm. Roughly two more hours to go. Normally he would not be checking the time as often but today was one of those days. He had to send at least fifteen boxes back to holding because they were not coded correctly, and either the computer or the network was really slow. He was hoping tomorrow he would end up in quality control. He had learned an awful lot since he began working at Digital Core Solutions. They could literally send him into any department on the floor and he would know how to do that job. He was what they called a floater. A person who was capable of performing all the job titles on the floor. Before that, he was what they called a filler. Someone who was limited in their ability to perform job titles. Everyone started out as a filler. Fillers learned different jobs on the floor of the plant in hopes of one day becoming a Floater. The company used it as a promotion system. Floaters are paid more per hour than fillers.

"Hey Richard, got a minute buddy, " he heard someone say standing behind him.

When he turned around Ronald Snyder was standing there. Ron, as everyone called him, was from the upstairs office. At Digital Core Solutions, there were only two kinds of people who work there. The big people and the little people. The big people worked in the upstairs offices where everything was planned and decided. The little people worked on the plant floor where everything was made and shipped. Ron was one of the big people.

"Yes Ron, how can I help you?" Richard asked.

"Well when you get a chance, I'd like to see you in my office," Ron replied.

"Computer's kind of slow, can I finish printing this batch of labels?" Richard asked.

"No worries, come on up when you finish," Ron said.

"I'll be right up Sir," Richard said.

Richard walked over to the printer as he watched Ron climb the steps going upstairs. He was worried and did not know what to think. Nervousness caused him to started feeling as though he had not eaten. He had no idea why Ronald Snyder would want to see him. After what felt like hours the printer began printing.

"Hey Rich, sounds like somebody might've put in a complaint on you," Leon said standing near a stack of boxes.

Leon worked in receiving. He was in and out of shipping all day long. He had obviously overheard Ron telling him to come up to his office. If it was one thing Richard hated, it was gossip, and Leon was the king of gossip.

"People get called upstairs for one of three reasons," Leon continued *"To get hired, fired, or promoted,"* he said giggling.

"Well, I'm not going to be negative about it," Richard said, holding back his scorn.

Chapter 4
New Beginning

As Daniel raced towards the person lying on the ground his thoughts were far ahead of him. He was wondering what could have happened. Was it his fault, or theirs? Why was the person lying on the ground? How bad were they injured? What would happen if it was his fault?

"911 what's your emergency?" The voice on the phone asked.

"My name is Daniel Carpenter. I just had a car accident and there's a person lying on the ground," Daniel managed to say in between breaths.

"Okay sir, where are you. Are you near the person?" The 911 Operator asked.

"Is she okay?" Daniel asked the woman kneeling over the one who was on the ground.

"Necesitamos una ambulancia!" The woman said desperately.

"Yes, I'm standing over her right now. I don't think they speak English; but I believe she's saying something about an ambulance," Daniel answered the 911 operator.

"What's your location?" The operator asked.

"We're right before exit 302 on interstate thirty-five," Daniel answered desperately.

"Ok sir, you have to calm down. Can you tell me if she's breathing?" The operator asked

"Yes, she's breathing and conscious but I think she's in pain. Her eyes are open and she has her hand over her forehead," Daniel told the 911 operator.

"Good, the police and ambulance are on their way.

32

I need you to stay on the phone with me until someone arrives. You mind telling me what happened?" The operator asked.

Daniel went about explaining in detail to the operator what had happened. However, for some reason as he watched the driver kneeling talking with her passenger something did not seem right. He could not put his finger on it but it wasn't adding up. He walked to the front of their vehicle and looked at what appeared to be the damage. It was a blue 2012 Honda Civic. The front panel on the driver side was all scratched up. He did not know anything about accidents but it was obvious what he was looking at was the result of some kind of collision. As he looked closer, he could see the paint from his truck inside the deep scratches that were on their vehicle. Seeing it made him feel at fault. When the police arrived he ended his conversation with the 911 operator. He put his cell phone back into his pocket and walked towards the police car.

It took over an hour and a half before the accident was cleared up. The passenger of the vehicle was taken to the hospital. Daniel and the other driver were both given and incident report and allowed to leave. It was 7:15 pm when he finally made his last delivery. He had called Beverly earlier and explained what had happened. He told her he would not be getting home until late. She was more worried about him being hurt than him getting home late. By the time he finished filling out the incident report for his job, it was 8:33 pm. He had gone all day without eating. He was so worked up after the accident he did not realize he had not eaten. He pulled into his driveway and looked at his watch, it was 9:15 pm. He was hungry, and both mentally and physically exhausted. He could not remember ever having such a bad day at work. He prayed tomorrow would be nothing like it. When he got to the front door Beverly was standing in the doorway waiting for him with a look of worry on her face. She gave him a hug without saying a word. Daniel walked into the house and flopped down on the couch. He kicked off his boots and exhaled.

"I didn't mention anything to the kids about the accident," Beverly confessed.

"Thanks. I've had enough explaining for one day already," Daniel replied.

"Are you ok?" Beverly asked.

"Yes, I'm fine. I just can't believe I had an accident that put someone in the hospital. I feel terrible," Daniel admitted.

"Was she hurt bad?" Beverly asked.

"I think she was more shook up than anything else. There wasn't any blood and I didn't see any kind of bruising. It was really strange. I spoke with the E.M.T. guys and they said head injuries are not always obvious," Daniel said.

"You're home now. It's time to wind down. I made lasagna. I'll heat some up for you so you can get something in your stomach," Beverly said getting up from the couch.

"That would be nice; but I need to get a shower first," Daniel said as he got up and headed towards their bedroom.

The next morning Daniel found himself sitting in his boss's office. His boss was taking him through a series of company liabilitie scenarios. Although Daniel was listening, his mind was somewhere else. His boss had informed him he would be working around the warehouse until the issue with the accident was cleared up. He could not believe what he was hearing. He had never had an accident in his entire life. For some reason, the boss didn't care about that. Everything was about insurance and getting sued. In so many words he was being told he was skating on thin ice. He could not imagine what the outcome would have been if someone had gotten seriously injured. He would probably be heading back home without a job.

His boss ended his lecture by saying, *"I understand things happen, but these types of situations have to be dealt with very delicately. Insurance companies don't care whose fault it is they only care about money. At this point, we don't know what they're going to claim. You have to try to put yourself in my shoes. I have to do what's best for the company."*

Daniel got home at his usual time. When he pulled in, he could hear music blaring from Heather's window. Beverly had not made it home yet and David was staying out for a football game. He went to the fridge and grabbed a beer. It was a Friday ritual. However, this Friday did not seem so special. He was beginning to feel this way more and more. It was not just the accident, he and Beverly were starting to lose a little of their flame. He realized no one stayed young forever, but the decline was faster than he expected. They were still attracted to one another, but the flame had lost some of its fire. As a result of this, their love life was starting to suffer. The satisfaction was starting to dissipate like fog in the direct sunlight. In the beginning, it was fresh and exciting. He could not get enough of her. She was nothing short of a human pretzel. She pleased him beyond belief. Now, they were slowly becoming two frogs on a log waiting for the next wave.

He quickly finished his beer and jumped into the shower.

He got dressed, went into the living room, and turned on the TV. The top of the news was something he always tried to watch. It was his opinion, you always had to know what was going on in order to know what to do next. News gave him that information.

"Hey, what's going on?" Heather asked coming downstairs from her bedroom.

"Just trying to get the top of the news," Daniel said.

"I didn't hear you down here. How long have you been home?" Heather asked.

"Long enough to drink a beer and take a shower," Daniel admitted.

"Do you guys have plans for tonight?" Heather asked.

"We didn't discuss anything, but you never know," Daniel confessed.

"I wanted to hang out with my friends tonight but I don't have enough money for the movies. Everyone's going to Larry's Place for a while, and then to the movies after that," Heather said with a slight frown on her face.

"How much do you need?" Daniel asked looking at her inquisitively.

"No! I didn't mean for that to sound like I was asking you for money. I was just explaining what my plans would have been if I had the money," Heather Complained.

"I understand. I'm not interpreting it like that. However, if I can help you out then that's what I'm going to do. Here is twenty-five bucks. It's been in my wallet for six days now, take it. It's yours," Daniel said, extending his hand out towards her with the money.

"I don't know, I owe so many people already,"

Heather whimpered.

"*Take it, pay me back when you can. No pressure,*" Daniel said.

"*OK, I promise I'll pay you back,*" Heather said taking the money

"*So, how's everything else going?*" Daniel asked.

"*Okay, I guess. Why do you ask?*" Heather asked with a strange look on her face.

"*I was wondering about you and Gary. You guys have been studying together for quite a while now. How's that working out. Is he a good guy?*" Daniel asked switching the conversation to something a little bit more serious.

"*You know how you guys can be,*" Heather said.

She looked at her phone, said "*Thanks,*" and dashed out the front door. He pressed play on the DVR and started watching the news from the top. It was always those who were getting shot, robbed, raped and killed who was at the top of the news. As he sat there watching it, he pulled out his cell phone and began making calls. He talked with his daughter along with her miserable mother. He called David to see what time he would be getting home. The game was over and he was just up the street at a friend's house. He ended his calls with a call to Beverly. She was revved up. She had an awesome day and was still feeling it. She was en route and would be home in roughly 30 minutes. He thought about how infectious Beverly's moods could be. Maybe she could get them all to commit to a night of bowling next weekend. She had done it one time before. It was after one of those revved-up days at work. It was actually a really good night together.

David walked in with a huge bag full of football gear. He was very broad for his age. Football seemed to fit him well. Along with becoming instantly famous, football had helped to build his self-esteem. David wasn't one of those boys who were easily influenced. He seemed to have a Sternness about the decisions he made.

"So, you're going to start this weekend's game?" Daniel asked with a smile on his face.

David could not hold back his own smile as he looked at his father and said, *"Yes, the coach told me after the game this afternoon."*

"I think it's awesome. You've taken enough pounding and have eaten enough dirt. You deserve to start. You've paid your dues," Daniel said.

"This is a really big game for us dad. These guys beat us twice last year. The team believes I respond better under pressure. Larry's been throwing too many interceptions. He freezes under pressure. He doesn't realize this is the age of the scrambling quarterback. He just stays in the pocket until it collapses. Instead of getting out of the pocket and looking for options he'll take the sack and lose a ton of yards. The coach said it was a team vote that I start this game. I think it's because the guys know I don't believe in giving up yards, even as the quarterback. I will scramble Dad!" David said, sticking his right arm out in front of him pretending to the blocking someone.

Daniel listened to David as he went on explaining why he was going to be the starting quarterback for this weekend's game. He was so full of excitement and amazement Daniel did not want to spoil the moment. He allowed David to enjoy his excitement by letting him explain everything that had happened leading up to him becoming the starting quarterback. Daniel himself was so caught up in the moment until he did not see or hear Beverly as she walked in the door.

"Is this excitement I'm witnessing?" Beverly asked while sitting her purse on the kitchen countertop

"David is getting the starting position for the upcoming game," Daniel blurted out.

"Is that so?" Beverly asked.

"Yeah, the coach told me after the game this evening. The guys believe they have a better chance at winning with me quarterbacking," David bragged.

"That's unbelievable David, we'll definitely be there cheering you on. Isn't that right, dear?" She asked looking at Daniel.

"Of course. We wouldn't miss it for the world," Daniel said agreeing with her.

"I have some good news of my own. I was offered the regional director's position. They like the way I've been handling all the local accounts. By consolidating all the accounts into a single database, I was able to manage them more efficiently. I was looking for a promotion; but the regional director was something I hadn't imagined," Beverly said with a smile that stretched from ear to ear.

"Wow, that blows mine out of the water," David said, tucking his football under his arm.

"I was thinking we could all go out and celebrate. Maybe get a bite to eat and head to a movie or the bowling alley. What do you guys think?" Beverly asked shifting her

eyes from one to the other.

"I promised the guys I'd hang out tonight. We're planning on looking at some old tapes to try and figure out the best strategy for the game," David said.

"I believe it's going to be me and you tonight dear. I spoke with Heather earlier and she has plans of going to Larry's, and then to the movies with her friends. She was a few bucks short so I gave her the twenty- five I had in my wallet," Daniel said.

"Well, you and I, it is," Beverly said sitting down and kicking off her shoes.

Daniel and Beverly ended up going to the Purple Mermaid. A place they had frequented several times before. It was not your traditional restaurant; it was more like a bar and grill. Daniel had made several friends since they had started going there. Like a lot of the other places they went to, Daniel was recognized as soon as he walked in. Before they could get settled in a few of the guys came up and asked him where he had been. Daniel knew it was the regulars who had a tendency to keep attendance. He shook a few hands and started listening to some of the jokes that were being told. Before he knew it, the beers he had consumed had him telling jokes of his own.

"Did you guys hear about the wife who took the husband to a strip club for their   20th   anniversary?" Daniel asked.

" No! What happened!" One of the guys standing at the bar shouted.

"Well, she decided to take her husband to a strip club for their anniversary. When they arrived the guy at the

front door asked, `Hey Frankie how you've been doing?`" Daniel continued with the joke. *"The wife looked at him and asked, how do you know this guy?" "I know him from the poker club, the husband told his wife. When they got to the bar, the bartender said,` hey Frankie are you having your usual?` Before his wife could say anything he said, he's from the poker club too. When he and his wife sat down one of the strippers came up and asked, will you be having your regular tonight Frank? After hearing this the wife grabbed him by the collar and headed out the door. She waved down a cab and both of them got in. The cab driver looked through his rearview mirror and said, `Boy Frankie, you picked an ugly one tonight,` It goes without saying, Frank's funeral is Monday night,"* Daniel said, laughing at his own joke.

Everybody else busted out laughing. One of the guys standing at the end of the bar shouted! *"That's some funny shit, Daniel!"*

Another guy chimed in, *"Did you guys hear about the guy who went fishing for the weekend?" "No, but we're sure you're going to tell us!"* Someone in the crowd shouted.

"Well, he told his wife he was going on a fishing trip with a couple of his friends for the weekend," The guy began with the joke. *"He asked his wife to pack his favorite silk blue pajamas set. When he got back from the fishing trip his wife asked, did you enjoy the trip? He told her he enjoyed the trip very much but asked her why she hadn't packed his silk pajamas set like he had asked. His wife looked him straight in the eyes and said, `I did pack them*

for you dear,` He told her he didn't see them anywhere. Without shifting her gaze, she said, `I put them in your tackle box.`"

"Wow, isn't that something," Somebody said laughing hysterically.

"I love fishing!" Someone shouted.

"It's time for another round," The guy at the end of the bar said holding up his beer.

Daniel and Beverly went through the night socializing as usual. The night was full of excitement. They laughed and drank with friends, and strangers. They got home shortly after 1:15 am and were both too intoxicated to try their luck at sex. When they first got together, they would have tried it anyway. However, things had changed and they both had low expectations. It had become something that happened if it did, and oh well, if it didn't. It was no longer the star in the sky that lit up the night.

In no time at all, their days of living together began turning into months, and months into years. Birthdays were falling from the calendar like leaves from a tree. They were now sitting at another football game two years after David had started as the quarterback. It was always nice watching him play. He was an exceptional quarterback. Not because he was Daniel's son but because he handled the ball with authority and controlled the team like a true captain. Daniel looked over at Beverly and like always she was cheering at the top of her lungs. Their relationship was still good. Everything except their sex life. Beverly had gotten too comfortable too quick. As a result, she had lost interest in pleasing him in their bedroom. She had fallen in love with their companionship and the security of having a man in her life. It left Daniel feeling neglected, and wanting. However, she was still a very loving person. She never forgot how to lift his spirits and bring a smile to his face. Nevertheless, behind closed doors, she was lacking.

The game was a tie score, 34 – 34. It was two minutes and fifteen seconds remaining on the clock. David 's team, The Texas Wildcats, had the ball and was on the 30-yard line attempting to score the last touchdown. It was hard to take your eyes off the game, but Daniel was caught up in something else. He had been watching the girl in the blue shorts ever since they had gotten there. She was beautiful. A little young, but gorgeous. The guy she was with was much older than she was. Daniel gave a fake cheer to throw Beverly off. He did not want her to notice him looking at the girl. He had been very careful. A few times in the past she had caught him looking. He looked at Beverly and began fantasizing about how it would be if he could have his way with her again. Not the one or two positions he was now restricted to; but the way it used to be when they first met. It had been quite a while since he experienced that with her.

It was one minute and seven seconds remaining. The Wildcats were on the 9-yard line. The running plays were not working. They got another 1st and 10 as a result of a penalty. David had been sacked twice already. The running back was getting crunched trying to come out of the backfill, and the wide receivers could not get open. It was a really tough game. The way it was looking the Wildcats might have to win by a field goal if it came down to it. They had possession of the ball and could run the clock down if they choose to. Every time he looked at the girl in the blue shorts, she seemed to be looking at him. The funny thing was that she knew he was looking back at her. She seemed to enjoy the attention. He smiled at her from the corner of his mouth while trying to hold a poker face in case Beverly glanced at him. It was funny how the younger ones seemed to be attracted to him. He would notice it whenever he was around Heather and her friends, or David and the girls who hung around him. As he looked over towards the girl one more time, the crowd went crazy.

Chapter 5

On the Edge

"Do you see anyone?" James asked.

"No, I don't see nobody," Michael answered.

"Let's walk around the back and knock, just to be sure," James said.

After they finally finished knocking on all the doors, and peeping through the windows, they decided to go in through the back door. The door was made out of a bunch of square glass panes, breaking the one closest to the lock would easily allow them to unlock the door. The house had a 6-foot privacy fence at the end of the backyard. It made it impossible for the neighbors to see the back door. Michael was nervous, but was doing a good job hiding it from James. He could not help but wonder if anyone had seen them and had called the cops who were on their way. What would his mother say if she had to visit him in jail? He did not have to worry about his father. His father was just someone his mother mentioned every now and then. Not a real human being that you could see and touch, just a name. Michael had not seen his father since Moby Dick was a tadpole. He wondered for a moment if there was ever really a Moby Dick. He caught himself smiling after remembering frogs come from tadpoles, and not fish. His personal humor took the edge off of his nervousness and brought his attention back to what they were about to do.

"You ready?" James asked.

"Yeah, Let's do it," Michael said.

James found a rock the size of his fist and broke out the window pane closest to the lock. Within seconds the door was open and they were inside. They both headed upstairs to the bedrooms. In the past, it was where they had always found the most valuable stuff. Michael kept asking James did he hear something. James finally said he didn't hear shit, and that he was too damn scary to be robbing houses. Whenever they robbed a house James was always like a maniac, going through almost everything in a matter of seconds. Drawers, mattresses, closets, cabinets, everything. Michael headed into the bedroom right off the main hallway. He went straight to the window, opened the curtains, and peeked outside. When he was satisfied, he didn't see any cars coming he closed the curtains and began going through drawers. James was right, he was too scared to be robbing houses. He kept hearing what sounded like someone opening the front door. He would search the room for a second, then dash out into the hallway to see if he could hear anyone coming in. He heard James call him and went into the room he was in.

"What's up?" Michael asked whispering.
"You get anything?" James asked.
"Yeah, what about you?" Michael Asked.
"Look at this right here," James said.

Michael looked down to see what James was talking about. James was holding a huge glass panther piggy bank. As he looked closer, he could see that it was filled with money, fives, tens, and twenties. By the looks of it, it had to be at least two feet tall. It wasn't just filled with money; it was stuffed with it.

"We'll take the whole thing with us but we need some kind of trash bag or pillowcase to carry it in. We don't want to be seen carrying this down the street," James

said.

"Let's get out of here," Michael said.

"You checked the other room already?" James asked.

"Yeah, that's where I came from," Michael said

"Let's look downstairs real quick," James said.

"Alright, I'll check the kitchen for a big bag to carry the bank in," Michael said heading downstairs.

"Okay, but hurry up because it doesn't seem like nothing is really down here. Too bad we didn't have a car cause they got some nice T.V's," James said pointing at what appeared to be a sixty-inch flat screen TV.

"I know. We could get some really good money for that one right there," Michael agreed.

Michael went into the kitchen and began going through drawers looking for trash bags. The kitchen was huge with drawers everywhere. He had no idea where to start looking. He opened the drawer closest to the sink to find it filled with all kinds of measuring cups, strainers, and graters. He quickly closed the drawer and opened the next one. It was filled with dishcloths. As he was going through drawers, he heard what sounded like a car door close. The sound came from the front of the house and this time he was sure it wasn't just his imagination. He ran to the front window and peeked outside. A man and woman were walking towards the front door, and the man was holding keys in hand. He looked towards the street and saw a blue Chevy Camaro parked in front of the house. He ran towards the back of the house and found James.

"Hey, somebody coming," He whispered to James.

"Who?" James asked with a tinge of fear in his voice.

"I think it's his parents," Michael said.

As they headed for the back door, they could hear laughter coming from the front of the house. Then the sound of a key being inserted into the lock. They would have to get out without being seen. It was going to be almost impossible. The front door was lined up evenly with the back door. Once you opened the front door you could look directly through the kitchen and see the back door. The only thing that would save them and give them enough time to get away was that the downstairs was not ransacked, and the back door had curtains. They wouldn't be able to see the broken glass pane until someone moved the curtain. However, when they got upstairs it would be a totally different story. If things went right, they would be at least three blocks away when that happens. The only problem they might have is being seen carrying a huge bank filled with money.

They eased out the back door and quietly closed it behind them. Then creped around the side of the house and listened for the sound of the front door closing. When they heard the door shut, they took off running. James was carrying the glass panther filled with money but it did not slow him down one bit. He was still faster than Michael. They ran about two blocks and then ducked into some bushes. They were thick enough and tall enough to block anyone from seeing them. James took off his tank top and tried to cover the glass panther so no one would be able to see what he was carrying. After wrapping it in the shirt they quickly realized it would not work. The shirt did not cover the entire bank.

"We need to wrap this up in something," James

48

said.

"*Yea I know, but what?*" Michael asked.

"*What about your shirt?*" James asked.

"*Let's just bust it open right here. We don't need to be seen carrying this big thing down the street. Plus we gettin ready to hit Broadway; and you know the police is always up and down Broadway,*" Michael said.

"*What else did you get?*" James asked.

"*I got two nice watches and a bunch of jewelry,*" Michael said pulling the contents from his pocket.

"*Nice,*" James said looking at what Michael was showing him.

"*I got a bunch of jewelry too,*" James said, reaching into his own pocket and pulling out what he had.

"*Okay, now let's look for something to break this open with,*" James continue talking while looking around on the ground for something he could use.

"*What about that rock over there?*" Michael asked.

"*Yeah, that'll work. We still need something to put the money in till we get to my house,*" James said.

"*Let's just put it all in my shirt and tie it up. When we pass the store, I'll go in and get a bag, and then we can just put everything in the bag,*" Michael said

When they got to James's House, they sat on the porch for a couple of minutes looking around to see if anyone had followed them before going upstairs. Even though they had been together during the entire burglary Michael was sure James had stashed some money and jewelry from him. No one ever split everything right down the middle. He had done too much crime not to know you always stash something extra for yourself. It was not a bad thing, it was just something everyone did. He really did not care about James stashing because today they had enough money for both of them. Judging from how much money he had seen inside the piggy bank alone, he knew there was easily a few hundred dollars in it. As for the jewelry, they would take it down to the Starfish Saloon. The owner of the bar liked buying hot stuff. He would love what they had because some of it looked really expensive. Michael remembered the time they had sold him an antique bracelet. He had given them four hundred dollars for it. It was probably worth a lot more but they just wanted to get rid of it because they were broke. Besides, Mark the owner of the saloon, never asked questions. The only question he would ask is how much.

James opened the bag they had gotten from the store and dumped everything inside of it onto his bed. They both started grabbing bills and straitening them out, putting them into piles of fives, tens and twenties. Michael was happy there were no one dollar bills. The Bigger the bills the more they would have to spit between them. The funny thing about counting money together after a robbery or burglary was how they paid close attention to one another. They both wanted to be sure the other one was not putting money somewhere it did not belong. Every time he would look at James, James would be looking at him. It was a game of cat and mouse, but in their game of cat and mouse, both the cat and the mouse wanted the cheese. Inside, Michael was getting happier by the minute. He could not help but think about the good time he would have with his girlfriend Renee. He would take her to the movies, and then out for something to eat. Most likely, they would end up at Pizza Hut because Renee loved their stuffed crust pizza.

After they had finished putting the money in piles James started counting it all. First the twenties, then the tens, and finally the fives. Six hundred and seventy-five dollars was how much it came up to.

"Boy, we gonna be rollin tonight," James said smiling.

"We can't roll tonight. I got to take Renee to the movies, remember?" Michael asked.

"Oh yeah, I forgot about that. What you gonna be doing after you take her home?" James asked.

"I'm hoping I can get her to lie to her parents about staying tonight with a friend so we can get a hotel," Michael admitted.

"Oh, that's what's up. You trying to smash that tonight huh?" James asked, laughing.

"You know it, but she be tripping, talking about that's all I want her for," Michael confessed.

"Boy you ain't never gonna get that; and if you do, she gonna have you chained to her hip," James said, pulling the side of the shirt as though he was hooked by something.

"That's alright cause believe me when I do get it, she gonna forget who her momma and daddy is," Michael bragged.

"Yeah whatever King-Dinga-Ling," James said Laughing.

"What time is it?" Michael asked.

"It's almost ten o'clock," James said looking at the time on his cell phone.

"Man, it's still early. Want to take this jewelry down to the Starfish to see if Mark is there?" Michael asked.

"Yeah, but we ain't gonna let him play us cheap

with this stuff here. Look at some of these diamonds in this necklace. You know it's real because they don't put no fake diamonds inside of real gold," James said pointing at the eighteen-karat gold stamp on the inside of the necklace.

"I agree, that's crazy nice. You think Mark is working this early though?" Michael asked, with a look of uncertainty on his face.

"Well, it's only one way to find out," James said as he got up off the bed.

They put the jewelry in a Ziplock bag James got from his kitchen. For some reason, it felt like a brand-new day when they got outside. It was either because the sun was now shining bright or because of the money he now had in his pocket. Michael was sure the feeling came from having money because on his way over to James's house he felt like he was under a dark cloud. Now that he had money, the cloud was gone and the sun seemed brighter. It gave him a pep in his step just knowing he could treat Renee to a movie, and perhaps spend the night with her in a motel. It had only happened one time before. He had bought a one-dollar scratch-off from the corner store by his house and had won five hundred dollars. It was the only time he had won any money from the lottery and the only time he had ever spent the night with Renee. Even though he and Renee did not do anything, he never regretted spending his money or his time with her.

When they got to Dr. Martin Luther King Jr. Blvd. they turned left and headed towards Old Dixie Hwy. In no time at all, they were standing in front of the Quick Fill on the corner of Avenue G and West 9th Street. Michael went into the store while James waited outside for him. When he came out James was talking to three girls who had pulled up in a gold Hyundai Santa

Fe. He could tell James had flashed some money on them because the girl who was driving kept saying, *"Why don't you jump in and hang out with us so we can get some loud."* Loud was what everyone called real good weed. It was called loud because it was some of the most potent weed you could get and it had a pungent smell to it.   You could literally smell it through almost anything you put it in. Therefore, everyone referred to it as loud. Michael leaned against the building drinking his soda while watching his homeboy in action.   It was always funny seeing how differently girls would act once you flashed a large amount of money on them. James happened to be one of the best at it. He would take a few twenties or fifties and wrap them around a stack of one-dollar bills. It would look like he had a couple thousand dollars or more.

After James finished getting the driver's phone number the girls pulled off and they walked the last two blocks to the Starfish Saloon. To their surprise, the White Mercedes belonging to Mark was parked in the parking lot. They looked at one another and smiled. When they reached the back door, James opened it and they both went in. It was always very dark inside. It reminded Michael of going into a haunted house in the daytime. When you first walked inside you could barely see anything. Your eyes had to adjust to the darkness before you could recognize what you were seeing.   As his eyes began focusing his mind started interpreting the familiar layout of the bar.   It had, two pool tables, a huge dance floor, a DJ's Booth, A VIP sections, a huge jukebox and the bar itself. He looked over to his right to see if anyone was playing pool at any one of the two pool tables that were there. Both were empty. He looked towards the bar and saw three people sitting on stools. Nobody was playing any music, so the silence was just as thick as the darkness. The three people sitting at the bar were all spread out which indicated they either did not know one another or did not want to be bothered.

"James," Michael said almost whispering.

"Yeah, what's up?" James responded stopping and turning around to face him.

"How much we gonna try and get for all this?" Michael asked.

"We got a lot of stuff here," James said pulling the zip lock bag from his pocket.

"That's what I'm saying. We need to come up with a price before we talk with him," Michael replied using his facial expression to emphasize his point.

"I don't know, what you think?" James asked looking unsure.

"We got like five watches, three necklaces, two bracelets, five rings, and about ten pairs of earrings. Everything is real. That necklace with all the diamonds in it is at least worth five hundred dollars alone," Michael bragged.

"So how much you think we should ask for?" James asked again.

"We shouldn't take no less than a thousand dollars," Michael said as he tried to express firmness with his tone of voice.

"For everything?" James asked.

"Yeah, but let's ask for fifteen hundred first and see if we can get that, but let's not take anything less than a thousand for everything," Michael said.

"Alright, that's cool," James said turning back around and heading towards the bar.

It took both of them by surprise when they got up to the bar and recognize one of the individuals sitting there as the owner. It was only after getting close enough to the bar and right before asking the bartender a question, did they realize Mark sitting there.

"Hey, what's going on fellas?" The owner asked before they could say anything.

"We came to show you something, you got a couple of minutes?" James asked.

"Sure. Let's sit at one of the tables over there," The owner said pointing towards the VIP section.

When they were seated, James pulled the bag from his pocket and placed it on the table in front of the owner. The owner unzipped the bag and looked at each piece of jewelry. Even in the darkness of the bar they still could see both the light that was captured by the jewelry, and the light in Mark's eyes as he looked over the contents of the bag. It was obvious he was very interested in what he was looking at.

"So what are you guys trying to get for all of this?" The owner asked.

"That necklace alone is got to be worth at least a thousand," James replied.

"We got watches, earrings, bracelets, and rings. We'll take fifteen hundred for everything, that's a steal for you," Michael said.

"Look, this stuff is hot so I'm going to either have to sit on it for a long time or have it broken down and sell it as scrap. Either way, I'm not going to get top dollar for it. You guys got to give me a better price if we're going to

work something out," Mark said while holding the necklace which was obviously the most expensive piece they had.

"So how much you talking?" Michael asked

"I'm thinking eight hundred for everything," Mark admitted.

"Come on Mark, you trying to play us like crack-heads. You know you can get way more than that for this shit, even if you have to melt it," James argued.

"I'll tell you what, if you give us six hundred apiece you can take all of it," Michael said pointing to all the jewelry that was now scattered about the table.

"Twelve hundred huh?" Mark asked while rubbing his forehead as though he was under a tremendous amount of pressure.

"Twelve hundred is a good deal Mark," James said agreeing with Michael.

"Let me make a few phone calls and see how much cash I have on hand. You guys sit tight for a couple of minutes; maybe even play a game of pool or something. I might be able to make something happen," Mark said as he got up from the table.

After putting all the jewelry into the bag James slid it back into his pants pocket.

"You see how much he was trying to give us for everything?" Michael asked

"Hell yeah! he must think we desperate. He got to be dealing with a lot of crack heads or something," James said frowning.

"Either that, or he remembered how cheap we sold

him that other stuff," Michael said referring to the time they had sold him the antique bracelet.

"Want to play a game of pool?" James asked

"If you don't try to cheat when you start losing," Michael demanded as he slid his chair back and stood up.

They got halfway through their game of pool before their patience ran thin and they ended up going back and sitting in the VIP section. Mark was still in his office in the back of the bar. They both sat there watching the two guys who had come in about 10 minutes ago and were now playing pool. The tall guy was putting a real beating on the short guy. They were playing eight ball and the tall guy had just the eight-ball left while the short guy still had four balls left, not counting the eight ball.

"Man, what's taking him so long?" Michael asked as his impatience chipped away at him.

"I don't know but I'm getting tired of waiting," James replied.

"You think we got too much jewelry for him?" Michael asked.

"This ain't like him at all. Why he gotta make phone calls just to see if he want it?" James asked.

"I don't know, but we need to let him know we getting ready to leave," Michael said.

Chapter 6

The Turn-Around

Richard placed the last shipping label on the box and logged off the computer. He was wondering if he had messed something up. Maybe the girl in casting who he did not get along with had put in a complaint on him. It had happened to a couple of other employees. Without warning, they were called up to the office and let go at the end of their shift. Looking at the clock, it was almost the end of his shift as well. His thoughts were racing so fast he could not hold onto a single one. He dreaded going upstairs to Ron's office. He only had one write up the entire time he worked there. It was when he refused to use a chemical compound that did not have a label on it. The supervisor took it personally and gave him a write up for refusing to perform a job. Richard began climbing the steps one at a time. Each step caused his body to feel heavier and heavier. It was the weight of fear coming down on him. He did not want to lose his job. It couldn't be a promotion because open positions were always posted first. He finally reached the top of the steps and suddenly felt dizzy.

He paused for a second and took a few deep breaths until the dizziness went away. He was falling apart and needed to get himself together. He steadied himself, cleared his mind, and fixed his clothes. When he reached Ronald Snyder office, he knocked on the door.

"Come in," A voice from behind the door said.

Richard turned the knob and pushed open the door. Ronald was sitting behind a huge oak desk. It nearly took up the entire back wall. There were Certificates of every kind hanging on both sides of the wall. It was apparent he had made some outstanding accomplishments in his life.

"Richard, take a seat," Ronald said pointing to a chair directly in front of his desk.

"I'm sorry it took me so long. The program for the shipping labels is running really slow today. It's taking a lot longer than normal to get them done," Richard complained as he sat down.

"Well, I'm confident you handled it, Richard. I believe it's the reason you are so good at working each of the departments on the floor. However, I would like to discuss something else with you," Ronald said looking directly at him.

"Digital Core Solutions believe in rewarding good employees. Especially those who exemplify the policies and attitude of the company. You're attitude and work ethics have been outstanding since you began working here. We wouldn't be a rapidly growing and profitable company if we failed to recognize our outstanding employees. With that said, we would like to offer you a permanent position in the quality control lab. As you know, it's a different pay grade so you would see an increase in pay. We wanted to offer you this opportunity before posting it. Is this something you would be interested in?" Ronald asked.

"A permanent position in quality control. I would love that!" Richard said, with his voice full of excitement.

"Well, the position is yours. You'll have to finish out the pay period in your current position. You will be promoted to Q.A. the beginning of the next pay period," Ronald said, as he got up from his seat and extended his hand out to shake Richard's hand.

"Thank you, sir. Thank you so much," Richard

said, clearly happy.

"Well then, that settles it," Ronald said

Richard could not believe it. When he walked out of the office everything suddenly felt different. He looked around the plant from the top of the stairs and felt a new sense of power. He now had a say in production. He would be able to approve or reject the quality of someone's work. He would be taught all the specs for each department. After his training, his job would be to simply go around the plant to each department checking the quality of work and making sure they were up to specifications. He would be a part of the quality control team. No more working on lines. He would have a tablet and a scanner. Four times a day he would take random samples from production into the quality control office for measurements and testing. Quality control had their own office. Full of all kinds of electronic gadgets for testing every single cable part made in the plant. He was filled with so much excitement he was still bubbling when his shift ended. He decided he would wait until the end of the week before letting anyone know he had been promoted.

When Richard got off work, he decided to make tonight special. It was time he treated himself. He pulled out of the parking lot and turned on the radio. To his surprise, his favorite song was playing. He cranked the volume up to amplify his mood. He was on top of the world. Faintly, he heard his cell phone ring through the music. He looked at the caller ID, it was his mother. He thought twice about answering it. He did not want her to ruin the moment. She had a special way of doing just that. He loved her dearly but she would not shut up about him being single for so long. She always made him feel pressured. He decided he would call her back later. He knew she would be happy for him being promoted, but she would somehow turn his promotion into him being single. It was always a disagreement, regardless of how subtle they sometimes were. It was him being single, versus her not telling him much about his father. Apparently, his mother was protecting his father's deep dark past. The only thing he knew about him was that his father had been in and out of prison several times. The reason why was being guarded by his mother until her last breath. As an only child, turning to his siblings for answers was not possible. He had tried pulling it up on the Internet several times but had no luck finding anything. He believed it was because it had happened over 50 years ago. There was not much of cyberspace back then.

Richard pulled into his driveway and noticed Ms. Kinsey struggling with a trash can. Ms. Kinsey was his 84-year-old neighbor. Tomorrow was trash day and she was having a difficult time getting her trash can to the curb. Most of the time, either himself or the guy across the street would take her trash out the morning of pickup. But sometimes, like today, she would try and gather up enough strength to drag it to the curb herself.

"Hey, let me get that for you," Richard said grabbing the handle of the trash can on the opposite side.

"Oh dear, thank you so much. There's not much in it, but it seems so heavy", Ms. Kinsey said releasing her grip from the can.

"I would've taken this out for you in the morning," Richard said, as more of a reminder than anything else.

"You and Larry are always taking them out for me. I just thought I'd save you the trouble and take it out myself," Ms. Kinsey said as she stood on the sidewalk in her nightgown watching him drag the can to its designated

place.

"It's not a problem," Richard said while wiping his hands on his pants.

"I just feel so bad not paying anyone to do this," Ms. Kinsey said looking helpless.

"You shouldn't feel that way, it really isn't a problem at all. Do you have anything else that needs to go out?" Richard asked

"No, that's it dear," Ms. Kinsey said.

"Alright then, let me help you back to the house," Richard said, putting his forearm under Ms. Kinsey's shoulder and leading her towards her front porch.

Richard rushed through his evening ritual of showering and eating as though he was late for an appointment. After cleaning up he turned on some music and jumped online. Tonight, he was going out. Where, he did not know yet. He found himself thinking about Helen. She seemed to interest him in a strange way. He could not quite seem to put his finger on it, but it was definitely something about her. Although he was thinking about her, he and she could never happen. He would never be able to overcome his fear of being with her sexually. He turned his attention back to what he was doing online. He would not be able to stay out too late or go too far because he did not want to be too tired going into work in the morning. He needed to do something in order to make tonight just as special as the promotion he had received earlier. There were a couple of places he wanted to check out. The closest one was about an hour and fifteen minutes away. The other was over two hours away. If he had the time, he would go to the one the farthest away, it was the one that was most promising. The last time he had gone there he really enjoyed the experience. He checked his e-mails to see if any of his contacts had emailed him about any new places. After finding none he decided he would go to the closest one. Besides, he did not feel like driving over four hours, then having to get up and go to work shortly after.

He suddenly remembered yesterday he had received his long awaited package in the mail. The one he had waiting on for nearly five weeks. It was a limited-edition tracking and hunting manual. It contained a special section about concealment of exotic animals in your home while living within city limits. It provided detailed instructions on how to build a soundproof bunker. The magazine claimed the bunker could be fortified in such a way that if it was built in the basement, someone visiting your home standing on top of it, would not be able to hear a sound coming from it. He had paid quite a bit for the manual, not to mention the wait. He was very excited over the idea of building a soundproof bunker in his basement. The good part about it was he did not have to answer to a landlord. Richard had saved up his income tax return for three years and used it as a down payment when he purchased his home. So instead of a landlord, he had a mortgage. Building the bunker would not be a problem.

He could not remember the directions to where he was going so, he looked it up and put the address into the GPS on his cell phone. He logged off the computer and went into the kitchen. He was still a bit hungry but needed to get moving. He wolfed down a bologna and cheese sandwiches, cut the kitchen light off, locked up and left. It was starting to get dark and his destination was over an hour away. He decided to stop by Dunkin Donuts and pick up a coffee from the drive-thru. He ended up ordering a large coffee with extra sugar and no cream. Although he was excited about where he was going, he did not want the drive to take a toll on him. The coffee would help to combat that, and keep him alert.

He remembered his mother had called him earlier so he reached in his pocket and pulled out his cell phone. He would have to call and talk with her before needing to use his GPS. Using a cell phone while driving in the state of New York was against the law. He decided to risk it, and turned the brightness down on his phone. He looked for the picture of his mom on his phone and pressed it. When he put the phone to his ear the dread of making the call gripped him.

"Hello," His mother's voice echoed through the phone.

"Hi mom," Richard responded.

"I called you earlier but it went to your voicemail," His mom replied.

"I know, I couldn't answer it I was driving," Richard said.

"I haven't heard from you in a couple of days. I was getting worried about you," His mom said with a hint of parental concern in her voice.

"I've been working long hours and getting home late," Richard lied.

"I just wanted to be sure you were okay. When I don't hear from you, I don't know what to think, and when it goes to voice mail it worries me even more," His mother said.

"Mom, I'm 52 years old. I have a job, my own car and my own home. It's time you stop worrying about me," Richard pleaded.

"I know, but you're still my son Richard, and worrying is something all moms have been cursed with. So, I'm sorry; I just can't help it," His mom said.

"Well, I called you to share some good news with you," Richard said changing the tone of his voice so his mom could feel his excitement.

"Oh, you finally met someone?" His mom asked with just as much excitement in her own voice as he had in his.

"No mom. I was promoted at work today," Richard replied while feeling his energy evaporate.

"That's nice. What are you going to be doing now?" His mother asked.

"I'm going to be working in the quality control department. Better pay and less work," Richard said feeling proud of himself.

"I've only been there three and a half years and I'm already in quality control," He continued. "They have a really high turnover with employees. A lot of the people I work with don't plan on staying because they don't see a future there. There's also quite a few there who are working through temporary agencies. I believe if I stick with it long enough, they're going to reward me again," He said with confidence.

"It sounds like you're really doing a good job. You've always been a hard worker, even when it came to things around the house. You'd stay on one thing for hours at a time. Doing your best to try and make it perfect. Sometimes I'd even make you stop because it was like you were obsessed with it. You've never had a problem with work, but all work and no play makes Jack a dull boy," His mother added.

"Mom, I really don't want to go there with this conversation. I just called you to check in with you, and *share my good news. Please, don't make it any more than that,"* Richard pleaded.

"Well, you know I'm not getting any younger Richard. Which means I'm not going to be around forever. Seeing you get married would be very nice, but having a grandchild would be even better," His mother stated, refusing to change the subject.

"Ok mom, it was nice talking with you. I'll talk with you again later," Richard said with a sense of urgency in his voice.

"I just wish you'd think about it. I'm not trying to pressure you but there's more to life than work. That's all," His mother said.

"I love you mom," Richard said before hanging up.

He knew it, nearly all their conversations ended with him being single. He could not understand why his mom was always pressuring him to get married and have children. He felt as though she was trying to relive her life through him. It was the same thing with the women at work. They made him feel the same way. He did not understand the programming but he did know that all women had received it. Probably the result of baby dolls and playing house. Those games little girls play while growing up. Whatever it was, it was capable of being passed from little girls to grown women. All of that was fine with him. What bothered him was when one of them tried to make him feel bad about being single. Other than that, he was fine.

This caused him to start thinking about Helen again. She never made him feel bad about being single. It was one of the reasons he enjoyed talking with her. On top of that, she was always able to bring a smile to his face. Of course, she wanted him in bed;

but he would avoid that at all cost. He wondered what she was doing at the moment. He wanted to call her. She had programmed her number in his phone a few months back. The thought of calling her opened the gates to his emotions. He did not know why, but fear was one of them. He was always lost when he came to Helen. The desire was there but he never had the balls to make a move. The more he thought about it the more he wanted to conquer his fear. Realistically, he did not have anything to worry about. Helen was always so sweet and kind when it came to him. He decided he would do a movie and dinner with her some time. However, both his place, and her place, would be off limits. He didn't want anything to do with that part of dating, at least not in the beginning. He continued to wrestle with the idea of calling her. What would he say to her? His mind quickly ran through a thousand different scenarios as to what he should say, and how she would respond. Neither one of them produced the courage he needed in order to make the call.

Instead of calling Helen, he placed his phone in its holder suctioned to the windshield and use the navigation. When he arrived at his exit the GPS announced his arrival at twelve minutes. He was making really good time. Although he could not stand being in crowds, the place he was going would definitely be flooded with people. However, it would be a different type of crowd. Onc in which he could disappear and not feel the pressure of being different. Everyone there would be minding their own business and doing their own thing. He would simply be one drop of water in the vast sea of people. It was one thing he loved about this particular crowd. For him, they provided the perfect camouflage. Blending in was as simple as joining the crowd.

The thought of getting there caused him to start speeding without realizing it. He eased the pressure off the gas pedal and watched the speedometer decrease in speed. He had to remember to keep his cool. He did not want any kind of attention. When he finally arrived, there were barely any spots left. He drove back and forth hoping to find a spot closest to the entrance. After circling the entire building, he realized that was wishful thinking. As much as he hated it, he would have to park somewhere in the back. The parking lot was huge. He wondered how anyone could remember where they were parked. People were coming and going in all directions. He drove very slowly to avoid hitting anyone. People were unexpectedly popping out from between cars. He ended up circling the parking lot for nearly 10 minutes before finding a spot. It was not what he wanted but it would have to do.

He entered the building and held the door for a young lady coming in behind him. The difference in temperature immediately brought his attention to what he was wearing. It made his long sleeve shirt feel like a sweater. He looked around to be sure he was not the only one wearing long sleeves. He felt a sense of relief when he observed others wearing similar clothing. The interior décor of the place was unbelievable. Obviously quite a bit of money went into the design and construction of the building. It was amazing. He started walking around looking at everything on display. He decided he would start at the top and work his way down. When he made it to the top, he looked down and could not believe the number of people there. If there was ever such a thing as a money generator, this was it. He stood there for several minutes looking around taking it all in.

"Beautiful isn't it?" A voice asked coming from the left of him.

He turned towards the direction of the voice to see who had

asked the question. Standing beside him was a woman holding a fountain drink in one hand and a bag in the other. To his surprise, she was absolutely beautiful. She had the deepest blue eyes he had ever seen. Her hair was a mixture of different shades of blond, cut short in what appeared to be something resembling a tomboy. She was very petite, standing no taller than the top of his shoulders. She was dressed in an all red silk dress. He had never been taken by the looks of a woman before, but he found himself lost between her deep blue eyes and the curves of her body expressing themselves through the silk of her dress.

"Beyond beautiful," Richard said, breaking away from the sensuality of her stare.

"Do you come here often?" She asked.

"Don't have much of a chance too," Richard answered.

"By the way, my name's Samantha, but my friends call me Sam," She said offering Richard her hand.

"I'm Richard," He said while shaking her hand.

"Excuse me for saying it, but you don't look like a Richard to me. I mean I know a couple of guys named Richard, and you look a thousand times better than either one of them," She said with a smile on her face.

The comment caused him to blush. He was not sure of it but he believed she was coming onto him. He found himself smiling, and was unable to hide it. She looked to be at least ten years younger than him. Easily somewhere between twenty-seven and thirty-five. She was drop dead gorgeous. However, she was not what he was looking for. The tomboy haircut and deep blue eyes were truly mesmerizing. Nevertheless, Richard was not interested.

He decided to end the conversation instead of standing there with her wasting his time.

"It was nice meeting you Sam, but I'm supposed to be meeting someone on the bottom level. I think I'm already a couple of minutes late," Richard lied.

"No problem," She said maintaining the smile on her face.

When he had gotten far enough away from her, he slowed his pace and started looking again. He could feel his blood warm when he finally saw it. There it was, right in front of him. He nearly lost his composure. His mind took off and started racing. *"Come on, think,"* he told himself. He could feel his body beginning to perspire. He had not come all this way for nothing. He needed to figure out how to go about doing it. His feelings were beginning to overwhelm him. Suddenly, he felt as though he was on stage getting ready to perform, and everyone was watching him, waiting for him to do something. He removed his cell phone from his pocket and turned on the camera. He closed the gap between what he wanted and himself, but there were too many people in front of him. He needed to make a move. If he took his time, he might just be able to do it.

Chapter 7

Changing Lanes

Everyone was on their feet screaming and yelling at the top of their lungs. Daniel got to his feet in time to see one of the boys from the opposing team run into the end zone for a touchdown. He could not believe it but the officials were holding their hands up signaling a touchdown. Sadly, there was no more time left on the clock. He looked over at Beverly and her face was full of disbelief. He figured it must have been a fumble recovery ran in for a touchdown. He looked out onto the field to see David take his helmet off and slam it into the ground. He wondered what exactly had happened. He did not want to ask Beverly because it would mean he was not paying attention. He overheard someone in the crowd say something about an interception. His mind could not accept the thought of David losing the game by throwing an interception. However, the look on Beverly's face and the way David had slammed his helmet into the ground caused him to think twice. When they got home, David locked himself in his room and refused to talk to anyone about the game.

Daniel had never been allowed to make any more deliveries after the accident. He had been assigned to the warehouse doing miscellaneous jobs. When he got to work that Monday, he had been assigned to the freezer. He could not understand why he had been assigned to the freezer. Working the freezer was for the new guys. He could not see himself packing meat in a freezer while having a bachelor's degree in math. When he applied for the job he was hired as a driver. There had to be some policy in place to protect him from being demoted to a laborer. He decided he would talk with his boss before leaving. He felt as though he was still being punished for the accident which had happened over 6 months ago. He had paid his debt. It did not make sense to him but he would find out something before the day was over. Meanwhile, his job description was to pack different cuts of meats in certain boxes and place them on the conveyor belt. Although the freezer was cold you could maintain a certain body temperature if you stayed busy. It was for that reason alone the new guys were placed in there. It was a work-or-freeze situation.

Before leaving work, Daniel spoke with his boss. In so many words he was told he would be working that position until the situation with the accident was cleared up. It was at that moment Daniel decided he would look for another job. He did not tell his boss, but he had come to that conclusion after their conversation. He was not sure what kind of work he would look for. Finding a job had never been difficult for him. Most of the jobs he applied for he ended up being overqualified. Having a Bachelor's Degree in math had a way of both opening doors as well as closing them. Before his divorce, he had worked for a Data Technology firm. His job was to tweak algorithms so they rendered specific calculations. It was a job that required undisturbed attention and concentration. Going through a divorce was a major distraction for him. His troubles started showing up in his calculations. He decided to resign and go with something which did not require concentrated thought. A delivery job was what he ended up with.

On his way home, he stopped by the store to grab a newspaper. The classifieds were an old and reliable place to start looking. When he got home, Beverly was sitting at the kitchen table going over some notes.

"Hi dear," Beverly said looking up from the table.
"Boy it smells good in here; what's for dinner?"
Daniel asked.

"I got home a little early today so I figured I'd put in a pot roast with some veggies," Beverly said.

"Any mail?" Daniel asked.

"Nothing but bills," Beverly answered.

"Would you believe they had me working in the freezer all day. Packing meat into boxes," Daniel said with a frown on his face.

"You can't be serious. Are you planning on sticking with that?" Beverly asked.

"Not at all, it's time for me to move on," Daniel said.

"What are your plans?" Beverly asked.

"I really don't know right now, but I can't see myself working in some deep freezer for god knows how long because of an accident," Daniel said.

"Honey, you've got an education. You're qualified to get almost any kind of job you want. Besides, you said making deliveries was something you were doing in the meantime. In my opinion, it's time you get back into the real job market; Or should I say, something in which you're qualified for," Beverly said with a look of inspiration on her face.

Daniel held up the newspaper and said, *"I agree. This is the beginning of a new direction"*

Three weeks after their conversation Daniel landed a job at the local high school as a substitute math teacher. When he was not filling in for an absent teacher, he had the math lab. They gave him a classroom and converted it into a lab. Daniel seemed to fit right in. Both the teachers and students loved him. Sometimes, he would find himself swamped by the number of kids coming into the lab. During normal school hours, students had to get permission from their teachers to come to the lab. However, when school was out students could use their own free time to come and study. The lab stayed open until 6:00 PM; roughly three and a half hours after regular school hours. It allowed students to get additional help if they needed it.

At first, Beverly was thrilled over his new job. However, shortly after a couple of teachers and students began calling him in the evenings, she started feeling differently. He tried explaining to her teachers sometimes called him about certain students, and students sometimes called him about needing help. A couple of times, he had kept the math lab open an extra hour because one or two students needed the time before taking tests. The nights he stayed late caused him to get home close to 8:00 pm. It was something Beverly was not used to. Despite the fact she encouraged him to find a better job it seemed as though she was regretting it. Going out to dinner with a couple of teachers who happen to be women, did not seem to help. Personally, he did not see it as a big deal. It was nothing more than socializing and fitting in. To Beverly, it was nothing short of cheating.

Tonight, was one of those nights he had kept the lab open an extra hour. He arrived home around 7:47 pm. Beverly was sitting on the couch in her nightgown sipping tea. Although he had called her and told her he was going to stay a little late, he could tell she was angry.

"Hi dear," He said putting his briefcase down and leaning over to kiss her on her forehead. She allowed the kiss to land where he intended, but the expression on her face told him it had no effect whatsoever. Kissing her was equivalent to kissing a coal

brick wall.

"Daniel, are you having an affair on me?" Beverly asked, turning around to look him in his eyes.

"What would ever make you think that?" Daniel asked in shock.

"Well, let me see," Beverly began. *"Since you started working around all those women you get a lot more phone calls at night. You leave the room or go outside to talk when you get them. You've gone out to dinner with them several times. There's a lock on your phone and you now make it a habit to delete your text messages,"* Should I go on Beverly asked.

"Honey, I think you're overreacting. However, I can understand why you may be feeling that way. Especially by putting a lock on my phone, and going out to dinner with a couple of coworkers, who happen to be women. This makes sense to me. But cheating, that's a little overboard. Deleting my text messages or leaving the room to talk on the phone really isn't a big deal," Daniel said.

"But why now, all of a sudden. After you started working at the school?" Beverly asked.

"Beverly, before we go any further with this conversation, I think we need to get past the most important thing first. If you don't remember what that is; it's called trust. At this point, I can't recall anything I've done to destroy your trust in me. If it's some kind of insecurity you have, causing you to distrust me then you're going to have to find a way to work through that. Because rather you realize it or not, you're trying to make me feel guilty about your own insecurities," Daniel said.

75

"Trust and insecurities, okay you can use those, but you haven't explained to me why there's a lock on your phone or why you're going out to dinner with other women," Beverly said with tears in her eyes.

"Ooh honey," Daniel said putting his arm around her neck and kissing her on the cheek. *"I put a lock on my phone because sometimes I leave it out on my desk at work, and I don't want any of the students getting into it. It's not because I have anything to hide from you. The dinners are nothing more than teachers getting together to socialize. Once a month the school picks up the bill for teachers to get together and share anything of significance. I was asked if I wanted to go and I accepted. It was just a coincidence I ended up going out with two teachers who were women,"* Daniel reassured her. *"That doesn't explain why you're always leaving the room in order to talk when you get calls at night,"* Beverly said wiping the tears from her eyes.

"I do that as a courtesy honey. Why would I want to sit in front of you discussing solutions to math problems with students or have a silly conversation with a teacher about a student?" Daniel said pulling Beverly closer to him.

"I don't ever want to be hurt like that," Beverly said allowing herself to be taken by his embrace.

"Now promise me we'll get back to trusting each other?" Daniel asked.

"I promise," Beverly said, leaning forward and kissing him.

When Daniel got to work the next morning, he was informed he would be sitting in for Ms. Wellinger. That meant the math lab would not be open until school was out. The availability of the lab was always based on the attendance of math teachers. When all the teachers were present the math lab was open all day until 6:00 pm. However, it was always closed during the hours in which a teacher was either late or absent. He thought about a couple of students who were regulars in the lab. They would miss him not being there until school was out. After leaving the front office he went to the lab and posted a note on the door informing students of what time he would be open today.

He could not help but reflect on the conversation he and Beverly had last night. It reaffirmed just how much she loved him. Yet, he refused to share with her just how much he was liked at school. How there were a couple of teachers who did not care about him being in a relationship; not to mention a few students as well. He could tell who they were by how they always came to the lab for nothing more than to visit with him. It just so happened Ms. Wellinger, the teacher he was sitting in for today was one of the teachers who had a crush on him. She had invited him to her place for dinner and some wine, even after he told her he was in a relationship. She had made it very clear that she really did not care. She told him that gossip was for kids and secrets was for adults; then said she was an adult, before asking him what was he. Daniel admitted to himself it was a hell of a pickup line and found himself laughing about it. His thoughts returned to last night and he decided that after work he would go by the cell phone store and buy another cell phone. He would have two cell phones, one that Beverly would know about, and one she wouldn't.

It had been two weeks since Daniel had bought the other phone. Beverly had told him how much she appreciated the way he had stopped the calls from coming in after work. She had no idea he had a second phone in which he was using for teachers and students. The second phone was kept in his car under the driver's seat. The ringer was always turned off so even when he and Beverly were in his car together and someone called him, she would not have the slightest idea. The extra phone had wiped away all the tension caused by him getting calls at night after work. Yet, the extra phone had caused him to alter his life a bit. Instead of staying in the house for the entire evening with Beverly and the kids, he had picked up a membership to the gym. Each night at 9:00 PM he would go to the gym. The phone that Beverly knew about, he would leave at home, and tell her he did not want to be bothered while exercising. That way, she would not think he was using the gym as an excuse to get out of the house, in order to make and receive calls.

Most of the time, instead of going to the gym Daniel would go to the park and check his text messages and return the calls he had missed. As he sat on the park bench going through his text messages, he came across one asking him where he was at. He looked at the name and quickly realized he was supposed to meet that particular student at The Panera Bread for a one on one tutor session. He remembered promising to be there around 8:45 pm. It was now 9:15 pm, making him thirty minutes late. He immediately pressed dial on the text message and listened as the phone began ringing.

"Hello," The voice on the other end answered.

"It's Mr. Carpenter," Daniel began. *"Look, I'm really sorry I forgot about our appointment. I usually set some kind of reminder but somehow, I didn't do that. If you'd like we could reschedule for tomorrow."*

"Mr. Carpenter, tomorrow is Saturday and I'm headed out of town with my family for the weekend. My

math test is Monday morning. Is there any kind of way you could still come tonight? We have over an hour before they close. I could really use your help," The student said nearly begging.

"I did promise you. If you're still waiting, I guess I could probably get there in about fifteen minutes," Daniel said.

It was after 11:30 pm when Daniel finally made it home. When he pulled into the driveway, he could see the lights in the living room, dining room and kitchen were all on. He did not think much of it because it was the weekend and everyone usually stayed up late Friday and Saturday nights. Before he could reach the porch, the front door flew open.

"Where in the hell have you been?!" Beverly asked standing in the doorway nearly screaming.

"Yeah dad, you left your phone here and we had no way of knowing if you were okay or not," David said sliding past Beverly in the doorway and walking onto the porch.

"Mom, calm down," Heather said to her mother standing in the doorway behind her.

"I decided to stay a little late at the gym. I didn't think it would cause hysteria," Daniel said, looking as though he was watching a house burn down.

"Are you trying to tell us we're wrong for worrying about you?" Beverly asked with a look of disbelief on her face.

"No, I'm not saying that at all. What I am saying is there is absolutely nothing wrong with me staying late at the gym on a Friday night," Daniel answered back.

"But dad, how are we to know what's going on when we have no way of getting a hold of you?" David asked.

"Okay, maybe I didn't take that into consideration, but there's really no need for all of this," Daniel said using his finger to point at them.

"I would've checked the gym already, but I don't have the faintest idea what gym you're going to. You think you would have at least let us know the name of the gym you go to," Beverly said turning around and walking back into the house.

"Dad, you've always stressed how important it is for me to be responsible. Right now, I can see why it's good to be that way. What would happen to me if I did the same thing; how would you feel dad. Do you really think this was fair?" David asked.

"David, I've already said it was inconsiderate on my part. I really don't know what else I can say to you besides offering you an apology," Daniel said.

"Just me dad, what about Beverly and Heather?" David asked.

"You're right, I owe them one also," Daniel agreed.

He found himself sleeping on the couch that night. Beverly refused to share the same bed with him. She told him he could have the bed and she would sleep on the couch. He felt guilty about what had happened and decided to sleep on the couch instead. The weekend was just as bad. He and Beverly were so distant it was as if they were living worlds apart. He tried everything within his power to apologize to her but she refused to give in. The last thing he wanted to do was try and explain to her what he had been doing. She would never understand. He even went so far as to buy her a card and a bouquet of flowers as a peace offering. She read the card put the flowers in a vase, and gave him a simple thank you. She had never treated him like that before. He would have to do something to bring their relationship back to where it was. He just didn't know what to do. Beverly was not the only one causing him to feel guilty. Both Heather and David were giving him the cold shoulder as well. However, they were not as cold as Beverly. They were simply slow to respond, and mainly quiet.

Monday came and the entire week went by in the same fashion. He tried to make the situation better by missing a couple of nights at the gym. It was not until Friday Beverly slowly started warming up to him. It was then she asked him was he going to spend another week on the couch. It was not until Wednesday night she finally cooked dinner. Before that, she had brought home take out for herself, Heather and David. He had been left to fend for himself. That Friday night, while laying in bed, he and Beverly had a very long talk. To his surprise, she was understanding about him staying late at the gym, but demanded that in the future he take his phone in case of an emergency. He apologized to her once again and promised to keep his phone with him and call her if he ever decided to stay late. After they had made up, Heather and David stop giving him the silent treatment. The next night he took them all out to dinner and a movie.

Although he was happy about making up with Beverly, the last thing he wanted to do was carry around both cell phones. He would have to figure out a way to get around it. Having his other phone would automatically put him under a time restraint. He decided he would start going to the gym directly from work. It would give him extra time to do one on one tutoring.

Daniel received a text message from Beverly while at work. She would be staying a little late at work tonight to go over a report. He closed the math lab up early and got home shortly after 5:00 PM. There was no one home. He decided to take advantage of the solitude by taking a shower and wearing nothing but his boxer briefs. He kicked back in his recliner and began flipping through the channels. He figured he would relax for the rest of the evening. He found a documentary on the discovery channel and fell asleep while watching it. The sound of the front door closing woke him. It was Heather. He did not realize how tired he was and that he had fallen asleep.

"I'm surprised to see you home this early," Heather said while going through the kitchen cabinets.

The layout of the house allowed one to walk directly into the kitchen or the living room once you entered the front door. They had used the couch and loveseat to make a petition between the living room and the kitchen.

"I decided to close the lab up early today," Daniel said.

"Do you know what time my mom's getting home?" Heather asked.

"Not exactly. She sent me a text while I was at work saying she'll be working a little late tonight. Apparently, she's going over some report," Daniel answered.

"Did you ever participate in any sports when you were going to school?" Heather asked.

"Yes, I wrestled and ran track. Why do you ask?" Daniel asked sitting up in his chair.

"Really!" Heather said coming into the living room from the kitchen.

Daniel recognized the surprise on Heather's face and realized it was because he was wearing nothing but his boxers.

> *"Oh, I'm sorry. I was taking advantage of being home alone. I fell asleep before I knew it,"* Daniel said.
>
> *"It's okay, I didn't know you were like that,"* Heather said.
>
> *"Well, we're family now so let's look at it like that. You sounded really excited when I said I wrestled in high school. What was that about?"* Daniel asked.
>
> *"It's my friend. I like him a lot, but he's on the wrestling team and he's very aggressive. How do I deal with that?"* Heather asked.
>
> *"First of all, you have to learn how to take him down,"* Daniel said getting up from his chair.
>
> *"What do you mean?"* Heather asked looking confused.

Before she knew it, Daniel had grabbed her and taken her to the floor. He was so strong she was powerless.

> *"You grab him just like this, dig your chin into his side and take him down,"* Daniel said as he brought her to the ground with his chin buried into her side.
>
> *"Oh my god, I can't move,"* Heather said while being held down on the floor by Daniel's bear hug.
>
> *"Exactly,"* Daniel said releasing her from his grip and allowing her to get to her knees.

"Now grab me any kind of way you want and I'm going to show you a couple of moves," Daniel said once they were both back on their feet.

"But I've got a skirt on, I should put on some shorts or sweat pants," Heather said.

"Don't worry about it. A couple more moves and you'll be tough as leather," Daniel said with his shoulders lifted high and arms extended out in front of him.

"Okay, but remember he's a boy and I'm a girl," Heather said.

Chapter 8
Endless Hope

Just as James was about to get up from the table the front door of the bar opened and two Uniform Police Officers walked in. One was Black and the other one was White. The last officer held the door open so the light from the outside could allow them to look around the inside before closing the door and letting the darkness reclaim its victory. Michael could feel his heart as it began beating to the exact intensity of his fear. He was sure the owner had called them about the jewelry they were trying to sell him. He had probably got caught up in a sting and was trying to save his own ass by snitching on anybody who came in with stolen property. James was scared too. It was all over his face. He was kicking Michael under the table and using his head to gesture toward the two cops who was now talking with the bartender.

" *Man, you see this?* " James asked

"Yeah, but we gotta chill. I think Mark called the police on us and had us to wait out here till they came," Michael said.

"What we gonna do?" James asked

"If they start walking over this way, we gonna have to run out of the back door," Michael said almost whispering.

There was no way in hell Michael was going to jail today. If he had to run, then running was something he would do. He hoped neither one of them would get caught. He also hoped the two cops were not there for them. However, in his heart, he knew they were there for them. Why else would Mark go into his office and not come out? He had never done that before. It was definitely a setup. They watched as the two police officers talked with the bartender. The white officer was doing the talking, while the black officer was looking around the bar as though he was looking for someone. After exchanging a few words, the bartender picked up the phone. After about a minute, he hung the phone up and said something to the officer, then went back to doing what he had been doing before they walked in. James kicked Michael feet under the table again and motioned towards the back door with his head.

Mark finally came from the back of the bar and motioned for the officers to follow him. For some reason, the police either did not see them, or just was not interested in them. Either way, it was strange because they definitely were not old enough to be sitting in a bar. He and James decided they would leave as soon as the cops were out of their sight. Before they could get up and leave, they noticed the bartender waving for them to come over. They waited until they heard Mark's office door close before walking over to the bar.

"What's up?" Michael asked the bartender.

"I don't know what kind of business you guys got going on with Mark, but being you guys are under age you might wanna hang out somewhere else until the cops leave," The bartender said.

"Yeah, we were getting ready to get out of here anyway," James said.

"Why is the police here?" Michael asked the bartender motioning in the direction of where the police had gone.

"Somebody tried to break in last night. The alarm scared them off, but not before causing some property damage," The bartender said pointing towards the back of the bar where a sheet of plywood had been placed over a window.

"Oh, that's why they hear?" James asked.

"Unfortunately that's why, but right now I need you guys to head out before I have to answer a bunch of questions about why you're sitting in here," The bartender said.

"Tell Mark we'll be back after the cops leave," James said to the bartender

"Sure, he sounded a little disappointed when I told him they were out here. I don't think he was expecting them to come as soon as they did," The bartender said.

They walked past the two guys playing pool and slipped out the back door. It had been so dark in the bar until the sun was almost blinding. In no time at all, they were crossing Old Dixie Highway on 10th street heading towards Australian Ave. When they left the bar, they decided to go and get some weed so they could smoke a blunt while waiting for the cops to leave. James called his man and told him they were about five minutes away from his house and wanted a twenty. They figured they could get two blunts out of the twenty. On the way there Michael stopped by the corner store and bought a couple of blunts so they would have them when they got the weed. Once they got it, they headed towards the Recreation Center off Avenue P and found a spot to chill and smoke their blunt.

"Man I'm taking Renee to a movie, out to eat and try to get her to spend the night with me," Michael said talking between puffing on the blunt and exhaling the smoke.

"Man that's like the fifth time you done said that.

You been with her all this time and you still ain't hit it yet," James said with a frown on his face.

"Renee ain't like them hookers you used to. She still a virgin. What you know about that?" Michael asked, smiling from ear to ear.

"If you believe Renee is a virgin, then you might as well buy Santa Claus phone number from me. I'll sell it to you for cheap," James said laughing and coughing from both the joke and the weed smoke.

"Ooh! So now you got jokes. Just for the record my girl is a virgin, and you mad cause you ain't never had one," Michael said while sticking up his middle finger.

"What hotel you trying to stay at?" James asked

"I don't know yet. Why, what's up?" Michael asked

"I've been talking to this shorty from Riviera Beach. If she's down maybe we can get a couple of rooms together," James said.

"I don't even know if Renee is going to be able to do it. Her parents is strict as hell. I'm hoping she can get one of her friends to say she's staying the night with them. I told her to tell one of her friends I'll give them like $50 if they do it for her," Michael said.

"Man, the police should be gone by now, don't you think?" James asked looking at his cell phone.

They made their way back to the bar and sure enough, the police car was gone. When they entered the bar, the owner was behind the bar talking with the bartender. When he saw them, he held up a finger indicating hold on. They sat down at the same VIP table they were at before and waited. When he had finished with the bartender he came over and sat down with them.

"OK guys, the best that I can do for you right now is a thousand dollars," Mark said reaching in his pocket and pulling out a wad of money, *It's only $200 short of what you guys asked for,"* He continued on, *" And I must admit what you guys ask for was fair, but right now $200 makes a big difference to me. Business hasn't been all that great this past week, and now I have to replace a window some punk busted out trying to get in here to rob the place."*

Michael and James looked at each other for a minute. $1,000 sounded good to both of them, but they knew that what they had was worth way more than $1,000. However, they really did not have anyone else they could take it to and sell it. Mark did not know it, but he was the only one they knew who had that type of cash for stolen property.

"That's kinda low, what you think James?" Michael asked.

"That's like dirt cheap," James replied.

"I'll tell you what, we'll take the $1,000 for now, but you still owe $200. What about that?" Michael asked.

"If you guys can wait a couple of weeks, we have a deal," Mark said.

"We could do that," James said looking at Michael.

"Yeah, we can do that," Michael replied agreeing with James.

The owner counted out ten $100 bills and placed it on the table. They gave him the bag of jewelry and split the money up between them. When they got outside, they started making plans about what they were going to do. James told Michael one of his friends had a nine-millimeter he was going to buy. Michael said he was going to pay his cell phone bill, check on renting a car, and go shopping for some clothes. After that, he was going to call Renee and see if she could get one of her friends to lie for her and say she was staying the night with them. James told him if he could get a good deal on a rental car, he would go in half with him, and if his girlfriend Renee was able to spend the night with him, he would try and get the girl from Riviera Beach to hang out with him too. Michael told him he didn't need a gun, and that he should spend his money on something else, but James was not trying to hear it. He said everyone else had one so he wanted to be sure no one else had the upper hand on him.

Unfortunately, nothing had gone as though he had planned. He ended up getting drunk early in the day and paying for a whole weeks rent at one of those pay by day hotels. For one whole week, he did nothing but splurge money and hang out with his boys. He did manage to see Renee on a couple of occasions but she acted as though she did not have time for him because he did not have time for her. Besides that, he was with a carload of homies when he had seen her so she really did not want anything to do with him. His week at the motel was now over and he was trying to make plans to finally take Renee to a movie, and hopefully spend the night together with her. The last couple of days he had been talking to her and apologizing. She said she loved and missed him, but wanted to see him without all his buddies being around.

Michael called his boy James and said everything was back on. He told him he was going to try and do the movie and hotel thing tonight. James told him it was about time, and everything was all good. Michael turned in his motel key at the front desk and hopped on the next bus.

School was just getting out so the bus was full of high school students. He called Renee to see what she was doing. She said she was still at school trying out for the track and field team. He asked her if she wanted to go to a movie tonight. She told him yes. He told her he wanted to take her out to eat first, and then to a movie.

He let it be known he wanted to spend the night with her. She asked him how would they be able to do that. He told her about his plan to pay one of her friends to say she was staying the night with them so they could get a motel together. She was interested in the idea but could not figure out which one of her friends would do it. Then she thought about her friend Myesha. Myesha would probably do it for her. He told her to offer her $50 to do it for her. His plan was to get a rental car, so James and his girlfriend could hang out with them. She said it sounded good but she would have to call him after her tryouts. Before hanging up, he insisted she talk with her friend first so she could let him know what was up when she called him back. She said her friend Myesha was already a part of the track and field team so she would talk with her after tryouts.

After his conversation with Renee, he decided to go to the mall instead of going home. Like always the mall was crowded. Mainly from kids hanging out after school. He was hungry so he headed to the food court to get something to eat. He gobbled down a whopper and some fries then went into the Top Shelf Clothing Outlet. They were having a clearance sale. He ended up buying three short sets, two pairs of sneakers and four fitted caps. While he was shopping James called and told him he had finally copped the gun he had been trying to get. He was bragging about how nice it was. After listening to him talk about the gun for a while he asked if he had got in touch with the girl from Riviera Beach. James told him he had, but she would not be done babysitting until about 8:00 tonight. He told James, Renee was still trying to get one of her friends to lie about her staying the night with them so they could get a hotel. They agreed to play phone tag with each other until they were able to get together for the rental car.

It was 5:38 pm when Michael finally got home. His mother had not made it home yet but his two sisters were there. When he walked in with all the shopping bags they immediately jumped up from the couch and began trying to look into his bags, while at the same time asking him for some money. It was a ritual, whenever he came home with shopping bags they would try and see what he had, and ask him for money. He put his bags down, reached into his pocket, and pulled out a wad of money. Like always, their eyes got big as they watched him count out money. He liked giving his sister's money because it made him feel like a big brother. He always gave his older sister a little more than his younger sister. It did not matter to his younger sister because she was happy to get whatever he gave her. He peeled a few bills off from the wad he had and gave each of them some. They both thanked him and told him his mother was on her way home.

His plan was to get a shower, change clothes, and leave before his mom got home. He did not want to be around to hear his mother preach about him stealing or robbing to get money. His plan was to leave her some money, but not be around when she got home. He would give it to his older sister and tell her to give it to his mother. After he had showered and changed, he went back into the front room and handed his older sister a wad of money. He told her to give it to their mother and tell her he loved her. She asked him where he was going. He told her he was taking his girlfriend to the movies. His younger sister let him know how good he looked and thanked him again for giving her some money. Before leaving, he told his sister to make sure their mother got all the money he had given her because he had counted it. She told him to stop trippin and make sure he answered his phone, because he knew their mother was going to be calling him.

He left home wondering how he was going to get a rental car. He would have to find somebody with a credit card because he could not rent one with straight cash. As he stood at the bus stop waiting on the bus, he called a couple of people to see if they had credit cards and would rent a car for him. He ended up calling his homeboy Rick and asking him to ask his sister if she would rent him a car if he paid her. Rick sister ended up getting on the phone and telling him her boyfriend said he would rent him his car for the night if the price was right. Michael told her he had $100 for a rental. She did not say anything, but he could hear her put her hand over the phone and say something to somebody. He figured it had to be her boyfriend because he had to be there to say he would rent him his car. She removed her hand from over the phone and said her boyfriend said $100 is cool. She asked him how was he going to get over there, and when he was planning on coming. Michael told her if her boyfriend came and picked him up, he had the money right then. She put her hand over the phone again and said something else to her boyfriend. She asked him where he was at. He told her they could pick him up at James' house.

He called James to make sure he was home. James told him he was at the store around the corner from his house, but was on his way back home. Michael told him about the car deal and James said it was cool and they would go in half when they got there with the car. He told James he would be there in about an hour, so if he was ready when he got there, they could just get the car and go. James asked him what time he planned on picking up Renee, because he could not pick up the girl from Riviera Beach until 8:00 o'clock. He said he planned on calling Renee after he called Rick sister back about the car.

Michael sat on the bus looking out the window with a smile on his face. Everything was coming together just as he planned it. He had spoken with Renee, and her friend had agreed to do it for her. Her mother was dropping her off to stay the night over her friend Myesha's house when he called her. Rick's sister and her boyfriend were bringing them the car at James's house in less than an hour. The bus would drop him off at James's house around 7:20 pm. That would give him and James enough time to go and get some weed so they would not have to be riding around all night looking for some. He was happy. Just thinking about spending the night with his girlfriend had him excited beyond control. As strict as her parents were, he did not think he would ever be able to have her again for one whole night. He was so charged up he felt like he could get there faster by getting off the bus and running there instead. A pocketful of money, a rental car, and a whole night with his girlfriend, life could not be better.

By 8:30, they had picked up both Renee and Breechelle, the girl from Riviera James had been telling him about. Everyone agreed on going to see the new movie, Black Panther, but not before getting something to eat. They went to a little Mom-and-Pop Buffet in Rivera Beach. James's girlfriend, Breechelle told them about it when they picked her up so they decided to try it out. To their surprise, it was well worth it. They decided to get the motel before going to the movies so they would not have to look for one when it was over. Michael and James had secretly bought a bottle of Hennessey before picking the girls up and hid it in the trunk. The plan was to drink it when they got to the motel after the movie. They would buy a couple of coke sodas, and on the down low, pour some Hennessey into them. He knew Renee would smell it on his breath but tonight he was treating her too good for her to fight with him about it. It was only when he was drinking and hanging with his homies and acting like a fool, she fought with him about it.

When they got to the mall the line for the movie was all the way out the door. Inside the theater, it was so crowded they could not find four seats in a row for them all to sit together. The movie itself was amazing. The special effects were out of this world. Michael could tell Renee was enjoying it also because she could not sit still. It was so intense he found himself on the edge of his seat quite a few times. He was glad they had chosen Black Panther.

He and James had got separate rooms. When they got back to the motel, they decided to hang out in James's room for a while. Renee and Breechelle both jumped on the bed and started whispering to each other, and giggling.

"Man, did you see the part when they were fighting to see who would be the next ruler?" Michael asked James.

"Yeah, homie with the dreads was brutal right?" James asked in return.

"I could watch that again," Michael said.

"I bet some of that technology really exist," Breechelle added.

"You better believe it," James said in response.

"Can you imagine the money they spent to make that movie," Renee said.

"Yeah probably enough to feed a small country," Michael said laughing at his own joke.

"No seriously, they had to spend big money to make that movie. Not to mention how much the actors cost," Renee continued on.

"Yeah, but did you see the line waiting to get in to see it? They gonna make a killin off it. Plus, movies out of Marvel Studios always make a lot of money," Breechelle said.

"I agree, cause my father is still into Marvel Comics movies, and he's in his fifties. When he talks about them, it's like he turns into a kid again. If I had to guess, I would say he was probably around when the very first one came out, and he's been going to see them ever since," Renee said.

"Well, I'm definitely hooked," Michael said.

"I am too," James agreed

"How can you not be with all the action and special effects?" Breechelle asked.

"I know that's right," Renee said.

"Alright homie, I'm about to go and chase Renee around our room," Michael said getting up from the floor and winking at James.

"Man is only 11:00," James said standing up too.

"Yeah well, me and my baby about to spend some alone time together," Michael said.

"Ok, but leave the car keys cause me and Breechelle might go for a ride to the store or something. Want me to call you in case we decide to go?" James asked.

"Naw, we good. We about to chill for the rest of the night," Michael said.

When Michael and Renee got to their room it was so cold it felt like they had walked into a deep freezer. Michael found the thermostat and turned the AC down. Renee sat at the end of the bed, grabbed the remote, and turned on the TV. Michael stood in front of her, placed his hands inside of hers, and pulled her to her feet. He looked her in the eyes and said he didn't think he would ever be spending the night with her again. He told her he wanted to be the one to make her a woman. Renee turned her head and started looking at the floor. Michael knew how shy she got when he said stuff like that to her. He placed his hand under her chin and lifted her head until her eyes met his again. He put both of his arms around her waist and asked her if she heard him. She shook her head up and down, and started looking at the floor again. He lifted her head up one more time and kissed her.

"I'm scared Michael," Renee said.

"Do you love me?" Michael asked.

"Yes," Renee answered.

"Then please let me make you my woman," Michael said.

"I am your woman," Renee said hugging the outside of Michael's arms.

"No, you're my girlfriend, but if you love me, you'll let me make you my woman tonight," Michael said to her as he kissed her under her ear.

"You promise not to hurt me?" Renee asked almost whispering.

"I promise," Michael said squeezing her and pulling her closer to him.

Michael and Renee lie in bed staring at the ceiling when

someone knocked on the door. Renee pulled the covers over her head and Michael jumped out of the bed and reached for his pants. After he put his pants and shirt on, he answered the door. It was James and Breechelle. They wanted to know if he and Renee wanted to go for a ride with them. Michael told him to hold on, then closed the door. He asked Renee if she wanted to go. She said, *"why not,"* and got out of bed and got dressed. Michael grabbed his cell phone off the dresser and looked at the time. It was 1:20 am. He did not have any idea where James wanted to go; but as he stood there watching Renee get dressed, he preferred staying there with her instead of going out for a ride. He went back to the door, opened it, and told James they are coming. James let him know they would be in the car waiting for them.

Chapter 9

Beyond Thoughts

Richard moved in closer, he was just about to make his move when his cell phone rang. He looked at the caller ID, it was Helen. He could not imagine why she would be calling him at night. He looked up from his phone and watched as his opportunity was swallowed up by the crowd. He stood there for a second as his thoughts and feelings darted between anger and confusion. Anger because she had called him at the wrong time, and confusion because he did not know why she would be calling. He let his phone ring without answering it. He noticed the time and decided he would head home. He could not stop wondering why Helen would be calling him at this time of night. His curiosity got the best of him. When he reached his car, he called her.

"Hello?" The voice on the other end answered.

"It's Richard, I just missed your call," Richard said.

"I'm sorry Richard I hope I'm not bothering you," Helen said.

"I'm out running errands. Did you need something?" Richard asked.

"I don't want to feel like I'm bothering you," Helen said.

"It's okay, is something wrong?" Richard asked.

"No. Not at all. I just wanted to tell you a Little Birdie told me you got a promotion," Helen said.

"Really?" Richard asked.

"Sure did, landed right on my porch and started singing its little heart out," Helen said.

Richard listened to Helen while thinking to himself, he was trying to figure out who could have told her. He had not told anyone, so he did not have a clue. The only other person who knew about it was Ronald, the one who had given him the promotion. He knew Ronald did not have time to be gossiping. His anger was suddenly replaced by his desire to know where Helen had gotten her information from.

"So is it true?" Helen asked.

"It doesn't seem like you have much belief in your birdie," Richard said.

"What makes you say that?" Helen asked.

"I don't think you would be asking me if it was true, if believed it, now would you?" Richard asked.

"Don't be a wise guy. Tell me if it's true or not," Helen said, wanting to know.

"I'll tell you what. I'll make a deal with you. If you tell me the name of your birdie, I'll tell you if it's true or not," Richard said.

"I don't want to get anyone in trouble Richard," Helen said.

"Why would they get in trouble?" Richard asked.

"Because of where they work, if I tell you, and you say something, they'll probably get in trouble," Helen said.

"What if I promised not to say anything?" Richard asked.

"You have to make me two promises, if that's the case," Helen said.

"What's the other one?" Richard asked.

"Promise not to say anything, and promise to tell me if it's true or not," Helen said smiling on her end of the phone.

"I can do that," Richard said.

"So, promise," Helen said.

"I thought I just did," Richard said.

"No, you didn't," Helen said.

"Okay. I promise," Richard agreed.

"Do you know Amy, the receptionist in the front office?" Helen asked.

"Of course, everyone knows her. She's the main receptionist," Richard replied.

"Well, that's my little birdie," Helen said.

"How many others know about this?" Richard asked.

"I believe I'm the only one she told so far. It's only because I've been looking for some overtime. By you being promoted it may give me a chance to get some in the department you're leaving. It was the only reason she called and told me about it," Helen said.

"It's true, but I had planned on keeping it a secret. Ronald called me in his office right before the shift was over and offered me a position with quality control," Richard said.

"Congratulations," Helen said, expressing happiness for him.

"Thanks," Richard replied.

"This calls for a celebration. Can I take you out to dinner?" Helen asked.

"I don't know, I've been kind of busy. Besides, if you're looking for overtime how can you afford the extra money to take me out to dinner?" Richard asked.

"I'm not trying to spend my rent money on you. I can afford to take you out and celebrate your promotion

with you. Who knows, I might have to ask you to babysit for me if I start getting overtime," Helen said.

"Babysit, you got to be joking. Right?" Richard asked.

"No, I'm not, but that's down the road. I'm still working on getting some overtime right now," Helen said.

"You have a nine-year-old son, don't you?" Richard asked.

"Yes, Mason. You'll meet him when we celebrate your promotion," Helen said.

"It feels like you're bending my arm, Helen. Do I have a choice?" Richard asked.

"Not at all," Helen replied.

Richard agreed on getting together the following Friday. He could not believe it but he was smiling when he hung up. It was her signature, to leave him with a smile whenever he talked with her. It was only when she attempted to get intimate with him; it caused him to feel uneasy. Deep down inside, he really liked her. She was always straightforward and did not appear as though she had anything to hide. Completely different from all the other women who sat in the lunchroom during break with them. Richard knew he was different, but with Helen it did not matter. He was slowly beginning to have fantasies about what it would be like being in a relationship with her. He wondered if she would be gentle with him if he let her have her way with him. He had never been with a woman before. Therefore, he had never really thought about it. However, Helen was causing him to think about it more and more.

Richard settled into his new job and the weeks began to fly by. After getting home from work he was spending his evenings building his bunker. He had sealed off a portion of his basement and turned it into the sound proof chamber illustrated in the magazine he had ordered. He had been very discreet and went to great lengths on keeping his neighbors out of his business. All building supplies were purchase at night, usually right before the store closed. The debris from the project was placed in black construction bags, put in the trunk of his car, and dumped at the landfill. It had taken him close to four months to build it. When he finally completed it, he had exactly what he wanted. A 10 by 12-foot bunker with a cast iron door and a bulletproof window.

Eight months had passed since Richard completed the building of his bunker. It was now being used for the exact reason he had built it. Lately, he had been going to a lot more Reptile Expos. He enjoyed looking at everything from snakes to alligators. It thrilled him knowing how dangerous they were. He was most fascinated by the King Cobra exhibits. The handlers worked some kind of charm on them and were able to put the snakes under a spell. Today, he would be taking Mason with him. He had started watching him for Helen shortly after he began working in his new position. He did not know it at the time but Helen had been serious about asking him to babysit when she got some overtime. The only reason he agreed to it was because she really did not have anyone else to watch him. Besides, it was only every so often. Mason was nine years old and very easy to care for. Since Helen had taken him out to celebrate his promotion, they had gone out together several times after that. They had also been to several movies together. He had even gone over to her house on a few occasions. Nothing ever happened, so he no longer feared it.

Richard's fascination with reptiles had rubbed off on Mason. He had a million questions whenever they talked about some of the different species. Richard found himself making up answers to some of the questions he would ask because he did not know them himself. For a nine-year-old he had to admit, Mason asked some really tough questions. However, Richard enjoyed his company, and the challenge of trying to answer his questions. It was the first time anyone believed in him with such conviction. It made him feel important. Mason had become very special to him. He enjoyed their time together. He was even starting to spend time with him when Helen was not working overtime. On a couple of occasions, he had gone by and taken Mason to the park and out for some ice cream. Helen was grateful because Mason's father was nowhere in the picture. She would always tell Richard about how excited Mason would get when he knew he was about to spend time with him. For Richard, Mason was the only person he could be with and feel as though he was in control.

Today was huge for reptile lovers. It was the first time Repticon had ever come to New York State. Repticon was the leader in Reptile and Exotic Animal Conventions. They produce reptile and exotic pet shows throughout the United States. In all the years of their existence, they had never held a convention in the State of New York. Richard imagined they would have everything there. He could barely wait to get there. He had first read about Repticon coming to New York when he received his tracking and hunting manual. That was over a year ago. At that time, it was still under consideration. There was a link under the article for anyone wishing to support the convention coming to New York. Apparently, they had received an outpouring of support, which made coming to New York a reality.

When he got to Helen's house, she informed him that she would only be working four hours overtime. She told him he could bring Mason home early if he wanted to. Richard briefly explained the magnitude of Repticon and told her not to worry, he would bring him home around the usual time. Richard asked her how was she doing, she told him fine, and she was happy it was Saturday. She went on to say how Mason had been nagging her about letting him have some sort of reptile. She told Richard she would not be able to sleep knowing there was a snake in the house. She did not care if it was poisonous or not. She was simply terrified of snakes. Richard told her if she ever gave it any kind of consideration maybe a lizard would not be so scary. She told Richard a grasshopper would be better. Mason came downstairs screaming Richard's name. He seemed to be more excited about going to the Expo than Richard appeared to be.

When he and Mason finally made it there, it was unbelievable. Cars were parked so close together that they could barely open their doors. Inside was even more jam-packed than the parking lot. People were going and coming in every direction. You could still move up and down the aisles, but you had to squeeze your way into each exhibit. There were hundreds of tables set up displaying all the exotic pets being sold. Repticon was truly the biggest Exotic Reptile Show he had ever gone to. The others he had attended were merely sideshows in comparison. As he thought about it, he realized his memory had failed him. He had been to a Repticon convention when he was on vacation in Florida, but it had been so long ago he forgot just how big it was.

"Can we go over there Richard?" Mason asked pointing in the direction of some tables displaying a variety of snakes inside of bowls and aquariums.

"Sure, let's see if we can get over there," Richard said turning around and walking in the direction of the snakes.

"Can we see one eat something?" Mason asked.

"I don't know if that's possible, but if it's feeding

time, we'll definitely be able to see something," Richard said.

"Can you buy a mouse so we can feed it to a snake?" Mason asked.

"Why don't we just by a snake?" Richard asked.

"Can we?!, Can we?!" Mason asked, almost screaming.

"Let's look around first, and then see if we can agree on something," Richard said.

They squeezed their way through the crowd and made it to the front of the tables. There were snakes everywhere, in plastic containers, terrariums, aquariums and glass bowls. If it was alive, it was there. Every size and every color. Richard and Mason slowed down when they made their way to the edge of the tables. They took their time to try and look at all the snakes on display. The owners were asking that no one pick up the containers holding the snakes. They did not want to put them under too much stress. It was only after making a purchase, you were allowed to pick up the one you had bought.

"Wow! Look at this one," Mason said pointing at a bright green snake inside a glass terrarium.

"It's almost like a fluorescent green," Richard said bending over and putting his face up to the glass.

"Is it the dangerous kind?" Mason asked.

"You mean is it poisonous?" Richard said returning the question with a smile.

"Yes, do it poison you when it bites you?" Mason asked, with his eyes full of curiosity.

"All snakes bite, "Richard said; "but it's the ones

with poison that's dangerous."

"Do this one have poison?" Mason asked with his face pressed to the glass of the terrarium.

"Let's find out," Richard said.

Richard lifted his arm over his head and started waving his hand back and forth to get the attention of one of the guys standing behind the tables.

"Can I help you?" The guy with the long mustache and dragon tattoo on his arm asked.

"We would like to know what kind of snake this is and if it's poisonous or not?" Richard asked.

"It's an Asian Vine Snake. They're sometimes called Whip Snakes. They're mildly venomous and what we call rear-fanged. Their fangs are not hollowed so their venom is actually chewed into their prey. Their native range includes Southeast Asia, Indo-China, Cambodia, Indonesia, Singapore, Thailand, Vietnam and West Malaysia. They mainly prey on lizards but on occasion are known to eat small rodents and birds. Depending on the level of care their life expectancy can range anywhere between 8 to 12 years. This particular species right here can grow anywhere between 4 and 5 feet long," The guy explained to them.

"So, in captivity can they live solely on a diet of lizards?" Richard asked.

"Absolutely," The guy replied.

"If he's poisonous how would someone go about cleaning the cage?" Richard asked.

"This particular terrarium has a detachable bottom just for that purpose. It allows you to clean up without ever

touching the snake," The guy said removing the bottom of the terrarium to show Richard exactly how it worked.

"Can we get it so we can watch it eat lizards?" Mason asked.

"Why don't we look around some more before we decide," Richard said grabbing Mason's hand and gently guiding him away from the table.

There was so much to see, they wouldn't have enough time to see it all. So far, they had petted a flying Lemur, held an Indian Domino Cockroach, and played with a Red-Eyed Tree Frog. Time had gotten away from him. He suddenly remembered he had not fed his own pet. He didn't like referring to what he had as a pet. The word pet, made it feel different. The excitement of taking Mason to Repticon had overwhelmed him. It had caused him to leave the house without feeding it. His guilt was replaced by anxiety. He needed to get home to feed it. He looked at his watch, it was 3:17 pm. He believed they had arrived somewhere between 9:15 and 9:45. He reached into his pocket and removed the parking receipt. It showed 9:42 am. They had been there for nearly six hours. He decided they had been there long enough.

"What would you say about us getting a snake?" Richard asked Mason.

"Yes! Can we get the Green Vine Snake you asked the guy about?" Mason asked.

Richard could not believe Mason had remembered that particular snake out of everything they had seen. He was really incredible for his age.

"Why not, let's see if he hasn't sold it," Richard said smiling while reaching down to grab Mason's hand.

"Yeah!" Mason said gripping Richards's fingers

Richard was surprised to find the same snake still there. The guy offered him a really good deal. He bought the snake, the terrarium and a few lizards all for under $200. After making his purchase he headed straight home. For a Saturday evening, the traffic was moving fairly well. In no time at all, he was pulling into his driveway. He planned on driving Mason home after going into the basement and doing the feeding. He unbuckled Mason's seat belt and helped him out of the car. Mason wanted nothing more than to see the snake eat a lizard. Richard would use the snake as a distraction. It would allow him to sneak downstairs without Mason asking a million questions. He grabbed the snake and terrarium and let Mason carry the lizards and wood chips used as bedding for the terrarium. When they got into the house Richard pulled the dining room table from against the wall and put everything on top of it. He positioned the table and one of the chairs so that Mason's back would be towards the basement door. He allowed Mason to dump the wooden bedding into the cage while he prepared the food he was going to take downstairs. When Mason had finish spreading the wood chips out evenly along the bottom, Richard dropped a lizard into the cage.

He left Mason staring into the cage waiting for the snake to eat the lizard. The door leading to the basement was in the kitchen. It was to the right of the refrigerator, and could not be seen from the dining room. He quietly opened the door and crept downstairs, disappearing into the darkness. He did not have a light switch at the top of the steps so it was completely dark going down. It did not matter what time of year it was; his basement was always cool and damp. When he reached the bottom, he walked blindly towards the middle of the room. After reaching up and grasping at the darkness he was able to locate the string connected to the light on the ceiling. When he pulled on it, the warm glow of light provided a temporary barrier against the cool darkness. His basement was completely empty, except for a small table and a chair in the middle of the floor. It was a very old house, made obvious by the old-fashioned cement sink on the opposite side of the room. Richard sat the food on the table, walked over to the door and flipped on the light switch. He pressed his face to the window and peered inside. It was something he had made a habit of doing. Although there was no way of getting out, he did not like surprises.

When Richard reached the top of the stairs Mason was standing in the middle of the kitchen waiting for him. He asked Richard what was the noise he heard coming from downstairs. Richard responded by asking him was he able to keep a secret, when Mason shook his head and said yes, he confessed and said he had an exotic pet he was keeping. At first, he begged Richard to see it. After he made it clear he was not going to let him see it right away, he pouted for a second then began asking a million questions about it. Finally, in order to get Mason to stop with the questions, Richard promised to let him see it once he trained it. Mason had told him whatever it was he had down there, the noise it made sounded funny, like he had heard it before. While taking Mason home Richard reminded him about keeping their secret. He had told him nobody could know about it, and that meant he could not tell his mother. He told him keeping secrets was how little boys turned into men. Mason promised he would not say anything to anyone because one day he wanted to be a man.

Richard could not put his finger on it, but the atmosphere at work had somehow changed. As he sat thinking about it while looking out the window of the quality control office, he could not make much sense of it. It was not a bad change. He enjoyed the feeling he was getting from his new position. He thought about how the women there used to make him feel different by the way they looked at him. Those days had somehow disappeared. He was now beginning to experience what it felt like being a part of the social blanket that covered Digital Core Solutions. He was as close to normal as he had ever been. He wondered if it had anything to do with his new position. Sometimes those who worked as quality control inspectors got treated better. It was probably because they had the power to accept or reject someone's work. However, he did not believe it was because of his new position. More than likely, it was a result of the relationship he had established with Helen. Not that they were lovers or anything, but because she had made it known they had been out on several dates together. He considered this more than anything else.

Chapter 10
Revelations

It was now Thursday and Daniel found himself sitting in the math lab thinking about Beverly finding the coupon in his pants pocket for 30% off his next meal at Jay's Restaurant. It had been two weeks since he began going to the gym directly after work and carrying both of his cell phones. Beverly had been doing laundry when she found the coupon. Everything had been going well after they made up, but he had now gone from the frying pan directly into the fire. He did not want to admit it, but it was true, the problems he and Beverly were having began when he starting working at the school. Nevertheless, he had given Beverly a lame excuse about being at the restaurant, and barely escaped another week of sleeping on the couch. However, if she knew the real reason he had gone, she would've been enraged.

He decided it was time for another job. The Teachers job had been his safety net from the previous job. But Daniel had a Bachelor's Degree in Math, and it was time for him to put that degree back to work. Numbers was something he loved working with. The possibilities were endless, having control of an infinite amount of results was nothing short of power. He loved it. He decided he would be hush-hush about searching for a job until he landed something. He altered his schedule just enough to fit in the library to do his job search. Within a week of submitting his resume and making calls, his phone began ringing. He was not just getting calls from some mediocre companies trying to low ball him but he was receiving calls from big-name companies acquiring about more past work history. One VyCal Technologies, one of the biggest, if not the biggest media firm on the East Coast. The other one, LifeCore Pharmaceuticals was another big name inquiring about more information. It was becoming almost impossible to keep it all hush-hush but he would keep his secret and wait.   He had also decided that he would not up and abandon the school, he would give them at least a one-month notice. Besides, there were a couple of students he would have to take his time with, because his departure would be unsettling.

There was something else amiss that Daniel was not telling Beverly about as well.   The rumor at the school. Apparently, a couple of parents had contacted the school about a teacher giving a student an expensive gift. The story was not clear, but one student told another student her beautiful necklace was a gift from a teacher at the school.   Allegedly, the school had vowed to find out if it was true or not. For now, though, no one knew who the students were or what direction it was headed. Daniel could not help but be bothered after hearing about this.   He had even gone so far as to slow down on the private sessions he had been providing. As he sat there thinking about it he quickly realized he had actually gone a bit too far. Taking students out to dinner and buying gifts was something he was not supposed to do.   More specifically, Female Students. Now the school had gotten wind of it and an investigation was underway. Daniel knew exactly who the student was, her name was Kimberly Jordan. He had bought her the necklace after she had snuck out of the house to be with him. He had been so caught up in the moment, he used his credit card to purchase the necklace.

He and Kimberly had been secretly talking ever since she accidentally told her friend about it. She told Daniel she had been drinking with her friend and made the mistake of telling her. She ensured Him that the necklace was put up somewhere nobody could ever find it. She also told Daniel that she was hearing something about him seeing other girls. She said the school did not ask her about this but some of the other girls that talk in secret were saying something to that effect. He told her that he tutored a lot of students but it's nothing to the story because it's all just gossip. He would always end their conversations by making her promise that she would keep the bracelet put up. Her promise was the only thing that mattered to him.

To his surprise when he reached home Beverly's car was in the driveway and the smell of food hovered around the outside of the house. He did not know what was going on but he took the smell of food as a sign of peace. At this point, he would take whatever he could get. He opened the front door, kicked his shoes off on the matt and peaked around into the kitchen. Beverly was leaning against the counter next to the stove with a wooden spoon in one hand and her cell phone in the other.

"*Hi Dear,*" Daniel said walking into the kitchen.

"*Oh, hi Hon,*" Beverly said, looking up from her cell phone and leaning in towards Daniel as he placed a kiss on her forehead.

"*What's all this?* " Daniel asked as he pointed his finger at what she was cooking.

"*Well, let's just say we're having a vacation from being upset at one another,*" Beverly said with a smile on her face.

"*I couldn't agree with you more,*" Daniel said as he gave Beverly another kiss, this time on the lips.

"*Knock it off guys*" You've got kids in the house, David said walking into the kitchen with a big smile on his face.

"*What's going on buddy?* " Daniel asked.

"*Nothing much, Got a break from school for a second. Figured I come home and catch a movie with you*

114

guys tonight," David Said, holding what appeared to be an energy drink in his right hand.

"*Hey! was this some kind of plan or something? If so, that would explain all the cooking and everything,*" Daniel said with a look of deceit on his face.

" *Cool your engines honey, you haven't been nowhere near your best behavior to deserve such a special get together,*" Beverly said with such calmness it snatched the air from under his feet.

"*So, where's the last of the pack?*" Daniel asked, referring to Heather.

"*Somewhere upstairs tucked away with her cell phone stuck to her face,*" Beverly said while stirring the huge pot of Swedish Meatballs and spaghetti sauce.

"*I'm going to get me a quick shower, I'll be right back you guys,*" Daniel said making his way through the kitchen and up the steps.

Before going into the bathroom Daniel knocked on Heather's door and waited to see if she would answer.

"*Yes, who is it?*" Heather answered the knock.

"*It's me,*" Daniel said answering her.

"*What's going on?*" Heather asked without opening the door.

"*I was just wondering if you had any plans on joining us for dinner and a movie,*" Daniel asked with his face practically touching her door.

Heather opened her door just as Daniel was pulling his face away.

"Did mom have you to come and ask me that?" Heather asked when she had finished opening the door.

"No. She doesn't even know I'm asking you," Daniel confessed.

Did I hear David downstairs?" Heather asked looking out her door towards downstairs.

"Yes you did, and he's staying home long enough to have supper and a movie," Daniel said as though he was encouraging her to do the same.

"Sure, I'll be down when you guys get settled in," Heather said while holding her phone to her ear.

"Great, sounds like a family night to me. I'm about to hit the shower. I don't know how long your mom has before dinner is ready, but maybe you could come up with some suggestions about a movie," Daniel said as he turned from her door and headed towards their bedroom to get a change of clothing.

For some reason Daniel sensed that this was all too good to be true, he could not understand why he felt this way, but he just could not believe the evening was turning out to be so nice. Perhaps it was the guilt he was feeling over everything he had been keeping a lid on. An accumulation of all the stress he had been dealing with over the last couple of weeks. First the ordeal with Beverly finding the receipt from the restaurant, followed by the talk going around the school about a student-teacher relationship, and finally the worry he had about the necklace being purchased with his credit card. He really needed an evening like tonight to relax and collect his thoughts about his next move. It was clear he would be changing jobs. He had already sent the additional information to both VyCal Technologies and LifeCore

Pharmaceuticals. Both wanted an interview. He had scheduled his first interview with VyCal on the following Monday at 10:30 am, and the interview with LifeCore was scheduled for two days later on Wednesday at 10:00 am. He had tried to schedule both earlier in the morning but apparently a couple of the so-called the big wigs wanted to sit in on the interview and they did not get in until after 9:00 am. Daniel considered tonight the perfect time to let everyone know he was changing jobs, but after thinking about it decided otherwise.

When Daniel arrived at work Monday morning he was told by Jennifer, the Principal's secretary, that the principal needed to talk with him. She secretly told him that teachers were being called in and interviewed about the allegations about the teacher-student relationship going around. Daniel asked her if the school was really taking it seriously. She informed him that today, where so much of this type of stuff is taking place, the school would do everything in their power to weed out the truth from the rumors. It was her understanding there was no one in particular they were looking at, but between her and him, Paul, the Gym teacher, might be who they focus on. In the past, he had been accused of inappropriate conduct regarding one of the senior students. She told him nothing ever became of it because that student's mother was on drugs and ended up in some rehab. Shortly after that, the student ended up leaving the state to go live with her father. Unfortunately, the girl followed in her mother's footsteps ending up in some rehab in Michigan.

As Daniel stood there listening to Jennifer run her mouth it was clear to him she was the gossip type. She appeared to be excited about all the drama that was going on. She had no problem telling him about the Gym Teacher's troubles. He could see her telling others about him if it ever came to that. He ended up cutting the conversation short by telling her he had a 10:30 am appointment; so, he would really appreciate it if she could relay that to the principal. She smiled and told him she would let him know as soon as he came out from the interview he was having.

Forty-five minutes later while sitting at his desk going over paperwork his phone rang. It was Jennifer from the front office calling to informed him the Principal had pushed back one of his interviews to accommodate him regarding his 10:30 am appointment, and he was now ready to see him. He told her he would be down as soon as he locked up. Daniel was really good at putting on a façade. He had come to master his outward appearance and could easily conceal how he was affected by something. At this particular moment, it was fear, and he managed his uneasiness by telling himself he didn't have anything to worry about. Trying to get himself to believe it was something he had been wrestling with ever since hearing about the investigation. Regardless of what he tried to convince himself to believe he knew it was him they were looking for. The funny thing about it was he did not feel any regret over the relationship he had been having with the student. In fact, they had seen each other a couple of times after the whole investigation thing had been started. In a twisted kind of way, he wished the laws dealing with sexual consent were different. It was a man's world, so men should be able to pick from any tree that bears ripe fruit.

When he walked into the office Jennifer pointed to the Principal's door and told him to go right in. He tapped lightly before opening it and walking in. Upon entering, Daniel nearly panicked when he saw Principal Paul sitting behind his big oak desk talking with two men. He did not know who they were but he was in shock and experiencing anxiety. While running her mouth the secretary never told him anything about outsiders being a part

118

of the school's investigation. Maybe Kimberly had come clean with her parents and told them everything. Jennifer the secretary was probably told to keep him thinking they did not have their eyes on him when in all reality they were getting ready to arrest him. He could literally taste the fear coming up from his stomach into his mouth. The two men there were definitely dressed like detectives. They were probably waiting on some squad car to arrive after they got him to confess everything. It would be just like television, perfect timing. However, unlike TV, he would not be confessing anything. He immediately reminded himself he did not have anything to worry about. This was the story he told himself that allowed him to maintain his façade, something he could not abandon right now, not when he needed it the most. He quickly shifted his belief into acceptance, which allowed him to gain control over his fear.

"Please come in and have a seat," The Principal said looking at Daniel and cutting his conversation short between the two men seated in chairs to his left.

"Daniel, this is Detective Ryan and Detective Matthew. They're here as a part of an investigation regarding allegations about a teacher and student having an affair," The Principal said when Daniel was seated.

"Oh," Daniel said turning his head to look at the two Detectives.

"Yes, we have a few questions we'd like to ask you if you don't mind?" Detective Ryan asked.

"Not at all," Daniel said

"Are you familiar with a student by the name of Kimberly Jordan?*"* Detective Matthew asked.

"Yes, I believe she comes into my lab for assistance," Daniel said.

"Have you ever had any contact with this student outside of the math lab here at the school?" Detective Matthew continued.

It was this question that caught Daniel off guard. In his mind he knew it would be how he answered it that would determine where he ended up in the investigation. If he lied and told them no, he would undoubtedly hang himself. If he told the truth and embellished a little, they may think he did not have anything to hide and consider him truthful, but meeting students after school on his own personal time might put him at risk. He was dammed if he did, and dammed if he didn't, tell the truth.

"I've met with several students who needed help for upcoming exams that couldn't make it into the lab during school hours. Some of them were behind in several classes," Daniel said looking Detective Matthew in his eyes.

"So I take it that's a yes?" Detective Ryan asked.

"I Can't say for sure if this particular student was one of those who were in need of this type of help. I mean I don't keep a record of who've I've helped in this regard, and I can't really put a face to the name, but I do remember the name because I log in everyone who visits the lab," Daniel said

"Roughly speaking, how many students have you helped with work after school on your own personal time?" Detective Ryan asked.

"If I had to put a number to it, I would say between fifteen to twenty," Daniel answered.

"Is this something every teacher does, or just something you do for students?" Detective Matthew asked.

"That's something I can't answer. I mean I don't know what other teachers do outside of school," Daniel said.

"So how would a student go about requesting additional time for personal tutoring if they were in need of that type of help?" Detective Matthew asked.

"Most of the time they'll either come by my classroom during lunch or between classes and explain their situation," Daniel Said.

"I would imagine in order to maintain contact with students you help off campus they would have to have your phone number. Is that an accurate assumption?" Detective Ryan asked.

"Yes, that's correct. However, I have a phone I use just so students can get in touch with me without having my private number," Daniel said.

"Does this additional tutoring come with a price tag or just something you do to help students?" Detective Matthew asked.

"No, I don't charge anything. It's something I do to help students who might be in danger of failing," Daniel said.

"Do you require permission from the parents?" Detective Matthew asked looking at a notepad he was holding in his hand.

"No. It never dawned on me that I should. I guess now that I think about it, it would be wise if I actually start doing that," Daniel said while looking at Detective Matthew scribble something in the notepad.

"Where do you normally tutor when off campus?" Detective Ryan asked.

"It's usually one of the local fast food chains, McDonald's, Burger King or Penera Bread," Daniel said.

"How do the students usually get to those locations?" Detective Matthew asked.

"I believe on several occasions they've been dropped off by their parents, friends, and some of them even have their own vehicles," Daniel answered.

"So you never actually go and pick up any of the students you tutor?" Detective Ryan asked.

"Not at all. If they need the help they can at least get to the location on their own; and if a student is a no call no show, I don't give second chances," Daniel said.

"Well, I think that about covers everything. Any more questions Ryan?" Detective Matthew asked his partner.

"No. I think that's about it," Detective Ryan answered.

"I think it's a really nice thing of you to help our students in that way Daniel, but you have to be very careful about how you go about providing that service. There are a few red and gray areas you need to consider," Principal Paul said giving him advice.

"Yes, I would say this interview has taught me quite a bit in such a short period of time," Daniel said in agreement.

"I understand you have an appointment so your free to go unless you need to ask a few questions yourself," The Principal said.

"No. I don't think I have any questions of my own," Daniel said getting up from his chair.

"If there's anything we forgot to ask, we may need

to talk with you again. In the meantime, if anything comes to mind that might be of help, please feel free to give us a call," Detective Matthew said while handing Daniel his business card.

"Will do," Daniel said taking the card from Detective Matthew.

It was 12:15 when Daniel walked outside from his 10:30 interview at VyCal Technologies. He could not believe they were offering him a salaried position in their Atlanta Georgia division. It was a dream come true, and a rescue at the same time. Although he was elated, he had told them he would have to think it over, as well as talk with his fiancée. The money was excellent. They would start him out at sixty-five thousand and increase it to seventy- five in six months, if he proved to be worth the hire. The only catch was he would have to relocate. However, they were willing to pay for the entire move. In his heart he knew he would take the position the minute he heard the numbers. The only reason he had told them he would have to think about it was that he had another interview at LifeCore Pharmaceuticals the next day. He was definitely interested in seeing what LifeCore was willing to offer. However, he was more motivated by the VyCal offer because it gave him the opportunity to move away from the drama that was drumming up at the school. VyCal said they would keep the offer on the table for a week before looking for someone else. The problem was going to be convincing Beverly to relocate. She had been promoted and was enjoying the money she was making. Nevertheless, she had been talking about going back to school and adding another Certification to her portfolio. This would be the angle he would use to convince her to relocate if LifeCore could not beat out VyCal's offer. He would offer to help pay for her tuition if she agreed to relocate.

The interview with LifeCore wasn't anything like VyCal. The pharmaceutical giant wanted him to intern for six months. After that, he would have to do another six months of probation. Finally, he would be hired on as Data Scientist that would help support their Risk and Technology teams with insights gained from analyzing company data. However, as an intern, he would have to show his ability to assess large data sets in order to find opportunities for product and process optimization while using models to test the effectiveness of the different courses of action. To Daniel, it was more like jumping through a ring of fire. It required too much just to get on board. With the internship and probation, it would be a total on one year before he could consider himself actually hired. Although the pay would be around twenty thousand more a year, it was not worth it after considering the fact that he would still be living in Texas. Right now, that was the last place he wanted to be.

Chapter 11
Sound of Silence

Michael and James pulled out of the parking lot and onto Old Dixie Highway. James was driving and Michael was riding shotgun. James and Breechelle wanted to smoke some weed but didn't have any blunts left. They wanted to find a seven eleven in order to grab some. When they came across one the girls got out with them complaining about being thirsty and needing something to drink. Four guys were standing outside the entrance of the store laughing and talking. A couple of them looked to be tipsy. Michael was not sure, but as Breechelle passed by them he believed he heard one of them say something to her. As he walked passed them he noticed the tallest one, to the left of the entrance, gave him a really nasty look. When Michael got in the store, he noticed Breechelle whispering something to James. As he watched, he could see James expression changed from happy to angry. After purchasing a couple blunts and sodas they left the store. When they got outside, James confronted the guy who Michael had overheard saying something to Breechelle. He let James finish saying what he had to say before calling him a fuckboy, and telling him to get the hell out of his face. James told him he had his fuckboy, before turning and walking away. As they got into the car, they noticed the four guys getting into their car as well.

James turned to Michael and said, *"I hope these clowns don't act up."*

"What did he say to you Breechelle?" Michael asked turning around in his seat to look at her.

"You don't wanna know," Breechelle said.

"It looks like they following us," James said

slowing down as he made his way out of the parking lot of Seven Eleven.

"*So why you slowing down?*" Michael asked.

"*I ain't tryin to get caught out there and be no victim,*" James said reaching under his seat and pulling out a gun.

"*Man! You been carrying that with you all this time?*" Michael asked.

"*Oh my god! Please just speed up,*" Breechelle said almost begging.

Michael looked out the passenger side rearview mirror and agreed that they were following them, and just like James, they had slowed down as well. James stopped the car, held the gun close to his right leg, and opened the door. That's when the sound of gunfire ripped through the quiet morning like thunder. Renee and Breechelle started screaming so loud they drowned out the sounds of the gunshots and made it impossible to tell if they were still being shot at. James managed to stick his arm out between the door, point his gun in the direction of their car and open fire. The sound of a bullet smashing into the side window let Michael know they were still shooting at them. Before he could tell James to drive off another bullet exploded into the back window causing it to shatter into a million pieces. James lifted his head up from the seat high enough to see over the dashboard, smashed his foot into the gas pedal, causing the tires to squeal as they burned rubber onto the asphalt filling the area with smoke.

Before getting back to the hotel James pulled onto a side street in order to calm down and stop the girls from crying. Michael was stuck, and could not seem to free himself from what had just happened. It was the sound of Renee crying from the back seat that finally brought him out of the shock he was in. When he looked back over the seat both Renee and Breechelle were crying and picking glass out of their hair. He looked over at James, and James was looking at him with an expression he had never seen on his face before. Michael was not sure, but he would bet everything he had on it, what he was looking at on James's face was murder. He turned back around, looked at Renee, and asked her was she alright. She was crying so hard she was shaking. He believed the shaking was probably from being shot at. Michael opened the car door, got out, and went to the back of the car. He opened the back door and Renee climbed out of the backseat. Tiny pieces of glass flickered like glitter all over her clothes as the light from the street lamp shined down on them.

"I want to go home Michael," Renee said between the shaking and the tears.

"It's after 2 o'clock in the morning Renee. There's no way in the world you can go home this late at night without your parents knowing something happened," Michael said.

"I'm scared Michael, what if those guys come back looking for us? What if they come to the hotel?" Renee asked.

"They don't know us, and we don't know them. They were just some idiots hanging out at the store drinking and looking for trouble. They have no way of knowing who we are or where we're at," Michael said taking Renée's hand and squeezing it.

Michael and James managed to calm the girls down enough

to get them back to the hotel where they were able to shower and clean up. He and James spent most of the morning trying to figure out a story to come up with for Rick's sister's boyfriend. The one who had rented them the car. They both agreed, regardless of how it went down, it could not involve the police. The more they tried to fabricate what to say the more they realized there were not a lot of stories you could tell that involved being shot at where someone was not trying to hurt someone else. After coming to grips with it they decided they would tell him the truth, pay for his windows to be fixed, and tell him to leave the police out of the picture. It was the only thing they could do considering the four bullet holes and the two broken windows that were left from the shootout.

Two weeks passed without Michael so much as receiving a single phone call or text message from Renee. He had been calling her almost every day since the night of the incident but she was not returning any of his calls. In his heart, he believed he had lost her. It caused him to feel empty inside. He could not drink or smoke enough to push the thought of her out of his mind, or numb his heart enough to stop him from feeling what he was experiencing over not seeing her. He had lost interest in everything. He wanted her back. No, he needed her back. She was the only thing in his life that truly mattered to him. He was lost, and he did not know what to do. He had thought about going to her house, knocking on the door, and asking for her, but her father would probably call the cops on him. He was some kind of big shot downtown, and according to Renee, he had zero tolerance for what Michael was considered, A Thug.

Personally, Michael understood how that night at the store could make a person think twice about things. It had changed him a little. He no longer wanted to hang out with his boys the way he used too. He started spending more time at home with his mother and sisters. He even went so far as to sign up online for G.E.D. classes. Coming face to face with death had a way of encouraging people to do what was right, at least for Michael it did. Rich had called him several times asking him did he want to hang out with him and the homies to play some ball and smoke some weed, Michael had lied saying he was helping his mother fix some stuff around the house she could not do herself. Another time he had lied and said, he was going to Belle Glade for a family get together. It was not until James had called him one morning asking him what was up with him that he finally hung out with his boys for the day.

Renee finally called him. She said she had been thinking about him but was afraid to be around him because of his lifestyle. She said she still loved him but did not want to be around anyone who put her life in danger. She told him he would have to choose what was most important to him. She asked him was it being with her, or being with his homies, because he would have to choose which one he wanted the most. She went on to explain how they could've all been killed that night, and that she did not believe he understood how serious it was. She made him understand that there was no way in the world she would have gotten in the car with him or anyone else if she had known they were driving around with an illegal gun. She ended what she had to say by telling him his friend James was bad news and he needed to stop hanging with him and find some new friends who do not smoke, drink and carry guns.

Michael waited until she had finished before he began telling her about how he had already started doing what she had said, and that he had even signed up to go back to school. He told her how much he missed her and how sorry he was that it ever happened. He said if he could take it all back, he would do it because the last thing on earth he wanted to do was to see anything happen to her. He told her how much he loved her, and how he had been down in the dumps over not hearing from her. He begged to see her again and promised to do whatever it took in order to show her how much she meant to him. He apologized to her one more time and asked her if she forgave him. After she said yes, they made plans to meet at the park later that night.

Two days later, Michael received a call from James. He told Michael he had found out who two of the dudes were from the night at the store. He stresses to Michael that they needed to take care of their business and give them back some of the bullets that they had given to them. He said they couldn't just let the shit fly because their reputation was on the line. He told Michael the rest of the homies knew what time it was, and was just waiting to see what he and Michael were going to do. He said he told them that they were going to handle their business because he knew that Michael wanted pay-back just as bad as he wanted it. Michael asked him how he came about the information. James said that two of the dudes were bragging about shooting up a car at a seven eleven off Old Dixie Hwy to a couple of girls that Daquan deals with. James said his cousin had driven him by the address the girls gave Daquan because he wanted to see if he recognized any of them. He said he couldn't believe it, but the tall one that was there that night was standing outside the house leaning against the fence talking to a girl. He asked James what he wanted to do.

When Michael hung up the phone, he could feel the pressure left from the conversation with James. In a way James was right. He could not have his name on the same list as cowards, that was equivalent to being a crackhead. Cowards and crackheads got no respect. He could not have that. He and James were going to have to do something, it was the code of the street, you did not let anybody do something to you and get away with it. They would have to retaliate, but then again, he had promised Renee he would stop hanging out with his old friends and start making better decisions. The last thing he wanted was for her to find out. He was sure he would lose her for good if she found out he lied to her. He was torn between his commitment to Renee and his loyalty to the streets. He could not understand how his heart and pride could be at war against each other. He was not sure if he would be able to manage the two. It felt impossible. Uncertainty and confusion wrapped his thoughts in a layer of doubt that kept him guessing for the rest of the day.

Michael intentionally avoided James's calls for nearly a week. He had been spending most of his days secretly attending G.E.D. classes and seeing Renee afterwards. He finally gave him a call when he got a text message from him saying call him it was an emergency.

"What's up?" Michael said when James answered his phone.

"What you mean what's up? You been dodging me ever since I told you I got them clowns address. What up with you, somebody shoot at us, and all of a sudden you got ice in your veins. You just gonna let this go? that's what you trying to say by not answering my calls? James asked expressing anger and disbelief.

"James, what you wanna do, pull up and kill everybody standing outside the house. I want revenge too, and I feel like everybody's gonna treat me like a coward if I don't handle my business, but I ain't feeling doing no drive by just to prove something to everybody," Michael said trying to convince James that it's really not worth it.

"Well, you can run from that, but Rick's sister called me and said the police got surveillance video of the shooting and they pulled up on her boyfriend and took him to the precinct to talk to him about the shooting. She said they was able to get his plate number from the video. She told me they even towed his car after they saw all the bullet holes. She wanted us to know it's only right that we step up and talk with the police because she ain't gonna stand around a watch her boyfriend go to jail for something he didn't have nothing to do with," James said with a little less anger in his voice.

"Are you serious, she said they got surveillance video. So, what about the dudes who was shooting at us? That's who they should have down at the precinct, not us. I ain't trying to go talk to no police. If they got the video then they know exactly what happened," Michael said.

"I ain't trying to talk with them either, but what's right is right. Plus it's Rick's sister and Rick is our homie so we gotta do what we gotta do." James said.

"If they got video, ain't you scared? Don't you think they gonna see you shooting out the door of the car?" Michael asked James.

"It is what it is. I'm going to deny everything they can't prove on camera, and even some of what they can prove on camera," James said laughing on the other end.

"So when you plan on going down to talk with them?" Michael asked.

"The sooner the better. I don't want this hanging over my head, we need to get Rick's sister's boyfriend out of this mess," James said.

Michael got to James's house around 9:15 the next morning. They had agreed to meet there before going to the police station together. He and James had to get their story straight so if they were separated and asked questions, they would not contradict one another. The police were experts with their divide and conquer tactics, so Michael and James had to be just as good, if not better, at their get together and corroborate, then the police were at their divide and conquer. They informed the officer at the front desk they were there to talk with someone about a shooting. From that point onward they were treated as first-class citizens. Michael figured it was probably because they thought him and James was there to snitch on someone. They finally ended up at the back of the precinct in a soundproof room talking with a Detective by the name of McCoy.

After admitting he had gone over the surveillance several times, along with having talked with Rashad Wilson, Rick's sister's boyfriend, Detective McCoy said it was clear we were not the instigators. He went on to say the driver of the other vehicle, Latrell Odem, was known to law enforcement for gang violence and possibly tied to several unsolved homicides. He told them Latrell Odem was someone they had been after for quite a while, but every time they thought they had him nobody was willing to testify because of his reputation. He said he was happy to finally see someone with enough balls to come to the precinct willing to testify and put this guy behind bars, where he belonged. After James told him they were not there to testify against anyone, they had only come to the precinct because they did not want to see Rashad caught up in something, he wasn't involved in. After Michael agreed with James, Detective McCoy revealed another side of himself.

Suddenly they had gone from friend to foe. He began

treating them as though they had been the ones who had open fire first. Not that he had mentioned anything about seeing James with a gun or shooting, but based on how the questioning changed. He asked them why were they at a seven eleven at 2 o'clock in the morning with two girls. He asked them did they have any weapons in the car and what were the names of both girls who were with them. He suddenly wanted to know why they were driving Rashad's car. He asked them both for a driver's license, and when they both said neither one of them had one, he said he could easily arrest one of them for driving without a license because the surveillance footage clearly shows one of them driving away from the Seven Eleven that night. He went on to say it was obvious based on the video that they must have known the other guys and perhaps it was some type of retaliation from something earlier. Clearly, he was angry over them telling him they were not there to testify on anyone. What was obvious was the fact that the video really did not show them a whole lot, because not one time did he mention anything about someone in their car shooting.

They walked out of the precinct knowing that they were considered the victims in the incident. Although Detective McCoy was angry, he could not get them to testify. James left the precinct happier than he had been before he got there. When Michael asked him why, he said it was because he now had the name of the one who had started everything by saying something to Breechelle. He said that he was the one he wanted the most, and he was going to make sure he gave him what he had coming. He asked Michael again was he down, or was he still gonna bitch' up and hide. Michael told him he could call it whatever he wanted to but sometimes a good run beats a bad fall. He told James to just let it go because he could bet everything he had, somebody else wanted him more than they did. James didn't want to hear it, and told

Michael, if you live by the sword you die by the sword.

Michael found his days being consumed by his G.E.D. classes, homework, doing things around the house for his mother, and spending time with Renee. However, it was the way his mother now smiled at him when she looked at him, and the hugs and kisses from Renée that was causing Michael to feel a lot better about himself, and life. He had given up drinking all together, but was still sneaking a puff or two off a joint every now and then. He was also doing good in school. His Teacher had told him if he could get a good score on the upcoming pretest, she would make sure he got into the next scheduled testing. She said she had been surprised about how high his math score had been because usually, it was math that caused students the most problems. His relationship with his two sisters had gotten better as well. He had invited them to the park one evening and let them meet Renee. His oldest sister Destiny, really liked her and had exchanged phone numbers with her threatening to snitch on him if he got out of line. When they got home, his sister told him how lucky he was to have found someone as cute and smart as Renee was. She said she was definitely a keeper, and not the dime-a-dozen type.

The following weekend Michael took Renee to the county fair. He managed to win her a giant teddy bear by throwing hopes with the basketball. They enjoyed the roller coaster so much; they rode it until their bodies still felt like they were on it even after they were done riding it. Renée loved cotton candy, and the fried dough smothered in sugar. Michael loved being with her, she was his cotton candy and fried dough all rolled up into one. He sat there looking at her as she was getting her palms read. She was beautiful. Her jet-black curly hair was throwing tiny sparkles of light towards his eyes every time she moved her head. Her golden brown skin had a look of sweet creamy caramel that begged for his kiss. The fullness of her lips seemed to stay moist with the flavor of strawberries. She was flawless. Michael loved everything about her. What he loved the most was the feeling he got whenever he was around her. She had a way of making him forget about everything. Nothing mattered when he was with her. Being with her, was where he wanted to be for the rest of his life. She always talked to him in a way that made him feel as though he could do anything he wanted. She was his guiding star, and he would follow her to the end of the world if she wanted him to.

Michael no longer communicated with any of his friends, except for James. For some reason, it was difficult for Michael to sever the ties with him. For that reason, they still talked to one another on the phone and would secretly meet up to smoke. Michael believed James no longer wanted the street life, and if he had a friend who was doing the right thing, who he could follow, he would leave it all behind. Michael knew their closeness came from him and James having the same family structure, along with them hanging out together most of the time. Lately, he had been trying to encourage James to enroll in the G.E.D. program with him. James never really said no, he just explained all the reasons why he could not enroll. Michael would listen to him and then turn around and ask him was he planning on hanging out doing nothing for the rest of his life. He would say no, and then say he had thought about going back a few times.

The last time Michael and James got together, James asked Michael if he told him something would he promise not to say anything to anyone. When Michael promised him he would not, he then told Michael he had shot a few dudes standing in front of the house he told him about. He said he was sure he got the one who had said something to Breechelle. He told him he had recognized at least two of them from the store that night. He bragged to Michael about how he had rented some crackhead's car and used it to creep up on them. He told Michael how good it made him feel, seeing them all run while he squeezed off shots at them. He wanted to know how Michael felt about him getting revenge for what had happened to them that night. It was something they had coming and it made him feel good knowing they got what they deserved. He wanted to know if Michael was on the same page with him about what he had done.

Michael could not believe what James was telling him. Stealing out of office buildings and doing burglaries was a long ways from doing drive-bys or gunning people down. Michael wanted nothing to do with it. He wondered what had caused James to go from stealing to trying to kill someone. Was he doing it because it was fun, or was he doing it because his intention was to hurt someone? Either way, it was wrong, and Michael did not want any part of it. He told James what he thought about it, and James responded by saying he had changed. He told James he didn't think it was good they hung out anymore because he was trying to avoid drama. He said he could call him if he wanted to but that was it. He told him he was trying to get his life together because he loved Renée and he wanted to do what was right for her. James told him he respected that, and they would always be homeboys because he was his brother from another mother.

Michael and Renée sat in the park holding hands and talking. There was something a little different about Renee that Michael could not put his finger on. Although they were talking, she seemed to be a little distant. Michael had asked her earlier if something was wrong, but she told him she was fine. However, he knew that was not true. After sitting there in silence' in what felt like hours, Renee finally told him she had not seen her period since the night they had been together at the motel. She asked him if he knew what it meant. Michael answered her saying he believed it meant she was pregnant. She told him they should have been smart and used some protection. Michael grabbed her by the hands got down on his knees and kissed her on the belly. He promised her he would stay in school, get a job, and take care of her and the baby. Renee looked down at him, started crying, and told him how scared she was. She reminded him that she was only 16, and he was 19, and she had no idea what her father would do if he ever found out. Michael told her he was not afraid of her father, and that he did not mean to get her pregnant. However, he was happy that she was and he wanted her to have the baby.

Michael picked up a part-time job at Popeye's Chicken. Although he was not making much because of his hours, it did not stop him from helping his mother out with bills and saving towards a car, and for the baby. The manager told him as soon as he graduates he'd give him more hours if he wanted them. A month and a half later, Michael did just that, he graduated with his G.E.D. The same night his boss closed 10 minutes early so everyone could celebrate his graduation. His boss told him he was proud of him, and he was a good worker. He encouraged Michael to consider college and said anything was possible at his age. It was something Michael had been thinking about ever since he had started attending the G.E.D. program. After hearing it from his boss, he knew it was something he was going to do.

Chapter 12

Open Door

He left the office and began making his rounds on the floor. It was time to collect samples for testing. He grabbed one of the pushcarts lined up outside of the office and headed over to section B. It was where all the coaxial couplers, splitters and extenders were made. When he got there, he looked at the monitor that tested the frequency of each piece being produced. It was his job to make sure the frequency stayed within a specific range. Brenda McMullen was the young lady operating the machine. Since he was promoted, Richard made it his business to memorize names. It gave the impression he was taking his new position seriously. Besides, he wanted everyone to feel as though he was getting to know them personally. Brenda waited until he had finished writing on his clipboard before asking him if something was wrong. She was one of the more attentive women, and went beyond paying close attention to her work to actually being meticulous about it. It was the reason they kept her in that department, where paying close attention to frequency levels was vital to production. Richard told her he was there to pick up samples for testing and everything was looking good from what he could see. She smiled at him and told him everyone was happy he had been promoted. Richard thanked her, grab some samples, and made his way through the rest of the day.

Shortly after getting off work, he received a text message from Helen. She wanted to know if he was interested in having dinner together. Their relationship had become more than what Richard ever thought it would be. He could not recall how it happened but he knew he now had feelings for her. It went beyond just liking her. She had come into his life, entered his heart and reserved space there for herself. When he first met her, he had no problems telling her no. Now, it was a struggle. In a way, caring about her made him feel lost. Aside from his mother he had never cared about any other woman before. Being lost and not having control troubled him deeply. At times he would get angry at himself. It would usually happen when he found himself thinking about Helen too much. He would get angry because his lack of understanding, created confusion. He could not understand how he had lost control over his emotions. It had happened to him, and he hated it. It did not bother him that he cared for Helen, it was the fact he allowed himself to be manipulated which got to him. He could not allow her to reserve too much space because if that happened, he would not be able to do anything but think about her. He would start by declining her invitation to dinner.

When Richard got home, he took a quick shower and threw the leftover pizza from the night before in the microwave. He thought about giving his mother a call, but changed his mind. Ever since he mentioned Helen to his mother, it had become difficult to get her off the phone whenever they talked. She could not express the level of excitement she had for him. She also shared with him how she thought he was gay. It was amazing how the thought of him seeing a woman had changed his mother. She was suddenly more interested in having him come over. More than anything she wanted to meet Helen and Mason. She even offered to foot the bill if she could take them all out to lunch, or dinner. His mother wanted to know everything there was to know about Helen. How old she was, where was she from, how many kids she had, what was her nationality, how far she had gone in school, if she had ever been married before, Richard could barely get her off the phone when he called her after he'd told her about Helen. The last time they talked she apologized for thinking he was gay, but said she did not know

140

what to think after he had never shown any interest in women.

The rest of the week went by without Richard giving in to any of Helen's invites. He promised himself he would be more careful not to lose more himself to her. Although she was genuine and sincere with him, he was afraid of falling in love. To Richard, falling in love meant losing control, and control was something he did not want to lose. He felt his phone vibrate in his pocket. He waited until he made it through the checkout counter at the store before pulling his cell phone out of his pocket. It was a missed call from Helen. He pressed the call button and waited for her to answer.

"Hey, you got a minute?" Helen asked, answering the phone.

"Sure, what's going on?" Richard asked.

"I want to know why you've been avoiding me?" Helen asked.

"I'm not avoiding you; I've been busy taking care of some things I have been neglecting," Richard said.

"For some reason, my heart is telling me that isn't true Richard," Helen said.

"I need to concentrate more on me. I feel like I'm losing myself to you. I'm not comfortable with that, it makes me feel weak, please try to understand this," Richard said, finally being honest with her.

"Are you saying caring about one another is a sign of weakness?" Helen asked.

"For me Helen, yes, it is. I've always been in control of myself, my feelings, and my life. Being in a relationship with you is taking me places I am not familiar with. I don't know what to expect from these emotions because I don't

have any experience dealing with them. I need some time away from us. I don't know how to make you understand this," Richard said, as his voice began trembling.

"If falling in love with me causes you to feel weak because you're losing control of your feelings, then I'm telling you it's okay. I want you in my life Richard, and if you let go and let your heart guide you, I promise you I'll be everything you need. But if you let fear push you away from me, you'll never know what it's like to love, and be loved," Beverly said.

"I want to be friends, but it's really hard to do that. I've never been in a relationship before, so I don't know where the line between friendships and relationships are drawn. The last thing I wanted to do was to lead you on, you are so different, you're a very special person to me. When I'm with you I enjoy our time together but I feel so lost, I just don't know what to do when we're together. I think it's best for me if I stop right now," Richard said.

"I think it's very selfish of you to only think of yourself. It's not only me who was falling in love with you, but it's Mason as well. You are all he talks about. It's too late for me to roll up my feelings like some rug lying on the floor, so I'll have to deal with this the best I can, but not Mason. I hope you'll give more consideration to him than you are to us. He deserves that Richard. If you're not sure about us, It's the only thing I ask of you right now," Helen said almost pleading.

"Helen, I'm not saying I don't want to spend any more time with you, I'm saying this is all new to me. I need to slow down a bit in order to understand what's happening to me. This has nothing to do with Mason. I enjoy my time

with him. I will continue to watch him whenever you need me to, as well as spend time with him like I normally do. None of this is going to change, please try and understand what I'm saying to you," Richard said.

When Richard ended the call he was more confused than he had been before talking with Helen. He was not only lost, but his heart was heavy. The last thing he wanted to do was hurt Helen, from what he could tell, he had done just that. Thinking about it didn't make him feel any better. In his mind, he had gone about it the best way he knew how. He hoped he had made it clear he didn't want to stop seeing her. He needed to slow down because of their friendship, or relationship, he wasn't sure which one they had, was going too fast. He had no experience with love but he understood a little about affection. From what he could make of it, he did possess that for her. He wasn't sure of his own feelings. He didn't desire her sexually but he had acquired an emotional bond with her. He wasn't sure if he would ever be able to have an intimate relationship with Helen. It was something he knew she desired. Regardless of how much time they spent together, thinking about her that way, rarely crossed his mind.

Helen sat on the couch thinking about the conversation she'd just had with Richard. She had never met anyone as complicated as Richard was. She couldn't figure him out for the life of her. Being afraid of getting in a relationship was one thing, but being terrified of one's own feelings was something she couldn't comprehend. From the moment she met Richard she knew he was different. However, she saw something in him that she wanted. Being that he was single and didn't have any children she threw caution to the wind. She took herself, and her feelings, out on the limb. In the past, it was something she had promised herself never to do again. Now she had feelings for someone who was doing more pushing than pulling. She couldn't remember a time they had spent together that they both didn't enjoy. Although they had never been intimate, holding hands and kisses upon the cheek, to her, meant it was something to look forward to. Maybe Richard did need more time. It was hard to believe he could be a 52-year-old virgin. In this day and time, there were no 52-year-old male virgins. Although possible, it was something she had a difficult time believing.

She decided she would be patient. She would take it slow and let Richard have as much time as he needed. However, she would let her son Mason grow on him, because he and Mason had a very strong relationship. Maybe in time, he would desire to have a son of his own. Besides, Mason loved spending time with him. She remembered Richard telling her he had mentioned her to his mother. She wished she had some way of meeting her. Helen was sure Richard's mother could help her understand the things she was having problems interpreting. Maybe that was something she could look into without him knowing about it. She would have to find out a little bit more about his mother. The more she thought about it, the more she needed to know why was he offended by his own feelings. She believed with the help of his mother she might be able to get him to accept what he was feeling about her. In her own heart, she knew she was falling in love with Richard.

Richard turned onto Delaware Avenue. Nearly 3 months had passed since he and Helen had their talk. At first, their relationship was a little strained. After a little while, Helen had told him she understood and would respect his wishes. Although they had slowed down on seeing one another quite a bit, since their talk they'd gone out on several occasions. Visiting the New York State Museum, and Jennings Landing. They had even taken Mason to

Huck Finns Playland, and went to the Palace Theater a couple of times. Richard was fine with it because Helen had come to accept him saying no when he wasn't up to going. However, he was now turning onto Morton Avenue from Delaware heading to Lincoln Park. He promised Helen he would meet her there in order to pick up Mason. She had managed to get on the schedule for some overtime. They had agreed to spend an hour or so in the park together before she had to go in for work. They planned on walking around the park for a little while before finding someplace to sit and talk, while Mason ran about the park as usual. It was turning out to be a good day so the walk would do him some good.

After spending time together, He and Mason walked Helen to her car and seen her off. To Richard's surprise, Mason had kept their secret about him having a pet in his basement. However, as soon as they were alone, like they were now, he would immediately begin asking Richard questions. Although Richard was heading home with Mason in the backseat, Mason hadn't been to his house since they'd purchased the snake and lizards from Repticon. Being that Helen usually picked up overtime during the evening shift Richard had been watching Mason at their house. That way, when he did fall asleep, he would do so in his own bed. Today was different, not only was it the weekend but Helen had managed to get some overtime on the early shift. Mason had started with the questions as soon as they hit the road. Richard told him to wait until they got home because he wanted to concentrate on driving.

Sure enough, as soon as they got into the house Mason ran to the basement door, grabbed the doorknob, and asked Richard to take him downstairs. Instead of telling him no, Richard asked him did he want to see the snake they had bought at the reptile show. Mason released the doorknob and said yes, showing very little interest. Richard decided to make Mason eat before allowing him to play with the snake. After he had Mason seated at the table he went to the refrigerator and took out baloney, cheese, and mayonnaise. He reached on top of the refrigerator and got the half a loaf of wheat bread that was there. After making the sandwiches he sat at the table with Mason. He always enjoyed the time they spent together. Mason was his best friend. He was able to keep secrets, didn't lie, and was someone he could trust. Although he was young, he was very intelligent for his age. Being that he could keep a secret Richard was comfortable with telling him things. He didn't have any hidden agendas so there were no worries about him being deceitful.

It was for those exact reasons Richard decided to be honest with Mason and told him the pet he had in the basement had died. He asked Richard why did it die. He told him he wasn't sure why it had died. He said he had given it everything it needed. It had water, shelter, and food. He said if he had to guess he believed it died from loneliness. He told him when he first got it, it wouldn't eat its food. It was only after he had gone into the basement three days in a row and held it, it had started eating a little. After a while, it stopped eating again and started losing weight. He had done everything in his power to try and get it to start eating again, but nothing worked. He said he had cuddled it and even tried giving it something different to eat. He told Mason he had cried when he went into the basement, looked into the window of the bunker, and realized it was dead. He told him how much he had gone through just to be able to keep it in the basement without anyone knowing. How much money he had spent building the bunker, and how long it took him to get it.

After he had finished telling him what had happened, Mason wanted to know if he was sad. He also wanted to know where Richard had buried it so they could have a funeral for it. He told Mason he was more angry than sad because he believed he could have found a way to make it eat. He also told him he had cremated it so he didn't have to worry about giving it a funeral. He went on to say the next time around he would make sure he got two of them. That way, it wouldn't be by itself and lonely. Mason reminded him that he never told him what kind of pet it was. The only thing he had ever said was that it was exotic. He asked Richard again what kind of pet it was. Richard smiled at him, and said if I tell you it's going to spoil all the fun. He told Mason he wanted it to be a surprise. He reminded him that grown men can keep secrets, so it's what he planned on doing in order to give him something to look forward to. He told him if he promised to be patient, he would let him see them as soon as he got'em. Mason smiled back at him and told him he could do that.

Richard sat in the break room looking at the calendar on his phone. He had exactly 8 more days before the beginning of his vacation. It was something he had been looking forward to ever since he had lost his pet. His vacation was all planned out. He knew exactly what he would be doing with his time. Ten days would be enough to accomplish what he wanted to get done. He had already reserved the van from U-Haul. He would be able to pick it up the day his vacation began. Unfortunately, he would have to drive all the way to Virginia. Given the date of the event and the time he had, it would be his first choice in finding what he was looking for. Three days after that there would be another opportunity in Ohio. Then it would be Pennsylvania and Connecticut. Richard hoped he would not have to drive to each state. He wished he could be fortunate enough to get one at the first exhibit, then turn around and get lucky enough to get another one at the next show. If it happened that way, he would be able to save quite a bit of time and money.

There were always so many cobwebs. It was as if the spiders in his mother's attic had photographic memories. Every year, the same spider webs over the same boxes. He took the broom and brushed away the webs from the boxes containing the Christmas decorations. Bringing the Christmas decorations down from the attic on Thanksgiving Day was just as important as the turkey that sat in the oven downstairs. Some of the ornaments in the boxes were older than Richard himself. Passed down from his grandmother to his mother, and perhaps from his grandmother's mother. He made it his business to handle the boxes with care because he wouldn't hear the last of it if anything were to break. Richard had been carrying these boxes down from the attic for decades. He was an only child and his mother had not been with anyone else since his father vanished into thin air. Helping his mother prepare for Christmas after Thanksgiving was a part of the holiday spirit they shared each year. As he made his way down the stairs the memory of doing the same thing last year made him feel as though it had only been a few months back. The older he got, the quicker the years seem to go by. The speed of which was now approaching what felt like months.

Richard couldn't understand it, although it was just him and his mother, for some reason each Thanksgiving, she always cooked enough to feed at least ten people. In the past, on a few occasions, she had invited a couple of neighbors over to eat with them. One had been his mother's best friend, named Mary. She lived on the same street, four houses down, and had eaten with them for the last two years. After her husband died, her daughters came from Arizona packed her up, and took her with them. He could tell by his mother's voice when she had called him and told him about it, she was heartbroken. Today, it would be just the two of them celebrating Thanksgiving together. Although having guess was fine, according to his mother, Richard was always more comfortable when it was only him and his mother. The food was always delicious. She always cooked the turkey until the meat was falling off the bones. Thanksgiving was one of the few occasions Richard got a chance to eat till his heart's content. When there were no guests he could eat until he was stuffed, then lay down on the couch and watch TV until he was able to eat some more. It was something he always looked forward to when Thanksgiving rolled around.

He finished bringing the last of the Christmas ornaments down from the attic in time to see his mother putting the last dish on the table. On his way over Richard realized this Thanksgiving was going be different. Not so much as not having any guest, or his mother cooking something different, but the talk they would be having over dinner. He knew it would be centered around his relationship with Helen. He figured the only way to go about the conversation was to be honest with his mother. He had decided this in spite of knowing his mother had a knack for asking very uncomfortable questions. It wouldn't be anything he wasn't used to. Hell, he had grown up with her being his mother his entire life. After they were seated, his mother gave grace, and Richard attacked the turkey.

"I can remember when you were just a little boy, all you cared about was that darn turkey leg. Did your best to get at it every single year," Richard mother said, as she watched him tear the leg off of the turkey.

"I guess some things don't change. When you like something, you're fond of it. Now when you love something, that's a whole another story. You just can't keep your hands

off it," Richard said looking at his mother and smiling.

"Well, I would have to say you love turkey legs. Make sure you save room to fit some of everything on this table inside that stomach of yours. I even made your favorite dessert," His mother said.

"Don't tell me you made banana pudding. If you made banana putting I'm going to get up from this table and hug and kiss you to death," Richard said clearly excited by the fact she had made it.

"I can remember the look on your face last year when I told you I hadn't made it. I don't think you were too happy about it. You didn't say anything, but when you asked me if I had made it, and I said no, I could tell it was something you were looking forward to," His mother said while watching him stuff his mouth full of food.

"No guests this year? I was thinking you were going to invite a neighbor or two. Did you decide otherwise?" Richard asked between swallowing his food and filling his mouth up again.

"Everyone's either got family visiting from out of town, or headed out of town themselves. The ones that are left, are the ones I prefer not to have in my home, sitting around my table eating my food. You should've invited your girlfriend and son over, I believe that would've made it a Thanksgiving to be thankful for," Richard mother said scooping a spoonful of stuffing out of the bowl in the middle of the table.

"To be honest with you mom, I like it better when it's just the two of us. There's nobody competing for attention, no one's walking on eggshells, and no acceptance contest going on. I get to be who I am with who knows me.

It's the only time of year I get to turn into one big pig, and still be loved," Richard said.

"So how is everything going between you two. It's been several months since you mentioned her to me. Are you still seeing her? You said you two had been going out to dinner and to the movies together. I think you even told me you babysat her son a couple of times, didn't you? You two must have really gotten close to each other if she's allowing you to watch her son. You must really like her a lot, do you?" His mother asked, looking at him as though she could see right through him.

"Helen's a very genuine person. She's much different than all the other women at the plant. I can actually be comfortable whenever we're together. She has a nine-year-old son name, Mason. I've watched him several times for her, usually when she's picking up over-time. She moved here from Michigan a little over four years ago. All of her family, as well as Mason's father, are in Michigan. I like her a lot, but I'm not sure about what we have. I think it's more of a friendship than a relationship, but Helen gives me the impression it's a relationship. It's just too confusing for me," Richard said looking at his mother as though he was lost.

"Is there any kissing and smooching stuff going on? Do you hold hands and go walking in the park? Do you talk on the phone with each other every day, maybe stay up late night talking sometimes? Is there something in her eyes that make you want to keep looking. Do you hug or peck after your night together? Do you think about her often when you're not together? Do you feel bad if you think you've done something wrong to her? Do you feel better when

you're around her then you do when you're all alone? These are the questions you need to ask yourself in order to figure out if your heart's in a relationship, while your mind is in a friendship," Richard's mother said while pouring gravy over the stuffing she had on her plate.

"There's a few yeses, and a few no's, if I ask myself those questions. However, I'm not looking for a relationship right now. I don't think I could ever be a part of the flowers candy and marriage thing. I don't want my life to become complicated. I've always been alone, I think I'm better at being that. I can already tell by the way I like her, falling in love's means losing control of your feelings. I don't want anyone in control of my feelings," Richard said.

"Well, God made Adam and Eve, not Adam and Steve. I think that means a man needs to have a good woman in order to make his life complete. Being afraid of sharing your feelings with a good woman doesn't make a whole bunch of sense to me. What's even more confusing is what the heck are you so afraid of?" Richard's mother asked looking up from her plate and into his eyes.

"Mom, I think I'm old enough to know what I want. What I and Helen have right now is good enough for me. I don't need to let her drag me into her bed to make my life complete. Besides, she already has a son, and that's almost more than she can handle right now. So, can we just let it go for now and enjoy the rest of our Thanksgiving together?" Richard asked returning his mother's look.

"Well, if that's how you feel about it, then there's nothing I can say that'll make you see any difference. But you got to remember, I'm not going to always be around to cook your Thanksgiving dinner. So, you better at least

consider her application as your future Thanksgiving cook," Richard mother said, smiling in order to remove the detention from their conversation.

"I never thought about it like that. You make a really good point. I don't think she'd be able to make a turkey leg like yours. You might have to give her some lessons in order to keep the turkey leg tradition alive," Richard said throwing in his own sense of humor.

"So, Helen's her first name, what's her last name?" Richard's mother asked.

"Helen... Helen McAllister," Richard said.

Chapter 13
Broken Promises

Daniel Finally broke the news to Beverly while lying in bed watching TV. He decided to discuss it with her before talking with David about it. Although he considered it equally important to both of them, her being promoted and David having the starting quarterback position, to Daniel it was more significant for him to first share it with Beverly. At first, she thought he was joking, just something he was saying to her to find out where her feelings about him were at. After he convinced her he was serious she laid in bed speechless for several minutes. She told him she could not just up and leave her job after investing so much of her time to get where she was. Daniel climbed out of bed got on his knees and begged her, she finally said she would think about it, and see what Heather had to say about the whole idea. It was a good enough answer for Daniel considering the fact that it was not a flat-out no. He was happy to know she was at least willing to entertain the idea. He didn't want to leave her, but in his mind, he had already decided he would go with or without her. He ended the conversation by telling Beverly he had exactly one week to give them his answer before they would offer the position to someone else.

David 's reaction was completely different than that of Beverly's. He told Daniel flat out he wouldn't go and he couldn't make him. At first, Daniel didn't know how to take what David had told him. He was lost in terms of what he should do. However, after discussing it with Beverly she reminded him he was the parent and David was the child. It was their conversation that brought him back around. Although it had been two days since David has stopped talking to him he stopped him on the way out to school and told him he would not tolerate what he was doing and he would have to go rather he wanted to or not. David stopped to hear what his father had to say, looked at him without saying anything and abruptly left after hearing what he had to say. Daniel knew it was going to be like pulling teeth getting David on board with relocating, but he would do whatever he had to do in order to make it work.

Two days later Daniel took Beverly, David, and Heather out for dinner. He decided to treat them to one of the most expensive restaurants downtown. In spite of where they were, David was still holding onto his anger. Daniel did not let David's anger dictate the mood, or discourage him. The expensive restaurant and dinner were a prelude to the kind of life they could have if they all agreed and got on board with him taking the position with VyCal Technologies. He waited until everyone was served dessert before he reached into his pocket pulled out a three-carat diamond ring, got on his knees, and proposed to Beverly.

"Beverly, I've been thinking about this long and hard. I've asked myself over a thousand times if I love you and could I be happy with you in my life until God calls one of us home. There hasn't been one time the answer ever changed. It has always been yes, yes and yes! I would like to know if you feel the same way about me, and if you do, will you marry me and allow me to take care of you?" Daniel asked looking up from on his knees into Beverly's deep blue eyes.

"Oh my god Daniel, I..., I Don't know what to say," Beverly said looking down at him.

"I want you to say what your heart is telling you," Daniel said looking up at her.

"Daniel, I love you, and I want to say yes, but I'm

155

so confused right now," Beverly said with tears running down her cheeks.

"If you can trust your heart, and allow me to be the man I want to be for you I promise you I'll take care of you, and Heather," Daniel said pleading with every ounce of emotion he had.

Heather and David both were blown away by what was taking place in front of them. Heather was sitting in her seat stiffer than a mannequin on display in a store window. If it wasn't for her breathing, she could have easily passed for one. Her eyes were as big as silver dollars with both hands over her mouth as though she was trying to muffling a scream. David, on the other hand, sat looking at his father propose with his lips closed so tight it forced the blood out of them causing it to appear as though there was a white ring around the outside of his mouth. It was the same with his fist, they were squeezed so tight white rings appeared around the outside of his knuckles. He couldn't believe his father had the nerve to propose to Beverly before he shared it with him. They had always talked about everything before either one of them made a decision. David believed his father had left him out of this decision because he didn't want to accept the new job his father had told him about. In his heart, he hoped Beverly would say no.

"My heart is telling me, yes, but I don't know if that's the right answer," Beverly said trembling.

"Just say yes, and let me do the rest", Daniel said taking her hand and kissing it.

"Daniel I've never been married before, and I don't want it to change us," Beverly said.

"I promise you we'll be the same people we were even after we're married," Daniel said with a smile on his

face.

"If that's true, then yes, I'll marry you," Beverly said placing her free hand on Daniel's cheek.

"You've just made me the happiest man in all the galaxy," Daniel said getting up from his knees and kissing Beverly gently on the lips.

Six months later they were married and had moved to Atlanta Georgia. David had fought with him all the way, using resentment and disapproval for both the marriage and the relocation. At first, Daniel had tried to be sympathetic towards him having to give up his starting quarterback position, but David seemed to be immune to any feelings he offered. After enough failed attempts Daniel decided to step back and allowed time to do what he couldn't. Finally, after meeting several friends at his new school, and making the football team, David was back to being himself. Heather was completely different. She was excited about both, moving to Atlanta and her mom getting married. It was her energy, that helped to motivate Beverly.

Inside of VyCal Technologies, Daniel had become a rising star. His ability to analyze information was amazing. His talent came from long hours of work on the job, and at home. He had turned one of their bedrooms into his office and used it for working late into the night and wee hours into the morning. Monday through Thursday he would normally get home in time for dinner. When he did, he would shower, eat, and spend an hour chatting with whoever was home before going into his office. In the beginning, he noticed Heather was always the last one to cut her lights out before going to bed. On a couple of occasions, he had gone into her bedroom and talked with her when he felt he needed a break. Over time, visiting Heather's bedroom late at night was something he started looking forward to. He liked the fact Heather never said anything to her mother about him visiting her late at night. At least Beverly had never said anything to him about it.

On a couple of occasions, Beverly had awakened from sleep and had come in to check on him. It caused him to feel some kind of way. The last thing he wanted was to get caught in Heather's bedroom. As a precaution, he made it his business to be sure it didn't happen again. After lying to his doctor about having problems falling asleep, he ended up with a prescription for sleeping pills. Unbeknownst to Beverly, he'd been dropping them in her drinks at night. If she complained about not being thirsty, he would encourage her to eat something. He would then crunch the pill up and put it in whatever she decided to eat. After slipping Beverly a pill, and before going into Heather's room, he had made it a habit to first go into their bedroom and attempt to wake Beverly just to be sure she was sound asleep. Several times, he had even gone so far as to slip some pills into both Heather's and David 's drink.

Daniel knew what he was doing was wrong, but had become capable of preventing himself from being controlled by the convictions of his morals and principles. It wasn't an easy process. The emotional turmoil was sometimes overwhelming. In the beginning, he wrestled with himself constantly. Submitting to his desires, then suffering the shameful feeling of guilt. It was a tug of war between right and wrong. A challenge in which good and bad pulled in opposite directions until bad dragged good, along with its virtues, over the line into the depths of immorality. Nevertheless, it was a conscious decision. One which caused him to reevaluate what he was taught. In the end, his heart and mind found an alternate reality, where truth and honesty gave way to deceit and lies. A place that allowed him to defy his own system of beliefs, shattering his chain of reasoning along with the teachings of society. A place to hide the monster in which he had now become. He desired the pleasures of sexual innocent. It caused him to yearn for the young and pure. It was this insatiable appetite which helped to free him from the chains of humanity, and being free of his feelings was the only way he could satisfy his appetite. The thought of being the very first always filled his loins with blood. Not only did it excite him, but it also caused him to become senseless and reckless. Like using his personal credit card to buy a teenage girl a 14-karat gold bracelet.

Although Daniel was now living in Atlanta Georgia he was still in possession of both of his cell phones. The one he used for his job and family, and the one he used to stay in touch with a few students back in Texas. The main one being Kimberly Jordan, the girl the investigators had questioned him about. He made it his business to keep in touch with her because the investigation was still lingering on, and Kimberly's mother was fixed on getting answers. Kimberly had made him promise that he would call her at least once a week. It wasn't a hard promise at all because he wanted to stay in touch with her anyway. Aside from being worried about someone finding out about the bracelet, his only worry concerned her falling for one of the younger boys in school. He often thought about going back to Texas just to see her. At times, the thought of it literally possessed him. It was usually after getting off the phone talking with her. She would tell him how much she missed him and wanted to be with him. However, lately, she had been questioning him about another girl who was secretly spreading gossip about being with him as well. When questioned about it, Daniel denied it every time she mentioned it. Nevertheless, he was always curious about the name of the girl spreading the gossip. The last time he had spoken with Kimberly she was furious. Apparently, the girl had said something that caused her to believe what she was saying was true. Daniel managed to calm her down by promising to fly her to Georgia to spend a day with him.

Before he knew it, the weeks started falling off the calendar like leaves from a tree during fall. Daniel continued to ascend inside VyCal Technologies like a rising star. His latest promotion had come as a result of his recent discovery. He'd been asked to run the numbers for the company's operational data in order to come up with a viable algorithm to save money. In the process, he had discovered 35 percent of the company's overhead was a direct result of operating on an outdated network. He suggested they migrate 85 percent of operations to the cloud in order to cut cost and save money. His suggestion resulted in a board meeting where he was able to show the savings that would result from such a migration. When the next quarter rolled around and the numbers supported his findings, he was offered the position of Assistant Chief Operating Officer. He gladly accepted the position, along with all the additional benefits that came with it. A big bonus, an increase in pay, and a personal expense account that included hotels, car rentals, and flight accommodations up to $10,000 annually.

Daniel's new position required him to have an intern under his tutelage at all times. It was something he took advantage of immediately. Shaving off some of his workload and passing out orders was a benefit he'd never had before. However, having authority over someone's career was a power he was unfamiliar with. Nevertheless, to his surprise, he was allowed to pick his own intern from the pool of those who had applied for internship. This was something that was right up Daniel's alley. Not because of the program but because of the age of those who chose to sign up for the program. The average age of interns who signed up for the program ranged between 18 to 21 years of age. They also offered a junior pre-enrolment program which allowed teenagers between the ages of 15 and 17 to get hands-on experience before actually deciding to enroll. This was the program Daniel was most interested in. Within six months of being in his new position, he had already gone through two of the pre-enroll students before ending up with a 15-year-old by the name of Hazel Wadsworth, along with his 18-year-old intern Patricia Scott.

He was extremely fond of Hazel Wadsworth. She had come from a broken home and ended up in the program from a lottery that involved less fortunate students. Daniel took full advantage of this and began secretly buying her perfumes and underwear. He even went so far as buying her several items of clothing for school. When she informed him that her mother was curious as to her being able to buy clothing, he told her to tell her mother he was paying her for doing work outside of the program. He told her to have her mother contact him if she needed to confirm it. When Hazel had come into work one day looking sad Daniel immediately pulled her to the side and questioned her as to what was going on. She told him her mother was trying to take her and her siblings to the State Fair in Marietta, but couldn't get the money to do so. As a result of it, they wouldn't be going to the fair this year. Daniel got up out of his chair closed his office door and sat back down pulling his chair directly in front of hers. He told her if she gave him a kiss and promised to wear a smile for the rest of the day, he would make sure they never missed a state fair again. The following week Hazel came into Daniel's office with a little figurine she'd won from the fair and told him it was something she wanted to give him for his desk.

His relationship with Patricia, his 18-year-old intern, was

suspicious at the least. Since taking her on, he'd began doing more late-night work at the office. Having Patricia stay late with him was raising a lot of eyebrows and becoming questionable. Not that anyone said anything, but it was the late-night office work with such a young female intern that seemed different. It just so happened Daniel was the only employee who would stay behind late at night to do work at the office with his intern. In the beginning, it didn't raise any red flags. Everyone in the company, and at home knew he was an extremely dedicated worker, oftentimes crunching out numbers and algorithms in the wee hours of the morning. However, it wasn't until Patricia became his intern he began staying late hours at the office. Before she became his intern, all of his late-night work occurred in his office at home. Now, he'd stay late at work at least two days out of the week. Added to this was the fact she had accompanied him on an overnight trip to one of the district offices.

Daniel finally peeled himself up from between the sheets and slowly made his way into the kitchen where Beverly sat at the table with her head down cuffed between her hands. It was Sunday, the only day he resigned himself to spending all of his time with his family. Most Sundays his son David was either at a football game or football practice. This Sunday was no different. After pouring himself a cup of coffee he sat at the table next to Beverly.

"Good morning honey, is something wrong?"
Daniel said reaching out with his hand and brushing some of her hair from her face.
"It's Heather. I don't know what's gotten into her. She's changed so much since we moved here. At first, she loved the house, her school, and being in Georgia. Now,

she hates everything. I can't understand it. She says it's all my fault and won't even talk to me," Beverly said lifting up her head and looking at Daniel through hazy eyes.

"You know there's quite a bit going on in her life right now. Between relocating, being a teenager, making adjustments to a new school, and new state, it's quite a bit if you think about it," Daniel said with a voice of reassurance.

"I could see if we had just moved here, say five or six months ago and she had just gotten into school and was new to everything, but we're talking nearly a year later. And it's not only her, I think I'm going through some kind of depression as well. I mean I'm sleeping all night long and I'm still waking up feeling groggy like I didn't sleep at all. I don't mean to be superstitious or nothing, but something just isn't right," Beverly said with confusion written all over her face.

"I can't see having a good night sleep as a form of depression," Daniel said, picking up his cup of coffee from the table and taking a sip.

"I don't think you're paying attention to what I'm saying here. Something is going on! Heather is acting out, and it's showing up in her grades as well. Ever since I can remember she has always maintained an excellent GPA in school. Now she's literally failing in math, barely getting by in English, and having problems in gym class," Beverly said exhaling a deep breath of disgust.

"Sometimes kids succumb to pressure, or maybe even boyfriend problems. Who knows what she could be going through at this particular point in her life? I mean if she won't talk to you how is there any way to find out,"

Daniel said reaching his hand out and taking her hand into his.

"If you think that's bad, what do you think about her asking me to put a lock on her door? It's like she wants to lock everyone out, It feels like she's punishing me for everything. I'm hoping she's not considering running away at this point. I don't know how much more of this I can take," Beverly said, in a voice laced with surrender.

Although Daniel was talking with Beverly about Heather's unexplained behavior, his mind was busy contemplating what he had already concluded about the situation. He would have to stop sneaking into her room and pumping Beverly full of sleeping pills. However, she had never said anything to Beverly about him going into her room since he first started visiting her. To his recollection, he had been in there quite a few times. He tried to ease his conscience by considering the fact he had always either given her money or bought her something each time he had been with her. The more he thought about it the more he realized he really didn't have to stop. It was only when he thought about how she avoided being around him that caused him to feel as though he needed to do something.

At the moment, Beverly wasn't aware of anything. However, he did have a few close calls that terrified him. He wasn't sure of it, but he was afraid David had heard sounds coming from Heather's room when he was in there with her. He had made up some silly questions, to test David, just to see if he had heard anything during the nights in question. Even now, thinking about it, put a thin coat of fear over his heart. He made up his mind that tonight would be the night he'd straightened everything out with Heather. Being that Beverly was already feeling depressed he would encourage her to take a couple pills to help with her mood, David had already asked for permission to stay at a sleep-over, so he would spend a little extra time in Heather's room tonight in order to help snap her out of what she was doing.

"Maybe I can try talking with her, or encourage David to give it a shot. He seems to be making pretty good grades, and friends, so I can't see it hurting anything if he tries as well," Daniel said.

"I'm open to anything at this point, I just wish it was some way I could understand what's going on with her. I'm just so lost right now. I don't even have any of her friend's phone numbers. What kind of mother doesn't have any of her daughter's friends phone numbers?" Beverly said looking at Daniel for some kind of answer.

"Well, I've been putting in so many hours at work I haven't really been paying attention myself when I know I should have been. I really apologize for that. If you believe some form of counseling or therapy is in order then you know you don't have to worry about the cost. My medical package covers everything you think you and Heather may need," Daniel said encouraging her by sliding his chair next to hers.

Daniel pulled into the short-term parking at Atlanta International Airport. He was there to pick up Kimberly Jordan, the student from Texas High. This was his fourth time flying her there. He'd been flying her back and forth since he first promised her nearly six months ago. He had worked out a system for getting her to Atlanta without running into any snags. Especially with the age restrictions, and her flying alone. He'd purchase her ticket online and paid the additional fees for flying an unaccompanied minor whenever it was an issue. The age limit was different according to what airline he chose. Lately, he and Kimberly had been arguing about the other girl at her school who'd been secretly telling stories about him and her having an affair when he was working at the school. Every time she confronted him about it, he would stick to his story saying nothing ever happening between him and the imaginary girl with no name.

On their last visit, he found out the real reason why she was furious over the rumor. It wasn't because of what the girl was saying, it was because the girl was Black. She told him the girl name was Shante Westbrook and she couldn't believe he would have sex with a black girl. When she mentioned the name, it sent chills through him. He remembered Shante very well. He had to grab hold of everything inside of him just to keep his composure, but the sound of that name rolling off Kimberly's tongue caused him to swallow so hard it forced air into his stomach. She had been so enraged he wasn't sure what she would do if she ever found out the truth about them. Deep down inside he hoped their visit together this time would not include the gossip of his past affairs.

Daniel made it his business to calculate everything as though he was dealing with math problems. This included how he went about renting their hotels, and getting Kimberly into the rooms without being noticed. He would make sure the hotels were big enough that no one paid any attention to what was going on. He would leave Kimberly sitting in the car in the parking lot while he checked in. After getting into the room he would call her and tell her what elevator to take and what room he was in. She would then walk right into the hotel get on the elevator and come directly to the room without ever being noticed. They would usually stay in the room from the time they arrived until the time they left. If they decided to leave and go somewhere, they would do their best to play the father-daughter role so no one caught on to them.

Chapter 14
Another Way

Michael decided not to tell his mother the good news until he had completed his enrollment at the community college. As soon as he got the news, he'd qualified for funding, he decided it was time to tell her. Since he'd stopped smoking marijuana, and started going to church with his mother and sisters, his life meant a lot more to him. He knew he needed to have a heart-to-heart conversation with his mother. In the past, he had never felt responsible enough to engage in a conversation like that with her, but now, his heart was dictating he do. He felt it was the right thing to do. Besides, he really wanted to know what she thought about what he was making of himself. He wanted to tell her about Renee being pregnant, about him getting his GED and enrolling in college, and how he planned on getting his Mechanical Engineering Degree. He was sure, she would be happy hearing about all of this. When Michael got home his mother was sitting on the couch folding clothes from a basket, and his two sisters were in the kitchen practicing their cooking skills.

Michael dropped the duffel bag he carried his books in at the front door, said hi to his mother, then walked over and kissed her on the cheek.

"You home a little early today ain't you?" His mother asked putting a perfectly folded T-shirt onto the pile of clothing sitting next to her.

"Yeah, I'm picking up a shift tomorrow after church," Michael answered.

"Do you remember Mr. Jenkins?" His mother asked.

"Over on 21ˢᵗ St.?" Michael asked.

"Yeah, on 21st St.," His mother said.

"Yeah, I remember him. Why, what's going on with him?" Michael asked.

"Well, he needs somebody to mow his lawn for him. Since his son moved to Alabama with his girlfriend, he's been needing a little help around the house. He told me to ask you if you'd be interested in making a few dollars, I told him you in school, and working," His mother said.

"Well," Michael began as he slid the three piles of neatly folded clothing to the center of the couch, so that he could sit on the far end, *"It depends on when he needs it done. If he could wait until Tuesday, I could get over there and do it."*

"I'll call him later today and see what he says," His mother said.

"Ma, I want you to know I'm sorry for everything I put you through. Dropping out of school and hanging with the wrong crowd. Acting as though I didn't care about anything. Using drugs and stealing from people. Stressing you out and causing you shame. Living here without contributing to the house. Everything I was doing, that I wasn't supposed to be doing. I want you to know that I apologize," Michael said looking over at his mother.

"Honey, we all make mistakes. It ain't a soul alive that hasn't stumbled and fell at some point and time in they life. But it' only after we realize we making a mistake that the choice to change comes. Some folks, happen to fall in love with doing wrong, and can't seem to picture themselves doing what's right. They are the hopeless few, but God did not intend for it to be that way. That's why we feel bad when we do what we know is wrong. I just thank

my Lord up above that he was able to see you through, because I never lost faith in seeing you turn into a good strong faithful young man," His mother said with conviction in her voice.

"Well, I want you to know how I feel. I also want you to know I finally got my G.E.D. and I start college in two weeks. I plan on staying in school until I get my Mechanical Engineering Degree," Michael said.

"Oh my God!" Michael mother said putting her hands over her mouth, *"You graduated, and you enrolled in college. When did all of this happen? I'm so happy, I don't know what to do. I need to bake you a cake or something don't I? Oh Lord, this is some really good news."*

"Ma, you don't need to do anything. You've done everything already. I just want you to know I love you very much, and I thank you for putting up with me for this long. Michael said with a very heavy heart.

"I love you too son, I'm so proud of you. I knew once you got from around bad company you was gonna to find yourself. Did you say you plan on becoming an engineer? And you already finish the GED program?" His mother asked with surprise still holding its grip on her expression.

"Yeah, I finish with my G.E.D. almost 3 weeks ago. I enrolled in the Community College right after that, but that's not it. My girlfriend is pregnant. You never met her but I know you gonna love her once you do," Michael said as he continued looking at his mother.

"Pregnant! Did you say your girlfriends pregnant? Lord have mercy son, you came with a bag of surprises today didn't you? What's her name and how old is she?"

170

His mother asked.

"Well Ma, this is where the problem comes in at. Her name is Renee and she's 16 years old. It wasn't something we planned, it just happened the first time we got together. I mean we've been seeing each other for over two years, but the first time we got together. You know what I mean. Now she's scared and don't know what to do. I don't know what to tell her because I don't know what to do either. I want her to have the baby, but she's saying her father will go crazy if he finds out. I want to know what you think?" Michael said, asking a question without actually asking it.

"Did you say she was 16 years old Michael? Son, that's kind of young for you, don't you think? If I was her daddy, I would go crazy too. What about her mother, did she say anything about her mother? Do her parents know how old you are?" His mother asked as her expression changed from surprised to disbelief.

"Right now, they don't know anything. They don't even know she's pregnant. That's why I'm talking to you, because neither one of us know what to do," Michael said.

"Son, this is a very complicated situation you dealing with. The girl's age is what I'm concerned about, not to mention her being afraid of how her father is going to act. Thank goodness tomorrow is Sunday because we need God more than anything right now. How far along is she, do she know when she got pregnant?" His mother asked.

Michael heard the question, but had pulled his cell phone out of his pocket and was looking at the text message he had just gotten. It was from James. He was texting him saying it was an emergency and he needed Michael to contact him immediately. He apologized to his mother for reading his messages while she was talking, but told her he needed to make a call and that they could finish talking later. She shook her head up and down, told him to make sure, and went back to folding laundry. He got up off the couch and went into his bedroom to call James.

James answered the phone and immediately asked Michael could he stay overnight. In all the time they'd been friends James had only stayed overnight two times. His mother had never pictured James as bad company because every time he had come around, he showed real good manners. Nevertheless, his mother was not friendly with the idea of any of his friends staying overnight. Michael asked him why he needed to stay overnight. James told him he believed the dudes he shot at had gotten his address. He said he went outside to empty the trash and noticed a car with four dudes in it parked across the street from his house. He said he had gone through the alley on the side of his house, all the way around the block and came out on the other side of the car. He said he was able to look inside the car. He told Michael even though the windows were lightly tinted he was sure he saw what looked like the barrel of a rifle. It was not only that, but they had been out there now for over two and a half hours.

Michael didn't want to see anything happen to his friends, especially not James. However, it wouldn't be as simple as just asking his mom could he stay overnight. It would have to be something significant, maybe even a little white lie. He told James he might be able to get his mom to allow him to stay overnight if James agreed to go to church with them in the morning. When he agreed to go, Michael put him on hold for a few minutes while he asked his mother. He came back and told James it was cool, he had lied and said he lost his keys, and his parents wouldn't be back until tomorrow morning. He told James to wear something presentable for church because he had also told his mother he was going to services with them in the morning. James must've thanked him at least 10 times before telling him he'd be over there in about an hour and a half. Michael forgot to ask him how did he think they got his address, but would be sure to ask him once he got there.

The next morning Michael's mother made breakfast for everyone before they headed out to church. James picked over his food and ate very little. Michael knew it was because his fear was causing him not to eat. His mother had allowed him to sleep on the couch, but every time Michael went out to check on him, he was wide awake. He told Michael he had no idea how they could have gotten his address. He asked James what made him think they were waiting for him, he asked Michael why would four guys in a car with tinted windows sit in front of his house for over two hours. He said he had heard through the grapevine one of the guys who were out there the day he did the shooting had died. He didn't know how true it was but it was what he had been hearing. Michael said it was funny because he hadn't heard anything like that, but James quickly reminded him that he no longer came around, and stopped talking to everyone, so he didn't have any idea what was going on. James told him he had been thinking about what he said about getting his G.E.D. He said he had called the number Michael had given him to see how to go about getting in the program. He promised that if he walked away from everything without going to jail, he planned on going back to school and doing exactly what Michael was doing.

Just like every Sunday, the music coming from inside Living Waters Baptist Church could be heard from the parking lot.

Once inside, one of the ushers escorted them to a row of seats that was completely empty. The choir was singing one of Michael's favorite songs, so instead of sitting down he continued standing and began clapping his hands in sync with everyone else. James sat there looking around but paying more attention to Michael than anyone else. He had never seen his homeboy act like this before. The funny thing about it was he looked like he was enjoying himself. He couldn't believe it as he scanned the church and noticed quite a few teenagers in there around his age. Most of them were doing the same thing Michael was doing, standing up clapping and singing. He couldn't understand how kids his age could get something out of being in church. He had to be missing something. Surprisingly, the music started sounding good to him. Michael's mother, who was standing and clapping as well, looked over at him and made him feel as though he should get up and do the same.

Michael sat down next to him after standing for a few songs, he told him today the preacher was going to spit fire. He said for him, it was the best part of the service. He told James sometimes he felt as though the preacher was talking directly to him. When he did deliver his sermon, sure enough, some of the things he said did ring true with James. When services ended, members congregated outside the church gossiping and talking about the message the preacher had given. Michael and James made their way through the small crowd, and onto the sidewalk in front of the church. James thanked Michael for looking out for him and said he was about to make his way home. Michael told him his mother would give him a ride home if he chilled until she finished doing her socializing. James said he was good, and that they had done enough for him already. Michael asked him was he sure, he said absolutely, stretching out his right hand so he and Michael could slap-five before departing. Make sure you tell your mother I said thanks, James told him before turning to walk across the street.

As Michael watched his friend walk away, he felt bad thinking about James situation. He wondered if they hadn't robbed that house, and James hadn't bought a gun, would things be any different. He found it hard to picture him having killed someone. He hoped in his heart it wasn't true. He reached in his pocket and pulled out his cell phone. He was hoping to spend some time with Renée today. The sound of someone letting off firecrackers startled him, causing his body to jerk, and his cell phone to go flying out of his hand. When he looked around to see who had set them off, he noticed people running towards the church from across the street. He heard tires squealing and watched as a blue car with tinted windows sped up the Street. It suddenly started making sense to him when the deafening screams coming from some of the women sliced through the confusion. After the car made a quick turn onto one of the side streets and disappeared, Michael looked in the direction in which everyone had run.

Lying on the ground was his friend James. Michael ran across the street and dropped down on his knees. He slid one hand under his neck and put his other hand on James' shoulder. He gently lifted his friend head off the pavement to try and hear what he was saying. He leaned in closer and put his ear next to James' mouth, that's when he noticed all the blood. James entire shirt was saturated with it. As he looked closer, he could see blood spilling out onto the pavement all around him. He kept trying to say something but Michael could not make out what he was saying. It seemed to be more mumbling than anything. Michael told him to wait that the ambulance was on its way. He began rocking his friend back and forth to try and comfort him. For some reason it felt like what was happening, wasn't real. It was like being wide awake inside of a dream, suddenly he could make out what James was saying. As he put his ear closer to his mouth to be sure he was hearing what he was saying, he heard his friend James say, *"I want my mama, I want my mama, I want my mama."* He kept saying it over and over. Then Michael heard what sounded like a deep exhale, and nothing else after that. When he lifted his head up and looked into James' eyes, it was obvious, he was gone.

Michael spent nearly the rest of the evening at the Police Department. He was questioned intensely about his relationship with James. They told Michael James' mother had no idea where he had gone. The same Detective, McCoy who had interviewed him and James previously was the same detective who questioned Michael. He wanted to know why James had asked to stay the night and decided to attend church with Michael and his mother for the first time. He told Michael it appeared as though James was avoiding someone. He let Michael know what puzzled him the most was how they knew he was at that church. He wanted Michael to explain that to him. When Detective McCoy left the room to get them some water, Michael thought about that same question, and was just as puzzled. How did they know James was at the church with him and his family? After Detective McCoy came back into the room Michael was honest with him and told him he had no idea how they could've known that. When Detective McCoy insinuated he was the only one who could've tipped them off, Michael was done with the interview. He simply told Detective McCoy James was his best friend and he would never have set him up for someone to kill him.

The shooting made the front page of the newspaper. The storyline was, *"Teen gets killed leaving church."* The Police Department and most of the local news stations were all over the story. It was used as an example to show just how bad gang wars had gotten. They went on to say the very place we hold to be the most sacred is no longer safe anymore. The Police Chief himself took it as an opportunity to gain face time by vowing to personally hold the individuals who did the shooting responsible. He went on to say if we can't be safe in our churches, then there's nothing much left to our communities. Michael had made the mistake of talking to one of the news crew while being recorded. Before he knew it, he was on the news inside of one of their storylines about the shooting. He couldn't recall giving them permission to air his picture on the news, but decided it was too late to do anything about it, and regretted ever talking with them.

Watching his friend die in his arms had affected Michael in ways he never thought possible. The first thing it affected was his sleep. He couldn't seem to get the picture of James's face out of his mind at night. It made him toss and turn for most of the night, and caused him to lose his enthusiasm in the very things he had just gained interest in. School, work and even church lost their significance to him. It had even affected his relationship with Renée. Although she was pregnant, he didn't seem to care if she called him or text him anymore. He had a persistent feeling of sadness that affected his behavior, appetite, energy level, and concentration. His mother told him he was suffering from depression and that she was going to look into getting him into some type of counseling.

Renée called Michael the day his picture was aired on the news. Their conversations had been very dry lately. In the beginning, she acted as though she couldn't understand why James would be going to church with him, or staying the night for that matter. After a serious argument between them, her heart prevailed, she had broken down and cried over what had happened. It helped

Michael to reattach to her because he was beginning to distance himself from her. She had called him to tell him her father, who is a City Councilman, watched the news clip featuring him and had commented on it calling Michael a typical thug. She said she had told her father he was stereotyping the guy on the news and it was wrong for him to do that. She asked Michael what type of chance would they have of her father accepting him as her boyfriend if the first picture he saw of him was someone on the news involved in a deadly shooting. She told Michael her father had gotten angry with her for defending someone who was involved in a shooting outside of a church. He had told her she was having some kind of issue with her morals and that he advised her to somehow straighten them out. Michael ended the conversation with her by telling her he didn't have time to listen to what her father thought about him without knowing him.

The day they put James in the ground was the saddest day of his life. A part of Michael was buried in the ground with him that day. Being a pallbearer didn't seem to help. It felt as though he was carrying the weight of the world. He did everything in his power not to cry but his tears flowed from the well within his heart. He watched as James mother cried out from somewhere deep in her soul. In between her sobs, she would scream No! No! No! then go back to crying. The only other funeral Michael had ever attended was his grandmother's. It had not been as sad as James. In old age, death was more welcomed by everyone. There was a tendency for people to look at it as a homecoming. When the person was young it was more of a tragedy than anything else. Acceptance came harder than the pain that walked alongside it. Denial was always sweeter in the beginning, it allowed one to push back the threat of reality until the bitter taste of acceptance could be tolerated. Michael held onto both the memory of James's face and his denial as though he was clinging onto a life raft.

Michael's mother convinced him to attend the Grief Counseling she had somehow arranged for him. At first, he didn't see himself as being depressed or suffering as a result of watching his friend die. However, after a couple of sessions with the therapist, he began to grasp an understanding as to what he was going through. She helped him to realize everyone experiences and expresses grief in personally unique ways. Those ways are shaped by family background, culture, life experiences, personal values, and intrinsic beliefs. He was taught it was not uncommon for people to withdraw from friends and family feeling helpless and sometimes angry. It was hard for him to believe it but he was taught some laugh while others experience strong regret or guilt. In the end, tears or the lack of crying can both be seen as appropriate expressions of grief. She helped Michael to embrace the belief everyone who grieves benefits from the support of others. Being able to make sense of the grieving process helped him more than anything. He was happy his mother had found such a nice counselor.

Michael finally saved up enough money to get his license and buy himself a car. It was what he needed to help boost his spirits. He began doing things and going places he hadn't been able to go, or do. He started taking Renée for long rides whenever their schedules allowed them to have several hours together. One day he had taken her to Fort Lauderdale Beach just so they could walk up and down the beach line bare feet kicking waves. They had driven down to Miami and walked around town admiring how beautiful it was. He had taken her to a couple of wrestling matches and sat so close to the ring until they were splashed with sweat from the wrestlers slapping each other. He even convinced her to go with him to a UFC fight, and after it was over, promised to never take her again because it was too gruesome for her. She was not the blood and guts type. Lately, they had been going bowling quite often. Renée was really good at it. She said her family bowled a lot and her father had taught her how to use the arrows on the lane when releasing the ball. Michael didn't like how Renée beat him, so he was bent on one day winning all of their games. That was another reason they had been bowling a lot lately. Michael had slowly pulled himself out of depression and his grades were reflecting it. He now had a 3.7 GPA. He was doing so good in his biology class he had been asked by a couple of students to consider getting together for a group study. They told him they thought it was awesome how he was able to quickly grasp most of the information the teacher was giving them. They offered to pay for the food at Panera Bread if he agreed to meet with them one night after class in order to go over some of the stuff that was going to be on the test. Not only was he doing great in school but he had also picked up a better paying job. He was now making double-digit wages working for an independent mailing company. He was responsible for digitalizing zip codes that would later be sprayed on the bottom of each piece of mail. The job was very easy and paid well. It involved nothing more than loading thousands of letters onto a machine that wisp them past a camera. The camera then took pictures of the addresses on the envelopes and looked them up within its database. When the addresses were located the envelopes would be reloaded into the machine and sent through a printer that put the address on the bottom of the envelope in the form of a digital barcode, all while traveling at unbelievable speeds.

In his spare time, Michael would volunteer his services to a few homeless shelters between Riviera and West Palm Beach. He started out unloading trucks and helping to prepare meals. Fortunately, most of the meals at the homeless shelter came cryovac. They arrived in vacuum sealed bags that only needed to be cut open and heated up. Some days he would help with laundry or other miscellaneous tasks that needed to be done. At the Riviera Beach facility, he was allowed to do intakes. Because of this, he had gotten to know quite a few of the residents there. After realizing that all of the shelters were networked, he was able to go into the database of each shelter and find out if each one was at its maximum capacity each night. After seeing there were always beds available between the three shelters he came up with an idea. He figured he could be of greater service if he started a street search program for the homeless. If he coordinated with whoever was doing intakes, he could ride around neighborhoods looking for the homeless. The person doing intakes would be able to tell him how many beds were available whenever he was out searching.

Chapter 15

The Other Side

Richard locked his front door, walked over to the U-Haul Cargo Van he'd rented and threw his duffel bag on the passenger seat. He climbed in, turned on the ignition, and put the address into the garmin he'd recently purchased. After it announced calculating route, he placed it into its' holder suctioned to the windshield. Eight hours and twelve minutes it would take for him to drive from Albany New York to Richmond Virginia. He had gotten a full night's sleep and was sure he would be able to make the drive straight through, minus a couple stops to use the restroom. The Navi had him calculated to arrive at 3:20 PM. After calculating a couple of stops, he figured it would be more around 4 o'clock when he actually got there. He had timed everything perfect. The event he was headed to was starting today and would last for two days, Saturday and Sunday. He really did not want to stay until Sunday. He was hoping he would be fortunate enough to get what he was going for today so he could turn right back around and come straight home. He avoided thinking about not being able to get what he was going for, especially after driving the entire way there. At this point it didn't matter how long he had to drive, he was willing to spend his entire vacation going from state to state if he had to. He closed the door, put the van in gear, and drove off.

Helen found it difficult to accept the fact he hadn't planned on spending any of his vacation time with her and Mason. She was crushed when he told her he would most likely be out of the state for the entire 10 days of his vacation. He couldn't figure out why, but it made him feel terrible inside after he had told her. The more he thought about it the more he realized she had really grown on him. He was no longer able to deny he cared about her. If everything went according to his plans, he would spend some of his vacation with her and Mason. When he got back he would surprise her by offering to come over and spend some time with her. He would even take his mother's advice and see if she wanted to have him over for dinner. That way, he would get a chance to see if her cooking was anywhere near what his mother was capable of making. It would also give Mason a chance to show off his room. He had practically begged him to come over just to see it.

Richard took Interstate 87 South to the New Jersey Turnpike. The highway was so congested he found himself becoming angry over the way everyone else was driving. The traffic was constantly slowing down, and he was having problems changing lanes when he needed to. He was happy when he finally made his way onto Interstate 95 South. After nearly 4 hours of driving, he stopped at a Love's gas station outside of Fieldboro New Jersey. After stretching his legs, using the restroom and grabbing a sandwich, he jumped back on the highway. Before long he was entering Maryland. Driving through Maryland was another part of the trip he dreaded. He could never get used to the Capital Beltway. The highway system had an Inner Loop in the Outer Loop. It didn't matter which one you were on, both of them were confusing. He used the 495 Express Lanes and paid the tolls in order to try and avoid some of it. After making his way back onto Interstate 95 South he pulled into Richmond Virginia two hours and 41 minutes later. In spite of all the traffic and senseless drivers, he managed to make it there in a little over nine hours.

He hadn't planned on getting a motel but he knew it would be almost impossible to drive back without getting any rest. He used his phone to Google information on hotels in the area. After making several calls he located one that had a room available. After checking in he got his key and made his way to the room. He didn't want to waste any of his time sitting in a hotel so he pulled up the address to Meadow Event Park, the place he would be going. After putting his duffel bag on the bed, he unzipped it and carefully went through its contents. He removed his wallet from his back pocket, pulled out the cash and counted it. He didn't plan on spending too much money so he took half of what he had and put it in the inside zipper of his duffel bag. After removing a few items from his bag, Richard changed clothing and left. He was sure the place would be packed with people, these types of events always were. He was actually hoping it would be. He enjoyed blending into crowds where no one was paying attention to him. It made him feel invisible. Not like at work, where everyone knew him and paid attention to the things he did.

Sure enough, the parking lot was at capacity. He found a patch of grass large enough to accommodate the van and parked. Some of the venues were too crowded for him to squeeze into. His enthusiasm motivated him enough to power him through the mass of people. He would not be denied what he had driven over nine hours to get. He pushed through the crowd of adults and was careful because kids were everywhere. He finally made his way over to the next exhibit and stopped to assess his options. He had come to the right place. In the 45 minutes since he'd gotten there, he had at least two opportunities to get what he had come for. He decided to be a little patient because it was still quite early. His prospects were looking good, the longer he stayed and visited the different exhibits, the more likely he would be able to get exactly what he wanted. Two hours and fifteen minutes after getting there Richard had gotten what he had come for and was now driving back to the hotel. The adrenaline coursing through his veins, and the excitement, caused him to grab his things from the hotel and head straight back to New York.

After getting back home Richard waited two days before

hitting the road and heading to Ohio. He wasn't as fortunate as he had been in Virginia. Instead of driving back to New York he stayed there sightseeing until leaving for Connecticut. Helen had convinced him to take pictures and share them with her via text messages. He had driven around to some of the landmarks and had taken pictures just for her. It had actually helped not to make the wait feel as long as it would have, if he hadn't anything to do. Fortunately, he didn't have to drive any further than Connecticut. On his second day there he ended up getting another pet and heading back home. He was happy all the driving was finally over. Once he got home, he would spend the next few days playing with his pets, and making the bunker comfortable for them. He had invested quite a bit of money and labor bringing everything together, it was time for him to enjoy it. He thought about Mason and wondered if he would ever be able to allow him play with them. So far, Mason had been able to keep a secret. That was a good thing.

It was after 1:30 in the morning when Richard finally made it home. He ended up sleeping until after nine. After eating a couple of pieces of toast and drinking some coffee he decided to feed his pets. The first one he picked up from Virginia hadn't eaten anything since he had gotten it. It was the same thing with the very first one he had. It didn't eat until it had been down there for nearly 5 days. He believed it had something to do with the stress and the change of environment. He opened the door to the bunker and took in enough food for both of them. He was happy to see that they were next to each other. It was a good sign. It made him believe they would be good company for each other. He had learned from the last time to keep the light on during the day. When it was off for too long it bothered them. From what he could see he believed one wasn't too much older

185

than the other. If he ever took them out to play, he wouldn't have to worry about one having more energy than the other. He stayed down there for quite a while trying to coax them into eating. When it failed, he locked up and left the basement. After three more days of trying, he was finally able to get them to start eating.

Before returning to work Richard ended up spending some of his vacation time with Helen and Mason. Helen told him the vacation must have done him some good because he seemed much happier. He agreed with her and told her it was the Thanksgiving dinner his mother cooked for him, and the vacation. She asked him what all his mother had cooked and Richard did his best to remember everything she had prepared. He asked Helen what she ended up doing for Thanksgiving and she told him, she and Mason were invited over to a couple of friend's houses for dinner. She told him they took advantage of it and got a chance to eat two different Thanksgiving dinners. She said Mason had gotten so full until he didn't want to see any more for close to two days. Richard ended up letting Helen have him over for dinner twice. To his surprise, she was a really good cook. His mother had always told him you could tell the quality of a woman by how good her cooking was. If that was true, Helen was definitely in the top 10. Both nights he went over for dinner, after they were done, all three of them ended up watching a movie. Mason always sat in the middle, it was where he loved sitting.

Helen knew Richard's feelings were growing for her. She also knew there was something causing him to hold back what he felt for her. She didn't want to go on playing cat and mouse for the next year or two, when intimacy was right there waiting for the door to open. She had to figure out what was stopping him from giving in to her. At 52 years old she couldn't believe he didn't have any experience with women. Maybe if he had lived his entire life in a monastery it wouldn't be so hard to believe. However, it didn't seem possible living in an open society where everyone was doing God knows what that he would be short of experience. She considered getting his mother's approval. Richard had given her his mother's name and address when she had told him she wanted to send her a card for Thanksgiving. Helen believed if she met his mother and talked with her, she would probably find out a little bit more about Richard and have a better chance of winning him over. Besides, there was nothing like a mother's approval to push things in the right direction. It was a good thing she had sent his mother the Thanksgiving card, she could simply say she was stopping by to make sure she had received her card. She would have to be sure to ask his mother not to say anything to him about her stopping by unexpectedly.

Christmas and New Year's had come and gone, and both of Richard's pets were still alive. For the last three weeks, he had been bringing Mason over on Saturday evenings to spend time together. It was done more so to keep him quiet than anything else. A result of him promising to let Mason see his new pets. Mason had a memory like an elephant, he would not let Richard forget that back in October he had promised him to let him see his new pets after telling him his first one had died. Although he hadn't kept his promise, he was sure Mason could keep a secret. He decided today would be the day. He wouldn't allow him to play with them yet, but he would at least let him see them. Helen had called him and said she would be dropping him off around two o'clock. It would give Richard enough time to go downstairs, tidy up the bunker, and feed them. He wanted Mason to understand having pets involved caring for them by keeping their area clean and making sure they had enough food. It was the reason they still had the Asian Vine Snake they had bought from the Expo.

Something that Mason had lost interest in. He told Richard he was hoping it got bigger, so they could start feeding it rats instead of little lizards all the time.

After taking care of what he had to in the basement and vacuuming the living room Richard heard the sound of a horn coming from his driveway. It was a little after 1:30 pm so he couldn't imagine it being Helen. He went to the window and pushed the curtains aside to see who it was. To his surprise it was Helen. The back door on the driver side was open and he could see Mason's little legs dangling from under the bottom of the door. Richard hurried up and went outside to meet them. Since he and Helen had started seeing each other and going out on dates she had never been inside his house. She had asked to come in on several occasions but he had told her he would invite her in after he did a little fixing up. She told him she really didn't care what it looked like inside she just wanted to see the layout. After getting her to accept him being embarrassed about her seeing it she agreed to give him enough time to do whatever he needed to do in order to let her come and visit. She said it wasn't fair that Mason was the only one allowed inside. Richard agreed with her and promised to use his extra time to get his house in order.

After getting inside and settling in, Richard asked Mason if he was ready to see his pets. Mason said yes, jumped up from the couch and threw both of his arms up in the air over his head. It made Richard feel good seeing how excited Mason got over the idea of going into the basement with him. Depending on how he acted Richard might even allow him into the room to play with them. Without Richard saying anything about secrets, Mason told him he would not tell anyone anything. This was all the more reason why he felt comfortable about letting Mason see what he had. It made Richard feel good knowing he had someone who he could trust. Although he was only nine years old, Mason had become the friend Richard never had. Richard got up from the couch, stood in front of Mason and kneeled down. He told him when they got down there, he would have to be calm so he wouldn't scare them. He told Mason it had taken him an awful long time to get them to start eating and calming down so the last thing he wanted to do was to stress them out all over again.

Richard went into the basement, found the string and pulled it turning on the light before allowing Mason to come down. He didn't want him falling down the steep stairs that led down there. The window on the cast iron door of the bunker was five feet up from the basement floor. Richard had to grab the chair and put it up to the door in order for Mason to be able to look into the room and see what was behind the door. After putting the chair in place, he lifted Mason up until his feet found the seat of the chair. He waited until he had his face pressed to the glass of the window before he flicked on the switch that turned on the light inside of the bunker. As Richard held Mason steady, he could feel his little chest swell as he sucked air into his lungs from the excitement of what he was seeing. Mason stared into the room for a long time without saying a word. After what felt like an eternity, he finally turned his head from the window, looked at Richard, and asked how did he get them. Richard told him he had to drive to three different states to get them. Mason asked him had he given them names, Richard told him no, he hadn't given them any names yet. He asked could he go in and play with them because he knew they would like him. Richard told him the next time he comes over he would let him go in with him to feed them.

The last several weeks at work had been different. He knew something was going on but he didn't know what. However, today he was about to find out exactly what it was. He had been told by

Ronald Snyder, the one who had given him the position, he wanted to see him at 10:00 am. His gut told him this time around it wouldn't be another promotion he wanted to see him about. When Richard finally made it up to his office he was told his performance as a quality inspector would have to improve, and that there had been a grievance written against him. Apparently, since he had been given his position there had been a spike in defects being returned, and the grievant claimed he was guilty of preferential treatment. It was alleged he never took any samples from Helen McAllister, who the grievant claimed was his girlfriend. Her production was allowed to pass without inspection. He was told the probationary period for that department was six months. Mr. Snider informed him it would be in his best interest to treat everyone equally in regards to testing production. He also advised him to become more familiar with the specs for each Department because QA work was a detailed -oriented position. He finished by saying the grievance would go through its normal channels so at the moment he didn't have much to say about it.

When Richard left Ronald Snyder's office, he felt deflated. Like someone had taken a straw and sucked all the life out of him. If he hadn't been on pins and needles while sitting in front of him, he would have found the courage to ask who had written the grievance. However, he had frozen and had only been able to listen. Nevertheless, he was sure he had been doing his job. He'd been meticulous when it came down to testing every part he took into the lab. There was no way imaginable the spike in defective parts was his fault. There had to be someone else responsible for it. Maybe there was someone who wasn't happy about him being a quality assurance inspector. As for the claim regarding him treating Helen differently, someone had definitely lied on him. He figured the best thing for him to do would be to return back to being the old Richard.

He rationalized with himself over his association with Helen. He still was not able to figure out if they had a friendship or a relationship. Personally, it didn't matter what they had, in his heart he felt as though he had made the wrong decision. He had long ago come to the conclusion she was causing him to lose control over his feelings and emotions. Now, he was on the verge of losing his job over her. He knew, in the beginning, he should not have allowed himself to open up to her. In no time at all, she had gotten close to him, and he had opened the door to both her and Mason. A doorway that allowed her in, and his feelings out. Richard felt his association with Helen was taking a toll on his life. It was something that would have to come to an end. However, severing the ties between himself and Helen meant cutting off his relationship with Mason as well. It was the thought of doing this which caused his heart to feel heavy. Nevertheless, it would be a weight he would have to bear.

After a week and a half of avoiding Helen by not answering her calls or returning her text messages, she approached him at work. It was obvious she was upset about him avoiding her and Mason and demanded he take lunch with her. Richard quickly agreed to meet with her because he didn't want her making a scene. It was bad enough someone had already written a grievance about him giving her preferential treatment. During lunch, Helen questioned him about why he had stopped answering her calls and texting her. She told him she doesn't know what to tell Mason when he asks her why he doesn't care about him anymore. Richard put his head down while listening to Helen express her feelings to him. It was difficult for him to listen to her and not engage his own feelings. He couldn't deny he had feelings for her and Mason. When she finished, Richard explained to her someone had written a grievance stating he treated her better than everyone else. He told her they were not happy with his job performance and that he was skating on thin ice.

Helen told him sometimes people get jealous and most often people will go to great lengths to inflict their jealousy upon you. She tried to convince him it was someone who was acting out of jealousy. However, she informed him she had met his mother and that they actually liked each other. She said they had enjoyed each other so much they ended up having coffee together on several occasions. Richard could not believe what he was hearing. How in the hell could she do such a thing without so much as mentioning a single word to him about it? For that matter, why hadn't his mother mentioned anything to him? There was no way she could have met his mother without him knowing about it. He figured it was just something she was using to get him back into her nest. Richard studied Helen's expression for a moment before saying a word. When he did speak, he tried explaining to her how he had let his feelings get away from him. It had not been his intention to open up to her and Mason in a way that caused him to feel vulnerable. He said he had thought about it deeply and came to the conclusion that it was best for him to step away from his feelings. He told her he understood about Mason and how he was an innocent bystander who was being affected by their decisions. He promised to spend a little bit more time with Mason in an attempt to explain to him what was going on.

Richard couldn't help but consider if, in fact, Helen had met his mother. There was no way for her to get in contact with his mother because she didn't know anything about her. Then he realized before the holidays Helen had asked him for his mother's address because she wanted to send her a Thanksgiving card. With that thought in mind, he realized she could have very well gone over to his mother's house and met with her. If she had done so, it would be all the more reason for him to sever his ties with her. To Richard, that was equivalent to going behind his back and doing something sneaky. If it was true, it would be all the more reason to be done with her, because she was proving to be untrustworthy. He would be sure to call his mother and asked her about it as soon as he got home.

Chapter 16
Ocean Deep

Daniel was not surprised that Kimberly was wearing the same attitude she had on the last time they had visited with each other. Not just her attitude, but the way she treated him as well. However, this time around she was colder and more distant than she was before. In so many words she told him she didn't think she would be coming back to see him again. She didn't come right out and say it, she just shaped her words in ways that implied it. Although he asked her what she was trying to say to him, he knew exactly what she was saying, and inside felt a sense of relief about her not wanting to come back. Personally, he was tired of hearing about the gossip going on at her school. He had moved on from it when he left Texas, but every time she came to visit him, she would bring Texas back with her. During the entire visit together, she would not stop going on about how much she believed the rumor, and how she could not be with any guy who had slept with a black girl. She said she just couldn't understand how people could date other races. She finished their visit together by telling him she refused to be with him because she believed he had been with the Black Girl Shante.

Three weeks later Daniel found himself pulling back into the same parking garage at Atlanta International Airport. This time around he was in search of a spot in the long-term parking. He and three of his coworkers had been ordained to attend a national convention on behalf of VyCal Technologies. It would be Daniel's second convention since being hired. After attending his first one he looked forward to any future offers that came his way. Besides processing a bunch of information over a period of two days, it was nothing short of a trip back in time to his college fraternity days. Unlike fraternity parties, his trips to the conventions was an all-expense paid trip. A trip in which he was allowed to take along his 18-year-old intern, Patricia Scott. Had he known this the first time around, he would have brought her with him then.

The flight from Atlanta Georgia to Orlando Florida international airport was so quick it felt as though they had been teleported there in a time machine. After gathering their luggage from the conveyors, they ended up waiting over an hour to pick up the rental car. Patricia was fascinated with the Disney themes that appeared all along the highway as they made their way to the hotel. All the lights, signs, and glowing rides made the night surrender to the feelings of great eagerness and excitement. Added to these attractions was the overwhelming traffic. Four to five lanes of congested highway with people going to Disney, coming in to attend the convention, to work, and God knows where. Daniel would easily agree that it had to be one of the most popular, if not the most popular tourist attraction in the world. It was definitely more than what the eyes could consume, so he had to be extra careful to pay attention to his driving and the road, not what the lights demanded of him.

VyCal Technologies spared no cost when it came to their accommodations, they had been booked into the Hyatt Regency on International Drive. Besides being one of the most expensive hotels in the Orlando area, it was literally a stone throw away from Orange County Convention Center, the second largest convention center in the US. Daniel and Patricia decided to meet up at the pool after they both had unpacked and showered. Patricia had a million questions and Daniel was sure he had the answer to half of them. Besides, he wanted to locate his coworkers to see what the seating arrangement was going to be while attending the convention. To Daniel, it really didn't matter, he preferred the get-in where you fit-in type of meeting that didn't require any type of seating accommodation. Nevertheless, it was the appropriate thing to do. Aside from this, he was interested in who was going to be hosting the party. The last time he attended he ended up going to a party in one of the executive suites. It was something he could not forget, and something he wanted more of.

Daniel and Patricia sat at one of the tablets reserved by VyCal Technologies listening to the guy on stage give his power point presentation on data mining. He had Patricia taking notes. Every once and awhile the guy would take a question from the audience. Daniel had asked a question himself and found the information to be something very useful in terms of the type of work he was doing. He didn't need notes on everything that was being presented so he had quickly worked out a system with Patricia that worked for both of them. By the end of the day, she was tired of writing and he was tired of listening. It was a good thing he had given her the heads up about how much information they presented during the two days of the convention because he had prepared her well. Instead of being overwhelmed, she was simply tired.

While standing in the lobby during the meet and greet, Daniel bumped into a couple of guys who had gone to the first convention he attended at McCormick's Place, The Convention Center in Chicago Illinois. They informed him there would be a get-together later that night in one of the presidential suites on the 11th floor. Daniel asked was it an open-door party, or by invitation only. He was told anyone from the top five companies listed on the convention portfolio were welcome. It was something he was happy to hear because VyCal Technologies was listed as number three. He just needed to know which Presidential Suite the get-together was being held in. He asked did they know the number of the suite. The tallest one of the two said he wasn't supposed to say anything, but because he knew him from their last acquaintance and because VyCal Technologies was within the top five, the room number is going to be 1126, and the password was going to be Blue Dot. He went on to say, just like the last time, the word is their planning on having two gold rooms.

Daniel and Patricia met up by the pool again around seven o'clock, kicked back in a couple of beach recliners and began talking about the highlights of the day while sipping Long Island Tea. Patricia had overheard some of the conversation between Daniel and the guys at the meet and greet. She was interested in the get-together and wanted to know what a gold room was. Daniel laughed, and told her before the night was over, she might end up finding out. For now, it was just something guys say to make a party sound special. Patricia looked at him puzzled and took another sip of her Long Island Tea. She told Daniel she understands if it's an all guy party, and if he needed to go alone, she would be fine. Daniel sat there for a minute without saying a word, he was trying to remember how many women he had seen at the first convention party he had attended back in Chicago. He did remember seeing a few, but he wasn't sure if they were invited or had come with one of the guys. He knew what the gold room was, but he wasn't allowed in the first time around because he was a new face, so to speak. He figured it was only one way to find out, he would take Patricia with him, if they turned him around at the door he would leave and come back by himself.

When nine o'clock rolled around both Daniel and Patricia were a little tipsy from drinking. They made their way up to the 11th floor and was both allowed into the party. For some reason, there were a lot more men than women there. It was the first time Daniel had ever been in a Presidential Suite. After looking around he understood why it was called a Presidential Suite, everything in it was elegant, from the ceiling to the floor. It was huge, nothing short of a palace inside of a room. As Daniel stood there looking around and sipping from the drink he had taken from the tray being passed around, a medium build guy wearing a white short sleeve shirt and tan khaki pants, who appeared to be in his early 30s, walked up to him. He stretched his hand out offering Daniel a handshake and said it was always nice to see new faces. He asked Daniel about Patricia and if he was planning on taking her into the gold room with him. Daniel told him she was his intern and that they had come there together. The guy then reached into his pocket and told him it was always better when you gave them this, pulling out a small white pill and handing it to him. Daniel looked at the pill in the palm of his hand and noticed the letters ROCHE and the number 2 etched it. He lifted up his head from staring at the pill in time to see the guy making his way through the crowd and slowly disappearing between a bunch of shoulders and arms.

Daniel slid the pill into his front right pocket and started looking for Patricia. He noticed her standing in front of the sliding glass doors leading to the balcony talking with a couple of guys. She seemed to be enjoying herself and not uncomfortable being the minority. After talking to several people Daniel looked at his watch and realized they had been there over two hours. After surveying the room, it became obvious that quite a few people had left. He decided it was time for him to satisfy his curiosity about the gold room. He made his way towards the back of the suite and bumped into the guy who had given him the pill.

"I didn't think you were going to make it back here," The guy said.

"Oh, curiosity killed the cat," Daniel said smiling.

"Yes, and satisfaction brought it back," the guy said offering the same smile back.

"My name's Zach by the way," the guy said extending his hand out offering Daniel a handshake.

"I'm Daniel," He said accepting the handshake.

"Me and a couple of the fellows were hoping you'd spice the party up a little. We were hoping you would give your intern the little treat I gave you and bring her into one of the gold room; unless she's one of the those who like to play without it," The guy named Zach said with a smile that suddenly seemed to stretch from ear to ear.

"Wow, I have met a lot of interesting people here tonight, and my curiosity about this gold room has kept me here this long. However, this has got to be the most interesting moment of the night. I mean, I'm curious about both right now. The gold room, and what exactly do you mean when you say, one of the those who like to play without it" Daniel said looking inquisitive.

"I think it's time for you to see for yourself. After that, you'll have the answer to both your questions. There's two rooms down the hallway. Look into the first one, then look into the second one. When you come back it'll all be clear," Zach said pointing to a narrow hallway.

When Daniel returned from looking into the rooms, he appeared to have an eagerness in his step. He walked towards Zack, slowing down just enough to smile, and wink, then went about looking for Patricia. He found her sitting in the living room talking with a guy who looked to be in his mid-50s. He could tell she was even more tipsy than earlier because she appeared to be leaning even though she was sitting straight up. He pardoned himself for interrupting their conversation and had Patricia to walk with him over towards the corner of the room so they could talk in private. He asked her was she enjoying herself. She told him she was, but didn't think she should drink anymore because she was really feeling it. He told her if she really wanted to enjoy herself, they were invited into one of the gold rooms. She told him it sounded interesting, but couldn't understand how it could be any different than being out there with everyone else. He told her it was where the grown folks went to play. He said they had nose candy if she knew what he meant, and everyone was getting to know each other on a much more personal level. He told her there were a couple of ladies already in one of the rooms so she wouldn't be uncomfortable if she decided to go with him.

Patricia was immediately offended by what Daniel was saying to her. She told him she had not come to Orlando or the convention to have sex, or an orgy, with a bunch of guys she didn't even know. She said if that was something he was into, it was fine, but she had never done anything like that. She told him she did not want to be a part of it and said she thought it was time for her to leave. Daniel quickly apologized and said he didn't mean to offend her. He said he really admired her and he was just being open and honest with her. He asked her could she accept his apology. When she said she would, he asked her could they at least have another drink together before leaving. She smiled at him and said of course, as long as they didn't end up in one of those gold rooms. Daniel looked at her, returning her smile, and said, I promise. He took her by her hand and led her to an empty loveseat that was on the opposite side of the room. He told her to take a seat and he would do the honors by going to the bar and getting them both something to drink. She told him nothing too strong because she had pretty much had enough already. He gave her the thumbs-up and headed over to the bar.

Daniel went into the bathroom, pulled a crisp $50 bill out of his wallet, along with the pill he had been carrying in his front pocket. He folded the $50 bill in half, placed the pill in the middle of it, closed it up and began crushing it into powder. He made his way to the bar and ordered two Long Island Iced Teas. He poured the contents of the $50 bill in one of the iced teas, stirred it up with an ink pen from his front shirt pocket, and gave it to Patricia. It wasn't thirty minutes before Daniel and Zach were lifting Patricia from the love seat carrying her back into one of the rooms. Zach told Daniel that before the night was over, they would have to carry her to her room. Daniel looked at Zach, shook his head, and said it made perfect sense to him.

Four days after returning from the convention Patricia suddenly quit the intern program at VyCal Technologies. When Daniel inquired as to her reason for quitting, he was told she offered no reason other than not showing up for the program again. This had Daniel on pins and needles for over a month, because he knew what had happened, he didn't know what to expect regarding Patricia. However, several months passed without anything becoming of it, so he was finally able to relax and concentrate on his work again. Nevertheless, he did try and call Patricia a couple of times on his own, but each time his call went straight to voicemail without her ever returning his call or responding with a text. In the days following the party, and before she had quit the program, they had never had a single conversation about that night. She had never brought herself around to asking him what he remembered about that night.

Daniel came home one day to find Beverly sitting at the dining room table drinking a glass of wine. When his eyes met hers, it was immediately obvious she appeared to be angry about something. She waited until he kicked off his shoes, put his briefcase on the couch, and took off his jacket before she asked him to take a seat at the table with her.

"Why didn't you ever tell me about the investigation over allegations of a teacher-student affair back at the high school in Texas," Beverly said looking Daniel straight in the eyes.

"I really didn't think it was a big deal, considering it didn't involve me," Daniel said looking back at her.

"If that was true, a Detective Ryan from Texas would not be trying to reach you," Beverly said, looking down on a piece of paper she was holding that she had scribbled something on.

"That's strange in light of the fact both Detective Ryan and Matthew have my cell phone number," Daniel said.

"Well, apparently he tried to call you several times but was unable to reach you. He said he left you a voice message yesterday but hadn't heard anything back from you. I told him it wasn't like you, you usually answer your phone unless you are in a meeting, and even then, you were really good about checking your messages," Beverly said folding up the piece of paper she was holding in her hand.

"Did he say why he was calling me?" Daniel asked with curiosity all over his face.

"Of course, and asked if there was any other way of getting in touch with you. I gave him your work number, and he said he was going to try it. I just can't believe you never mentioned a word of it to me. I feel as though you were hiding this from me," Beverly said with the anger

holding fast to her expression.

"I assure you there's nothing to hide. I'm not the only teacher who the detectives spoke with, all the teachers were interviewed over those allegations. If I had to guess, I would say they were calling me to inform me that the story was probably made up, and the investigation was over," Daniel said getting up from the table and pushing in his chair.

"Don't you think they would've told me that, and had me to relay the message to you?" Beverly asked looking up at Daniel.

"Well, I'll try returning his call after I get out of the shower and unwind a bit," Daniel said, ending the conversation by walking out of the kitchen.

As Daniel walked away, he felt as though he was being carried by a force beyond himself. He could not determine if it was the result of all the thoughts running through his head, or the pull of his emotions toward his feelings. Whatever it was, it temporarily suspended reality. His thoughts prevented him from focusing on the present as soon as Beverly told him Detective Matthew had been trying to contact him. The more he thought about it, the more he realized it was the fear causing him to experience what he was feeling. He didn't know how he had done it, but while talking with Beverly, he had managed to hold himself together although confusion, panic, and uncertainty was colonizing his heart and mind. He couldn't understand why he had not gotten the message Detective Matthew said he had left him. He reached into his front pants pocket and pulled out his cell phone. He scrolled through his missed phone calls, and looked to see if he had any messages, there was nothing.

It suddenly dawned on him. He had given Detective Matthew the phone numbers to his other cell phone. The one he had not touched since Kimberly had visited. After she had gone back to Texas, he had decided he would avoid the drama for a little while by putting that phone up. She had left with an attitude, and he didn't want to hear any more about the rumors the girl Shante Westbrook was spreading around the high school back in Texas. He would have to get the phone from the trunk of his car and give Detective Matthew a call. It was something he dreaded thinking about but knew he had to do it. Beverly told him she had given Detective Matthew the phone number to his job, but apparently, he had not called. Being that it didn't appear an urgent matter, Daniel found a sense of relief when he thought about it.

Daniel pulled into the parking spot reserved for him by VyCal Technologies. Turned the ignition switch off and pressed the call button on the cell phone he was holding in his hand. He had been trying to reach Detective Matthew since leaving home. Once again, the call went to voicemail. This time around Daniel left a message, pressed the end call button, and put the phone on vibrate. He couldn't afford to be late today, there were three meetings scheduled and unfortunately, he had to attend each one. It was days like these he missed his intern, Patricia. She had been there to shuffle his papers around, take notes, and remind him of what he might be forgetting. For now, he was out of luck because the next round of interns was six weeks away. Junior interns were not allowed to take on the full workload of an intern, so Hazel, his 15-year-old junior intern was out of the question.

Chapter 17
Night and Day

Michael got the okay from both the Riviera Beach and the West Palm Beach homeless shelters and made it his business to do street searches at least once a week after school and work. This gave him a new sense of value. Helping the less fortunate had a way of making him feel good about himself. He actually looked forward to that one day of the week in which he did this. He had even gone so far as to take Renée out with him one time. It didn't work out well because she complained about how poor their hygiene was and said she couldn't take seeing people that way. None of that bothered Michael, he always got something out of anyone he could help. Like the one time he came across a homeless lady and her eight-month-old baby sleeping under a bridge. She had no food or money and was feeding the eight-month old sugar water from a baby bottle. She had taken a handful of sugar packets out of IHOP and was feeding her baby sugar water to stop her from crying. She told Michael everything her and the baby owned were in the two backpacks and a grocery cart that she pointed to next to them. He immediately went to the store bought some powdered formula and bottled water for the baby. Before it was over, he For some reasowas able to get them into the shelter that night. n, Michael began feeling as though he was being followed. He couldn't be sure of it but it had become a persistent feeling. He also noticed he was now seeing more and more police on the routes he normally took to work and to school. He knew he didn't have anything to worry about with the police because he had stop misbehaving a while back. He changed some of his routes to see if it made a difference in terms of feeling that way. He knew he wasn't going crazy or his mind playing tricks on him, he was sure of that. It was after James had been killed, he became aware of it. He couldn't imagine why someone would be following him, especially the police. He wondered if he was actually paranoid. He decided he wouldn't worry about it. If he was being followed, he would find out one way or the other.

One afternoon while riding through his old neighborhood looking for the homeless, he ran across Tony, one of his old homeboys. He was hanging out on the side of a corner store drinking beer. Michael pulled up to the curb, parked his car and got out. When Tony recognize it was Michael he lit up like a candle. It was obvious he was happy to see him. Michael was just as thrilled seeing him as well. It had been a long time since they had seen one another so a hug was definitely in order. He told Michael he heard he had gone back to school and was in college. He said a lot had changed since he had stopped hanging out with them. A couple of the homies were in jail, and Rick stopped hanging out after his girlfriend Alicia had the baby. He said everybody wanted to do something to Rick's sister for giving James up. Michael asked him what he meant by giving James up. He said the dudes James had shot at found out through the crackhead he rented the car from that it was him. He told him they had Rick's sister's boyfriend under pressure because they found out it was his car that got shot up at the seven eleven that night.

Michael could not believe what he was hearing. It was starting to make sense though. So how did she give James up, he asked Tony. He told him once they found out it was James, they threaten to do something to both Rick's sister and her boyfriend if they didn't help them get James. They said she had started texting James telling him she had somebody who wanted to spend a couple hundred dollars on some product. She even knew where James lived from the time when they dropped the car off to you and him at his house. We found this out because James texted

Steve and asked him did he know anything about the person Rick's sister was talking about. He told Steve she had somebody who was trying to spend a couple of hundred dollars with him but he was leery because she was acting desperate. That was the day before he was killed. Everybody figured she had to be texting him the whole time he was with you. As Michael listened to what was being told to him, the story of what actually happened crystallized in his mind.

As he replayed the events of that day in his mind, he clearly remembered seeing James texting while sitting in church with them. It also explained why he chose to walk home instead of taking a ride from his mother. He was probably under the impression they were going to meet him somewhere not far from the church. She had given them his address as well. It was the reason they had been sitting outside of his house waiting for him. It was a good thing for Michael she didn't know his address because she would've given them that as well. Tony said she had done it because they threatened to do something to her and her boyfriend if they didn't help them get James. Michael wondered how could she have done that, and how she must feel knowing she was responsible for James getting killed. Then again, she probably felt like it was better him than her or her boyfriend. It was so sad it made Michael felt as though he needed a drink. He told Tony it was nice seeing him again, gave him a hug, got in his car and left. Drinking was something he definitely wasn't going to be doing.

Michael decided to participate in the study group his classmates were having. Instead of meeting at Panera Bread he had convinced them in choosing a less expensive restaurant off A1A. It was his third time studying with them since he had been offered the opportunity. Being he had a test coming up at the end of the week he studied with them a little longer than he normally did. He got home around 8:25 pm. He was surprised that he hadn't heard anything from Renée throughout the evening. She would usually text him asking how was his day going, where was he or what was he doing. He had texted her earlier asking heard the same, but he hadn't heard anything from her. He wondered what was going on with her.

After talking with his mother and messing around with his sister he jumped in the shower and went to his room to study some more. While removing his books from his bag his phone rang. It was Renee. When he answered his phone the voice that came back through his speaker didn't sound like Renée. The person on the other end was hysterical. They were crying and calling his name at the same time. When he finally recognized the voice, it was Renee. She managed to calm herself down enough for him to understand what she was saying. She told him she had run away and wanted to come over. Michael looked over at the clock on his dresser, it was 10:15 pm. There was no way in the world his mother would let her stay overnight with him. It was out of the question. However, if he sneaked her up the back way, he would be able to get her in without anyone knowing. He asked her where was she, when she told him where she was, Michael slipped out the back door and into his car. When he got there, she had stopped crying, but the evidence of her tears was upon her face. She got in the car and closed the door without saying a word.

"You okay baby, what's going on, Why did you run away?" Michael asked, reaching over and putting his hand on her thigh.

"It's my father. He's trying to make me put the baby up for adoption. He says I'm too young to know what to do with a baby because I'm a baby myself. He's constantly

asking me for the name of the boy I got pregnant by. He says he needs to talk with his parents because he's not raising another child, especially no bastard child," Renée said as she started crying again.

"Did you tell him?" Michael asked.

"No, why would I do that," Renée answered.

"Well he won't be raising our baby, that's for sure. We don't have to worry about that. It sounds like he's angry, but that don't give him the right to tell us what to do with our baby? It's our baby Renée, not his," Michael said with a hint of anger in his voice.

"Yes Michael, but I think you keep forgetting I'm only 16. My age is something my father is constantly reminding me of. He told me he refuses to allow his daughter to make him look like some irresponsible father. He said getting pregnant at 16 does just that. There's nothing I can say to him he wants to hear," Renée said wiping the tears from her eyes with the back of her hand.

"What about your mother, what does she have to say about it. Have you talked to her at all?" Michael asked.

"My father runs everything in that house. Whatever he says goes. I don't think my mother has the nerves to stand up to him. It's always been that way," Renée said.

"Well, if your mom's not going to say anything, and he's not listening to anything you have to say, then maybe it's time for me to try and talk with him," Michael said, rubbing Renée thigh.

"Michael, you just don't seem to understand. My father will press charges on you. I'm 16 and your 19. I'm underage Michael and you could go to jail for us having sex. My father is a City Councilman and he's stuck on this

thing about his public image. I just want to get as far away from him as I can. I don't want to have to give my baby away," Renée said as she put her head down crying much harder than she had been.

Michael leaned across the seat and did his best to put both of his arms around her. He was lost. He didn't know what to say, or what to do. There had to be something that could be done to make everything better. He just didn't know what it was. For now, his hug would have to be the solution. He needed to provide some type of comfort and security against what she was dealing with.

> *"Renée, I promise you, you're not going to have to give the baby away. If you could just trust me I promise you I'll do everything in my power to make sure that doesn't happen,"* Michael said looking through the tears and into Renée's eyes.

> *"I don't want to give it away. I can feel it moving around and everything. It's mine and I want to keep it,"* Renée said looking back at Michael.

> *"Just stop crying, and let's work on figuring this out together,"* Michael said taking one of his hands and wiping the tears off her cheek.

The next morning Michael received a phone call from Detective McCoy. He wanted him to come back down to the precinct to answer a couple questions for him. Michael said he was willing to answer them over the phone, but McCoy insisted he come down instead. After finishing his shift at work, he headed to the precinct. He had told the detective what time his shift would be over with, so when he got there, Detective McCoy was waiting on him. Like before, he was escorted to one of the interview rooms at the back of the station.

"Thanks for coming down," Detective McCoy said once they were both seated.

"No problem," Michael said in response.

"What's going on is we need to make sense of why we have two dead teenagers in less than a month. Let me add to that by saying three shootings, and two dead. We need you to help us understand why this happened," Detective McCoy said looking up from a folder he had opened in front of him.

"I don't know why this happened. Like I told you before we were at that store with our girlfriends the night those guys shot at us. We had gone to see a movie and had two hotel rooms. It just so happened the girls got thirsty so we decided to take a ride to the store. When we got there, they were drinking hanging out in front of the store," Michael said looking at Detective McCoy.

"So, what's the problem with giving us the names of the two girls who were with you the night this happened. Is it because one of the girls might have been seeing one of those guys who were at the store? Maybe this all came about as a result of jealous rage. Is that why neither one of you guys wanted to give us the names of those girls?" Detective McCoy asked.

"If you look at the video, you'll see neither one of them knew any of those guys. There wasn't a single word pass between them. One of them said something to James's girlfriend that upset her. That's what you'll see. Apparently, they were just waiting for somebody who they could start

some shit with. We happen to come to the wrong place at the wrong time. That's what happened," Michael said.

"Okay, I got that part. What I don't have is how the same guys who shot at you that night ended up being a target of a drive-by which leaves one dead. Then less than two weeks later your best friend gets killed outside of a church you and him had just attended. That's the part I don't get, and it's that part I need you to help me with," Detective McCoy said.

"I don't know what to tell you. I don't have the answer to that. I go to school and I work. I'm not a part of a gang, and I stopped hanging out with my bad friends a long time ago," Michael told the Detective.

"For some reason I just don't believe you're telling me everything you know. Maybe it's that, no snitching thing, keeping you from being honest with me, but you should be aware that this whole ordeal here is far from over. If you think these guys are going to be satisfied just because they got your friend, you have another thought coming. We're not going to stop until we get to the bottom of this, because we know they're not going to stop until there's one more body lying in the street. Hopefully one of them won't be you," Detective McCoy said closing up the folder.

"I haven't done anything to anybody. I don't know what my friend James had going on because I had to stop hanging out with him as well. The only reason we were together that morning was because he had called me that night needing a place to stay. He believed somebody was outside of his house waiting for him to come out. It had nothing to do with me. Why would I have to worry about

somebody wanting to do something to me?" Michael asked.

"Are you telling me you can't see the connection here, or are you just blowing smoke at me. Personally, I believe you know exactly what's going on, or at least got an idea of what's going on from what some of your old buddies have probably already told you. All I could say is it's not going to be me out there dodging bullets. If this is how you want to go about it then it's all on you. Until either your conscience grows a pair of balls, or truth escapes from its prison, you have a nice day and feel free to call me if you need to," Detective McCoy said getting up from his seat clearly frustrated from the conversation.

Thanks to Detective McCoy, Michael left the precinct with a completely different outlook. It was undeniable he needed a solution to the problems that were now accumulating. More than anything, he realized there was no quick fix for Renée's situation. Not so much as even a Band-Aid, and it seemed as though what James had done was now threatening to eventually spill over into his own life. He felt as though he needed to escape and take Renée and the baby right along with him. That's when it hit him. He would enlist in the military. That's what he would do, he would join the Army. It was the solution to all his problems. He would start out by enlisting for a year or two at first. It would be enough to get him away from the situation James had created while continuing his education and working on a future for Renée and the baby. He had heard about all the benefits the government gives its veterans. If he enlisted in the military, he would be a veteran when he finished his service. It was his only option for everything that was going on. The more he thought about it the better it made him feel. He decided right then and there it was what he was going to do.

Michael met with Renée the following Friday and took her to the ice cream stand. He figured he'd wait until they were able to spend a little time together before telling her his plans. He hadn't told anyone about it yet, not even his mom. Renée would be the first. He bought her a huge cone filled with butter pecan, her favorite ice cream, with nuts sprinkled all over the top. It was obvious she was pregnant now. Not huge, more like a half of basketball tucked under her shirt. Michael loved her, and he was willing to do whatever it took to take care of her and the baby. He was glad she had stuck with him when he was acting like a fool getting high and robbing people. He considered himself blessed because God had looked out for him. He had given him an angel who had stuck with him through everything. He knew he would one day marry her. He had given up his other two girlfriends and was happy with only her in his life. He just needed to prove himself to her father so that her life would be better as well. There was no better way to do it than going into the Army and serving the country. Michael was sure there was nothing her father could say to make bad out of that.

He waited until Renée had eaten half of her ice cream. That's when he told her his plan to enlist in the Army in order to make everything right. He explained to her how it would get him away from everything going on regarding the shooting. How his benefits would take care of her and the baby, and how her father would be able to accept him once he found out he was in the military. He told her it was a win-win situation for both of them. It made him feel good to show her how he had come up with a solution to their problems. Renée wasn't as open to the idea as Michael thought she would be. She said she didn't want him to leave her. She told him she wouldn't know what to do once he was gone. It was bad enough she had to deal with her father every day who now looked at her as though he wanted nothing to do with her. She told Michael she felt so alone. Both at school, and at home. She said he was the only one she could talk to, the only one who cared. If he left her, she would be lost. Michael reasoned with her and was able to get her to see how going into the service would help them. She did not want to accept it, but was able to understand, in spite of her rejection.

Chapter 18

Shattered

Helen finished the conversation by expressing to Richard how much Mason has been asking about him. She told him she could respect him wanting to step back from the relationship, but said Mason did not deserve to be abandoned. She said all he does is talk about seeing those darn pets he has. After hearing this, Richard realized he couldn't just up and walk away from him. Mason knew about him having the exotic pets in his basement and he was starting to leak that information to his mother by mentioning the fact he had them. Then again, there was the snake and the gecko lizards he had as well. At the moment Helen had no idea what pets Mason was referring to. Mason was holding onto his secret and Richard had to be sure no one found out about it. He would have to keep some type of relationship with Helen in order to prevent Mason from saying anything to anyone. He was suddenly angry with himself for allowing everything to get out of control. It had to be something he could do to fix it all.

The following Saturday Richard picked up Mason and brought him home to spend time with him. Mason talked about going into the basement from the time Richard picked him up until the moment they pulled into the driveway. Once they had gotten inside Richard had Mason sit on the couch and he explained to him once again how much trouble he could get in if someone found out about what he had in the basement. He asked Mason did he want to be the one who got him into trouble by saying something to someone. Mason shook his head no and said he wouldn't say anything to anyone. Richard told him as long as he didn't say anything, he would let him help, and play with them whenever he came over. He reminded Mason to be careful about what he said to his mother because she was afraid of all kinds of animals, especially the reptiles. He said he hadn't told her anything so she didn't know. Mason promised never to tell anyone.

Richard ended the call with his mother and decided she was another one he was going to have to start avoiding. It was true she and Helen had been seeing each other. According to his mother, Helen was a very sweet girl who she enjoys spending time with. They had exchanged phone numbers and were now talking with one other regularly. Although Richard had managed to pull himself away from Helen. His mother and Helen were now meeting once a week for coffee. At least meeting for coffee is what they both claimed. However, Richard knew it was a lot more to it than that. He didn't care how much they visit one another, He and Helen would never be. By the looks of it, He and mother were heading down the same road.

Helen stood in the hallway listening to Mason playing alone in his bedroom. He apparently had two imaginary friends in which he was playing with. She overheard him telling them he needed to give them names. As Helen listened more closely to Mason playing with his invisible friends, she was amazed by how real a child's imagination could be. She took notice of him telling them he would make sure to give them pretty names. But it was something about him telling them he knew their parents were probably looking for them, but he would take care of them them, that bothered her. As Helen stood by the door taking it all in, she wondered just how long her son would go on having fun pretending to be playing with two imaginary friends. However, she couldn't shake the thought of him having friends whose parents were looking for them. She listened closely as he began naming all the things he would bring them.

The urge to peek into Mason's room overwhelmed her. She lifted one of her feet from the floor as though it was a feather, and placed it back down in front of the other distributing her weight back onto it as slowly as possible. She lifted her other foot and did the same thing before stopping in her tracks and listening to see if he had heard her. When she was sure he hadn't heard her, she continued creeping towards his doorway.

When she heard Mason say, *" I don't like how dirty you are, I'm going to give you a bath because Richard promised me to let me help him clean you up."* Her body stiffened.

It was difficult to comprehend what she was hearing because it was now suddenly beyond her son just having a couple of imaginary friends. It was something involving Richard. Immediately, her mind went into question mode, but the questions were coming too fast to recognize which ones were the most important.

She peeked around the corner and looked into Mason's room. He was sitting on the floor playing with two stuffed toys. Helen eased her way into his room and sat on the edge of his bed. When Mason finally heard her, he turned around and looked up from the floor and smiled at her.

"What's going on buddy?" Helen asked looking down at him.

"Nothing just playing with my friends," Mason said turning back around and looking at the stuffed toys he had been playing with.

"What were you guys talking about?" Helen asked with a smile on her face.

"We were talking about the playground at school," Mason said, as he sat one of the stuffed toys down he was holding.

Although Helen knew he was lying, she was considering what it was going to take in order to make Mason tell her the truth. She wasn't the type of mother who believed in jacking up her child in order to get the truth out of him. Fear and violence was something she did not employ when it came down to her son. She preferred being firm, fair and consistent while using logic, reasoning, and persuasion. Not only did it instill good values in him, but it helped her as well. She decided she would use the very cause of the problem, as her solution.

"Mason, look at me," Helen said, waiting until he was turned around and facing her before continuing. *"You wouldn't be lying to me would you?"*

"No," Mason said turning his head and not being able to look at her.

"Well, I know you're not being truthful. If you're going to keep secrets from me and lie about it, then I guess I'm going to have to stop you from going over to Richard's place," Helen said looking at Mason who was looking at the floor as though he was looking through it.

"No! No! Please no!" Mason said turning around and looking up at his mother. *"I was only talking about the pets Richard has in his basement,"*

Looking at her son it was now obvious he was telling her the truth. Not so much as the pleading, but the look in his eyes and the sound of his voice confirmed it. If he was lying over some dumb pets Richard had in his basement, then she really had nothing to worry about. How could she allow herself to get worked up over Mason playing with a couple of stuffed toys and mentioning Richard? He had actually taken really good care of

Mason each time she asked him to babysit. She reacted like he was some horrible monster. As she thought about it, it made her feel bad that she would think of him in such a way.

"So, you didn't want me to know Richard allows you to play with his pets?" Helen asked, going from a straight face to a smile.

"He didn't want to get in trouble, so he told me not to say anything to anyone," Mason said turning his head up from the floor and looking at his mother.

When he saw his mother smiling, he asked, *"Are you mad at me?"*

"Why would I be mad at you?" Helen asked.

"Because I didn't tell you the truth," Mason said.

"Well, you're telling me the truth now. That's all that matters," Helen said.

"Is Richard going to get in trouble?" Mason asked.

"As long as he's just letting you play with his pets, I think I can keep it a secret," Helen said, reaching her hand out and rubbing the top of Mason's head.

Helen slowly made her way up the steps of Richards mother's house. Over the last several months, they had developed a very close relationship. It was more than what she could say about her in Richard. Although she was awfully fond of his mother, Helen realized She and Richard would never be. She had decided today would be her last visit. It was time for her to slowly start severing the bond between Mason and Richard. In her heart, she knew it was going to be one of the hardest things she would ever have to do. Mason thought the world of Richard. Breaking her son's heart was not an easy feeling to embrace. If only she could point the finger at Richard, but she couldn't, she had played a part in it as well. After all, it was her idea to go after him in the first place, and not the other way around. It was a chance she had been willing to take. Thinking only about herself, she had dragged her son right in the middle of it all.

Helen sat listening to Richard's mother while sitting at the dining room table sipping on the hot tea she had poured for her. According to his mother, Richard had never shown any interest in women. Helen had been the first. His mother thought he was either gay, or had something against women. She told Helen if she had not been his mother it would have been easy for her to believe he had been abused by a woman. She went on to say she didn't have anything against gays and homosexuals, but she was happy when Richard started spending time with her. She thanked Helen for bringing him out of his shell and showing him he could be happy spending time with a woman. After cleaning off the counter and pouring herself a cup of tea, she sat at the table across from Helen and said, she couldn't understand how he ended up being the shy and lonely type. As a child, she had always taken him to all kinds of places and had even gone so far as to trying to get him involved in sports. It was her way of trying to replace the emptiness that was left from him growing up without a father.

Helen asked his mother had she ever been over to his house. She told Helen that in the 3 ½ years in which he'd lived there, she had only been over twice. The first time was when he first moved in, and the second time was when he had been really sick and she had brought him over dinner because he sounded terrible. She said that was when he had given her a key to his house to hold onto. He said he wanted her to keep it in case one day he accidentally locked himself out. She told Helen she had often times thought about going over to his place when he was at work just to see how he was living, but changed her mind because she knew if he ever found out, he would stop talking to her. She looked at Helen with her eyes full of sorrow and said, who would've known he would stop talking to me because we became friends. After a few moments of silence, she went on to say for some reason she believed Richard had forgotten about ever giving her a key. After taking a sip of tea, she set her cup down on the table, looked at Helen, and asked her had he ever invited her in. Helen told her she had been over several times to either drop Mason off, or to pick him up, but had never been invited in.

It had been nearly three weeks since Richard had seen Mason. However, he was now sitting in front of his school waiting for it to turn out. Helen had called him and asked him would he watch Mason for a little while so she could pick up some overtime. Deep down inside he was happy about doing it because truth be told, he had actually missed the little fella. However, he could never bring himself around to picking up the phone, calling Helen, and asking her to allow him to see Mason. Not only did he lack the courage to do such a thing, but if he had done it, it would have been equivalent to slapping her in the face. Besides, he knew eventually they would no longer be a part of his life. It was the only way for him to get his life back. Today, however, he was going to make the best out of the time they had together.

Richard sat in his car looking through his windshield at all the tiny little faces that began flowing from the front doors of the school. Both his eyes and his mind were doing the best they could at using face recognition in order to find Mason in the sea of faces. Richard had made it his business to be one of the first to arrive. His past experience taught him he would have to get out of his car in order to get Mason if he didn't get there super early. Getting out of his car was something he did not want to do. He couldn't stand being in crowds. It was something he avoided at all costs. Unless however, he was using the crowd itself as camouflage.

Richard noticed some of teachers walking out of the building holding some of the students by hand. As he looked closely, he could see a kid who resembled Mason pointing in his direction. He squinted his eyelids against the sunlight in order to block out the rays. It was Mason's hand the teacher was holding, and they were now walking towards his car. Richard knew the policy of the school was to escort a child to the vehicle of the person who was designated to pick them up for a day or two days in place of the parent, or the person, who normally picked them up. The procedure insured two things. First, that the child actually knew the person who was picking them up, and second, it allowed the teacher to remember both the face, and vehicle of that person.

After they had driven off, like always, Mason immediately began his interrogation. Richard did his best to answer his questions as slowly as possible instead of being bombarded. He knew they would slow down once they got home. Therefore, being patient with his answers would buy him more time. It was obvious by the questions Mason was asking him that he was missed as well. Although he wanted to know how his pets were doing, he was more concerned about why he hadn't called or came by. He said he had asked his mother the same question but she had told him to ask Richard those questions the next time he saw him. It was the first time he had felt what he was feeling as he listened to Mason talk, but something inside of him would not let him answer certain questions, they made him feel as though he was vulnerable. Getting Mason to his house was the only answer. Sure enough, as soon as they entered the house Mason ran to the basement door, unlocked it, and asked Richard could he go downstairs. It had been a while since Mason had been over, and he had done a good job at keeping their secret, so Richard didn't hesitate to say yes.

The time seemed to have gone by faster than he wanted. Before Richard knew it, it was time for him to take Mason home. Except for having gone upstairs to grab a couple of sandwiches, they had spent all of their time in the basement. He had let Mason help brush, washed, and feed them. At first, Mason told Richard they looked really sad; but after feeding them, cleaning them, and playing with them he said they were now happy. Richard agreed with him and told him it was going to take a lot more time before they got used to being down there. Mason wanted Richard to promise him to let him help to take care of them until they were happy being down there. It was something he could not promise. The precious time in which they had spent together, would be nothing more than a memory sometime in the near future. Especially, if he was fortunate enough to close on the property he had made an offer on.

Since finding out about Helen and his mom's secret rendezvous, Richard very rarely accepted Helen's phone calls, completely ignore her text messages, and did everything within his power to avoid her at work. As for his mother, he hadn't spoken with her since he had found out. Nevertheless, he knew his mom and Helen were still meeting up to have their little coffee and talk. At first, he couldn't stop thinking about why they were still seeing one another, but soon consider it a waste of time burning up valuable calories wondering about it. The one good thing that had come out of him and Helen breaking up, if you wanted to call it that, was the fact that the situation at work had gotten a lot better. He hadn't been told it officially, but Mr. Snider was now smiling at him whenever they saw each other. He had even gone so far as to give Richard the thumbs up on a couple of occasions.

Helen sat in the break room staring off into space, with an

expression of disbelief on her face. She had just got off the phone with the school talking with Mason's teacher. Apparently, Mason had been caught stuffing two pairs of shoes that didn't belong to him into his backpack. His teacher said when she questioned him about it, he told her he didn't know why he was taking them. The more Helen thought about it, the angrier she became. She put two and two together and suddenly realized Mason had mentioned getting shoes for his imaginary friends the day she had eavesdropped on him. It was clear to her that all of this was stemming from those darn pets Richard was allowing him to play with. For the first time since they had stopped seeing one another, Helen was actually glad it had happened. The last thing she wanted was for her son to be influenced by someone like Richard.

She thought about confronting him, but quickly changed her mind because he had actually been a good babysitter. Not to mention, she didn't know anyone else who would watch Mason when she wanted to pick up some overtime. She didn't want to take the chance of upsetting him by confronting him with it. Knowing Richard, he would take it as though she was blaming him for what Mason had done. In all actuality, he was to blame. If it wasn't for him allowing Mason to play with his pets, he would not have got in trouble for trying to steal. Nevertheless, she knew there had to be a solution. She decided she would have a talk with Richard's mom, she had always proven to be very understanding over the short period of time she had come to know her. If his mother didn't know how to handle it, Helen doubted if anyone else would. The last thing she wanted was to add fuel to the fire by making things worse right before Richard's birthday, which was less than two months away.

Richard shook the hand of the real estate agents who had been showing him properties. It was the second one he had shown him that he was mainly interested in. The house sat on 2 acres of land and was on the outskirts of town. It had three bedrooms, 1 ½ bathrooms, a full basement, and an attic. It was just what he was looking for, and the price was negotiable. According to the agent that particular house had been on the market for quite some time, which meant the owners were more than willing to lower the price. It was the size and location that got Richard's attention, they were the very things that made him start looking for a new property in the first place. He needed to get out of the city and away from Helen and Mason. Now that he no longer felt threatened about his new position at work, the extra income would allow him to be able to afford the new property comfortably. That was, as long as his mortgage payments stayed under $1000.

On the drive home, Richard started reflecting back on how his life had changed. It wasn't until he allowed Helen in and started spending time with Mason. That had been over a year and a half ago. Everything in his life had always been in order before he allowed them in. He was used to being in control of everything. Now, he had lost his privacy, his relationship with his mother, and some of his feelings along the way. It wasn't because either Helen or Mason were terrible people, but because he had learned to live without other people being in control of his life. Losing that made him very uncomfortable and insecure. In the beginning, he had actually enjoyed spending time with them. Especially the times Mason and him had spent alone, like the very first time he had taken him to a Reptile Expo. He could still recall the expression of excitement that was all over Mason's face. However, those memories were quickly replaced by the thought of him not having spoken with his mom in over two months.

Although Richard had no clue about electrical or wiring, he was able to go online and follow the directions on how to install a junction box and wire a light switch at the top of the basement stairs. A couple of weeks ago he had nearly fallen down the stairs. He was tired of trying to find a string dangling from a light in the middle of the ceiling. At first, he didn't believe he would be able to do it. But as he made his way through the project, he slowly gained the confidence needed to complete the job. When it was all done, he had a professionally installed light switch at the top of the basement stairs.

Mason had never stolen anything before. Helen couldn't figure out why he would try and take something that didn't belong to him. Whatever it was, she was going to be sure to get to the bottom of it, and she was going to start with Richard. She had already questioned Mason a little bit more about the kind of pets Richard had. He had told her Richard had live monkeys in his basement. Helen couldn't believe it, but after hearing it A lot of things began making sense. Like why she had never been invited inside his house. She couldn't think of anyone who ever kept monkeys in their house. All the secrecy was probably due to the fact that they were probably illegal to possess. She knew for certain that some species of monkeys were in fact illegal. It also explained the reason Richard had made Mason promised not to say anything to anyone.

It was obvious that all of the secrecy and disregard for morals and rules were affecting Mason in a negative way. If it wasn't, he would not have lied to her and believed it was okay to take something that didn't belong to him. The more she thought about it, the more it heated the blood flowing through her veins. She knew if she continued to dwell on it, it would be just a matter of time before her blood boiled. If that happened, self-control would be the first thing out the door. However, teaching her son how to break the law was something she would not stand for. At that moment, it was only one thing she wanted, to see what kind of monkeys Richard had in his basement.

The real estate agent called him to tell him his offer had been accepted. However, Richard was already ahead of the game. Before he had heard anything back from the agent, he had gone to his bank and applied for the loan that would allow him to purchase the property. The only thing the bank needed was all the information regarding the new home. Richard could barely contain himself. It meant if everything continued to go the way they were going, he would be able to move into his new home on his birthday. It would be his birthday gift to himself. If only his mother had not gone behind his back and befriended Helen, he would have been able to share his joy with her. Even though they had their differences about him being single, or him not having any children, she was still his mother and the only person on earth he truly loved. Lately, he was really starting to miss her.

Chapter 19

Below the Surface

When Daniel got back to his office after the second meeting, his secretary informed him he had missed a call from a Detective Matthew out of Texas. His secretary gave him a sticky note with Detective Matthew scribbled on it, it was a different number than the one he'd been calling. Daniel went into his office, closed the door, and dialed the number. Detective Matthew picked up on the second ring. Daniel started the conversation off by apologizing for not returning his call earlier and attempted to justify it by lying about how busy he'd been. Detective Matthew allowed a brief moment of silence to occupy the space between the conversation before going on to tell him about new developments in the investigation, the one involving him. Apparently, Kimberly Jordan's mother had gotten a hold of her phone and downloaded her call list onto her computer. After doing so, she had provided a copy of that lists to him and Detective Ryan.

Detective Matthew was now calling him because one of those numbers on that list belonged to him. He needed Daniel to help them understand why the daughter would be calling him after he's been gone from the school for so long. As he sat there listening to the Detective talk on the end, the fear running through his veins caused him to feel as though he had taken some kind of drug. He didn't know what kind of drug, but it was definitely a feeling of being drugged. Although he was hearing the words detective Matthew was speaking, it was as though they were going through some type of filter, and only the words that scared him the most was getting through. The most terrifying word at that moment was, list.

When he became aware of Detective Matthew asking him if he was still there, he snapped out of his trance and let his fear do the talking. He said she had first called him complaining about not getting the type of help she'd gotten when he was working in the math lab. He told Detective Matthew that on a few occasions she had called to ask him what it was like living in Georgia. Apparently, some of her friends had told her about places in Georgia she was curious about. Places he had not been. He remembered her calling him asking him to explain the Pythagorean theorem to her. He said he had spent over an hour on the phone with her on two different occasions trying to explain Euclidean Geometry and the relationship of the three sides of a right triangle. He told Detective Matthew those were the only times he could remember talking to her since moving to Georgia.

After hanging up with the Detective, Daniel started to dial Kimberly's number but quickly realized they could not talk on that phone ever again. He was going to have to call her as soon as possible, but he was going to have to call her from a payphone. The thought of how hard it was going to be to find a payphone; in a day and time where everything was wireless, would probably be equivalent to finding a baby dinosaur running across someone's yard. Luckily, they were still out there, far and few in numbers, but still around. He found one about 4 miles away from his job on the side of a corner store. He needed to talk with Kimberly, they had to coordinate their stories before she talked with Detective Matthew. He pushed his two quarters into the opening on the top of the payphone and dialed her number.

After Kimberly answered the phone, Daniel found himself running out of breath several times trying to explain to her everything he needed her to say, in regards to the investigation. In the course of feeding her instructions, he would stop every now and then to ask her if she was still there. When he had finished going over everything he asked her did she understand. To his surprise, she told him he didn't have to worry about anything. She told him she was done with him. She didn't want him to call her anymore because her mom had found out she hadn't stayed overnight at her friend's house when he had flown her down to see him. Her mom was now threatening to send her to live with her grandmother because of it. She said her mom had ransacked her room, and now she could not seem to find the bracelet he had bought her. She told him she wanted it all to be over with, before hanging the phone up on him.

Daniel was still numb a weak later from the phone call with Kimberly when he got home from work to find a small U-Haul sitting in his driveway. His first thought was someone had ended up at the wrong house and was probably being told that as he was driving up. However, when he pulled in behind the truck, he noticed the back of the truck open and recognized several items from the house. He quickly exited his car and walked in through the front door that someone had left wide open. He looked towards the back bedroom and saw Heather walking towards him with her arms full of clothes that were still on the hangers. He opened up his mouth to asked her what was going on but was silenced by the sound of Beverly's voice coming from behind him.

"So, is this what you married me for, you needed a cover?!" Beverly asked, holding a stack of papers in her hand, with a voice that was somewhere between a loud cry, and the expression of painful emotion.

"What are you talking about?" Daniel asked walking towards her and reaching for the stack of papers she was holding out in front of her.

"Well, I refuse to be your cover Daniel, and to believe you married me because you loved me. I must have

had fool written all over my forehead. I should have been smart enough to recognize this when you had students calling you all times of night, or when you would leave the room in order to talk when you got a call from one of them. Even your late-night excursions to the gym without me being able to get in touch with you, all the signs were there I just never paid attention to them. I wanted to believe I had someone I could love and trust so I jumped over all of the signs, not paying attention to a single one," Beverly said throwing the stack of papers in Daniel's face.

"Beverly, will you please calm down, I don't have a clue as to what you're talking about. Can we at least talk about this, do you really need to be stuffing your things in a U-Haul truck? What have I done so terribly wrong to cause you to suddenly up and leave me? I don't think I've done anything bad enough to deserve this," Daniel said bending down and reading the papers on the floor as he picked them up.

"Oh! you don't, well maybe no one else can see the terrible monster hiding behind this marriage, but I can! All those charges on your credit card you've managed to hide by burying them in your paperwork are proof of just how horrible you are. Extra cell phones bills, a gold bracelet, purchases from a woman's boutique, hotels and flights for unaccompanied minors. What the hell does all of this add up to? There's obviously things going on I can't even begin to imagine. Just pray to your dear God you don't have anything to do with why Heather has been acting out," Beverly said in a voice saturated with fury.

Although Daniel stood there begging for Beverly to let him

explain, her words were draining him of strength and power. The things she had said to him prevented him from feeling normal. She had opened the box with all his secrets, causing him to feel naked and vulnerable. Without warning the anger of betrayal begin to swell inside of him. He suddenly felt as though he wanted her out of his life. She had gone behind his back, dug through all of his personal information, and was now using it against him. He didn't want, or need, a woman like that. She had become more of an enemy than a wife. This caused him to experience a sense of relief watching her load their things into the truck. However, he would play along with the situation and not let her know he was actually happy she was leaving.

"Beverly, could you please just stop one minute. I'm telling you I can explain all of this to you. You have to at least give me a chance to shed some light on what's going on. You're jumping to conclusions without understanding what's going on," Daniel said putting the papers on the table and watching Beverly walk out the door with a suitcase in one hand, and a bag of cosmetics in the other.

Beverly put the suitcase and the bag in the back of the U-Haul truck, walked back in the house, stopped directly in front of him, looked him straight in the eyes, and said, *"The only thing I have to say to you, is stay the hell out of my way, and don't hesitate to sign the divorce papers once you get them,"*

By the time David got home from football practice, Beverly and Heather had packed up and gone. He looked around the house and immediately noticed several things missing. he walked into the kitchen and found his father sitting at the table going through some papers. David wasn't sure what it was but there was a certain mood in the house that caused him to feel unsettled. When his father looked up from the table at him, his expression reassured David something had happened. Aside from the sound of his own breathing the house was unusually quiet.

"Dad, is everything all right?" David asked, removing his book bag from his shoulder.

"No, it isn't. I came home to find Beverly and Heather loading up a U-Haul truck. She up and left me without ever giving me a warning. I never knew she was so unhappy," Daniel said in a voice that betrayed what he was really feeling inside.

"Her and Heather are gone?" David asked in total disbelief.

"Yes, they're gone," Daniel said.

"Why would she up and leave you like that dad. Did you guys have an argument or something, I mean I don't understand. Didn't she at least tell you why she was leaving?" David asked while scratching his forehead from the confusion.

"It had to be a combination of things. Me being consumed by my job, which caused me to accidentally neglect her. She was missing her family, and not feeling significant after giving up her job and moving to Georgia. Heather had turned into someone totally different, getting bad grades and becoming antisocial. She said she couldn't take it anymore," Daniel said while lying to David as though it was the truth.

"Is this just something for the time being, or are you guys getting a divorce?" David asked.

"I really don't know right now son, all I can do is keep an open mind about all of this," Daniel said getting up from the table with the stack of papers tucked under his arm.

The next morning when Daniel arrived at work, he was informed by the secretary that his boss wanted to see him as soon as he got in. He immediately went upstairs to find out what Mr. Westheimer wanted of him. After about a five-minute wait in the lobby, he found himself sitting in a chair directly in front of his boss's desk. Mr. Westheimer had gotten the word about Detective Matthew calling the company trying to reach Daniel. He was very concerned about the phone call because to him detectives were usually the byproduct of investigation. He wanted Daniel to know the company had a zero tolerance for lawbreakers. He needed to be reassured there were no laws being broken inside the company, or outside the company. He wanted to give Daniel the opportunity to make clear anything that might affect his employment with the company. He said transparency was VyCal Technologies policy in all matters of business.

Daniel finished listening to Mr. Westheimer's spiel regarding zero tolerance for lawbreakers, and reassured his boss by lying about why the detective was trying to reach him. He told his boss he and his wife were going through a divorce, and she had hired the detective to do her leg work because she was in another state and wasn't there to do it for herself. He said the detective had paperwork he needed him to sign. He told his boss besides that, it was nothing else to the matter.

Before Daniel realized it, three weeks had passed since Beverly had left, and just as long since Detective Matthew had tried to reach him. Back then, it felt as though his world was slowly crumbling in on him. Now, everything was a lot better. Today was one of those, three-meetings-in-a-day, work days. Daniel had finally been able to get in touch with the guy named Zack he had met at the last convention. He contacted him because he wanted some of the pills Zack had given him. When he did finally talk with him, Zach told him they were called roofies. After they had agreed upon a fair price, he sent Daniel 30 of them. Things were looking up at work as well, he now had a 20-year-old female intern who had begun working for him a little over a week ago. His personal life had taken a turn for the better as well. He had met a 22-year-old beautiful brunette by the name of Ashley McLeod who had been over to the house a couple of times for drinks. He hadn't gotten anywhere with her, but that was before he received the pills Zack had sent him.

As he sat there in the middle of his first meeting, he couldn't help but feel anxious about everything he had set in place. Today was Friday, and his weekend was booked. Saturday his friend Ashley would be coming over for drinks. David was spending the entire weekend with one of his buddies. He had gone to great lengths and spent quite a bit of money bringing it all together. He had convinced Hazel Wadsworth, his 15-year-old Pre-intern, to drop a couple of pills in her mother's food or drink so she could sneak out of the house tonight and meet up with him. He had learned his lesson about buying jewelry with his credit cards so he had given her five crisp $100 bills and told her to hide them and spend them a little at a time. This weekend was going to be one of the best weekends he'd ever had. He was beyond himself with excitement, and it was causing the time to feel as though it was dragging on.

As Daniel sat there consumed by his thoughts, and barely listening to what was being said, he happened to look up from his folder and through the glass window of the conference room. His thoughts froze as he looked directly into the eyes of Detective Ryan. Standing next to him was Detective Matthew. The secretary got up from behind her desk and began escorting them towards the conference room. Before his mind could fully process what was going on, the door to the conference room burst open. Everyone inside went motionless, and a brief silence took over the room. Both Detective Ryan and Detective Matthew entered the room with faces hardened by cases that sometimes took the life out of them. Daniel Carpenter, Detective Ryan called out Daniel's name reaching behind his back and removing a pair handcuffs. You're under arrest for the rape of Kimberly Jordan, the detective said as he lifted Daniel up from his seat placing his hands behind his back and putting the handcuffs on. Daniel felt the cold metal of the handcuffs grip his wrist as he watched the crowd outside the conference grow in size. In no time at all, what started out as a promise to be the best day of his life, suddenly turned into the worst day he could ever imagine.

Chapter 20
No Chances

When Michael passed Palm Beach Gardens and pulled onto PGA Boulevard, he heard the sound of sirens behind him. When he looked in his rearview mirror he realized it was him who was being pulled over. He took a left onto Old Palm Drive and came to a stop. The officer came to Michael's window and asked for his license, registration and proof of insurance. He reached into his center console and pulled out his registration and proof of insurance. He asked the officer could he reach into his back pocket and grab his wallet. When he had given the officer all three documents, he asked him why he had been stopped. He told Michael to sit tight for minute and he would explain it to him when he came back. Michael looked over at Renée, it was obvious she was nervous. He told her to relax they had nothing to worry about his insurance and everything was up to date. She told Michael the last thing she needed was for her father to find out they had gotten pulled over by the police. When the officer came back, instead of telling Michael why he had been pulled over, he asked Renée for identification. She told the officer all she had was her student ID. He told her it would do, and waited until she passed it to him.

When the officer returned, he handed both of them their documents. He informed Michael he had been stopped because his car fit the description of a reported hit-and-run incident in the area. He apologized for the delay and told them they were free to go. As Michael pulled away from the curve, he knew the officer had lied to him. However, he couldn't make any sense of why the officer had stopped him. He hadn't been speeding or anything. When he looked over at Renée, the thought occurred to him it was probably because of Detective McCoy. Most likely, he was bent on finding out who Renée and Breechelle were. He wasn't going to be satisfied until he talked with everyone who was in the car that night. It was a gut feeling he had. It was like the feeling he had about being followed. He wasn't one to believe things happened by accident. If it was true, he now had Renée's name. It was nothing to worry about, besides Renée's father being a city councilman. He decided to keep that thought to himself and not say anything to Renée about it.

Michael decided to talk with his mother about his plan to enlist in the military. When he got home, she was sitting in her favorite recliner watching television. It was some show he was unfamiliar with. He asked her did she have a minute, she said of course, grabbed the remote and turned the volume down. He finished telling her about Renée being pregnant and how her father was irate. He let her know what Detective McCoy had said to him, and how he had been stopped for nothing earlier that night. He shared with her how he wanted to be able to take care of his girlfriend, and their baby. He told his mother the benefits from being in the military would allow him to do all of that. He also let her know how he felt it was a good idea if he left in order to get away from the drama the shootings had created. He believed it was just a matter of time before they would try to get him as well. He told her he planned on enlisting for a couple of years at first. By then he would know if it was meant for him or not. He finished up by adding he would also be allowed to continue his education.

Just like Renée, his mother wasn't receptive to the idea as well. She was more concerned about him being involved in a war than anything else. She told him America always seemed to be fighting in somebody's backyard. She let him know she wanted the best for him, but she didn't know how she would be able to handle him being involved in some war. She asked him had he spoken with Renée's mother or father about her being pregnant. When

239

Michael told her no, she told him that was equivalent to having an open sore and not putting a Band-Aid on it. She asked him had he considered Job Corps or anything else that might be available for him. Michael told her he believed he was too old for Job Corps, and even if he weren't, he still preferred the military over Job Corps. In the end, his mother told him he had to live his life according to what satisfied him. She told him she was happy he was still making decisions to better himself, so that was what really mattered to her.

When Monday rolled around Michael skipped his morning classes and instead went to the recruiting office of the Marines. Over the weekend he had gone online to check out the benefits and requirements of all four branches of the US Military. After reading up on each one of them he decided the Marines was what he wanted. He spoke with a recruiting officer by the name of Nicholas O'Reilly, who was a Private First Class. He spoke with Michael in great length about what the Marines were about. They went over a bunch of information about his education, health and citizenship. He explained to Michael he would have to take both and aptitude, and initial fitness test. It was only after he passed the requirements, he could look forward to being recruited. After that, every recruit had to make it through 12 weeks of intense training in order to determine if they were capable of becoming a Marine. After watching a couple of videos and going over the signing bonus Michael filled out all the necessary paperwork he needed to in order to start the process. He walked out of the recruiting office feeling a sense of pride and accomplishment. He was going to become a Marine.

Two days later, while at work, Michael received a call from Renée. She told him her mother and father were getting ready to take her down to the police station. Apparently, some detective by the name of McCoy had come to their house while she was at school. He was looking for her to interview her about a shooting. She said her mother had called her father, who left work early in order to take her down to the station. She told Michael she heard her father on the phone talking with the family lawyer. He was apparently going to meet them downtown. She said her father was hysterical. He couldn't believe she was involved in some kind of shooting. She said the detective didn't tell her mother much, because the only thing her mother could tell her father, was that it was about a shooting. She told Michael she loved him, and he hadn't heard from her because her father had taken her phone. Renée stopped talking for moment, said her father was coming, and quickly hung up the phone before Michael could say anything.

For the rest of the day, Michael could not seem to shake the feeling of nervousness and anxiety. He was on pins and needles from the time he received the phone call from Renée until he laid down in bed that night. Even then he was restless. The last thing in the world he wanted was for Renée's father to find out she was in a car while someone was shooting at it. Even though he was preparing to go into the military he felt it would not matter to a father who was afraid for his daughter's life. In spite of remembering they had been the victims that night, it did nothing to hold back the feeling of hopelessness he was now experiencing. His chance of redeeming himself in the eyes of Renée's father had now been destroyed. He found himself wrestling with his misfortune and distress in hopes of breaking free from his emotions. He was able to cling onto the reality that what had happened, was not their fault. It was this truth which helped him to push back sorrow and disappointment. It allowed him to appreciate the realization that neither he nor Renée had been shot, or killed that night.

Even while sitting in class trying to take notes, Michael was worried about what Renée's parents had found out about that night. He knew they had probably found out everything. How Renée had actually stayed the night with him at a motel and not over a friend's house in which she had lied about. How no one had a license, even though they were out riding around at 2 o'clock in the morning. How his best friend James, the boy who had been killed leaving church, had an illegal gun in the car. He was sure when her parents left the police station they knew everything Michael and Renée had tried to keep secret. He had no idea how long it would be before he heard from Renée again. He suddenly hated the night that everything happened. Why did they have to go to that store?, out of all the stores they could have gone to. It didn't seem like it was fair. He put all his effort into focusing on what the teacher was explaining. He needed to concentrate.

In between classes Michael checked his cell phone for messages. He had a habit of muting it while in class. He had three missed calls and one voicemail. Two of the calls were from his mother, and one from a number he didn't recognize. He also had a text message from his mother, telling him to contact her as soon as possible. There was nothing from Renée. He knew after their visit to the police station yesterday it would be a long time before Renée got her phone back. He decided to call his mother first because she rarely sent him text messages. When she answered the phone, she told him two detectives had come by the house looking for him. She said she couldn't remember the other detective's name, but the detective named McCoy had given her a card. He told his mother it was about the shooting because Detective McCoy was the one he had spoken with at the station. She said she wasn't sure, that's why she had called him. Before hanging up, she advised him to give the detective a call because apparently he wanted to talk with him again.

The voicemail left on his phone was from Detective McCoy. He wanted Michael to contact him as soon as possible. After he listened to the message, he dialed Detective McCoy's number. When the detective answered, he told him who he was, and said he was returning his call. He was asked to come back down to the station in order to clear up a few things that had come to light. Michael agreed to meet the detective at the station as soon as his last class was over. His shift at work started two hours after his last class, so he would have plenty of time to make it to the station before having to go to work. Michael already knew what the detective was talking about when he said, a few things had come to light. Renée had known his reason for lying to the police about what had happened that night. Michael was protecting James by leaving out the gun. Hopefully, Renée had tried to do the same for him. Detective McCoy was probably going to question him about why James had a gun on him that night. It was the only thing Michael had withheld from him.

When Michael finally made it to the precinct, he ended up waiting over an hour before Detective McCoy arrived. Even though he told the detective what time he would get there, he was not there when Michael showed up. When he finally arrived, Michael sat back listening to what he had to say. His assumption had proven to be correct. He wanted to know why Michael had failed to mention anything about the gun James had on him that night. He told Michael if he had been honest with him about what had happened he would not have made the situation worse for himself. He said he would not have had to interview the daughter of a City Councilman, who had no idea his teenage daughter was involved in a shooting. He went on to say honesty, regardless of how difficult it may be, is often times the best course of action. He told Michael he was surely to blame for the additional troubles resulting from his attempt to hide the truth. Michael asked Detective McCoy what did he mean by that.

Detective McCoy sat back in his chair, raised his arms, interlocked his fingers, and placed both of his hands on top of his head. He sat there looking at Michael without saying a word. After what felt like forever he finally spoke.

"If it wasn't for your girlfriend coming down here helping us out by telling us exactly what happened, we would still be trying to find the pieces to the puzzle. It's always the ones who are willing to help, who justice depends on. Do you realize by not helping us, you actually caused yourself problems?" Detective McCoy asked.

"How did I do that?" Michael asked sitting up in his seat.

"First of all, your girlfriend who's pregnant, is 16 years old. By law, she's still a minor. Second of all, her father is a City Councilman who wants nothing short of having your head on a platter. You don't seem like a bad kid, just somebody who hung out with the wrong crowd at one time. However, my hands are tied in this matter. Her father is pressing charges on you for statutory rape and endangering the welfare of a minor," Detective McCoy said taking his hands down from the top of his head.

"Rape, endangering the welfare of a minor. Are you serious, I never raped Renée. How did I endanger the welfare of a minor? Her father is making this up because Renée ended up getting pregnant by me. He's lying. Just because he's a City Councilman he can come down here

and put false charges on me?" Michael asked clearly angry over what Detective McCoy had said.

"Because Renée was in the car with you that night, and she's a minor, you can be charged with endangering the welfare of a minor. By the statement given to authorities by Renée, that you are the father of her unborn child, and through your own admittance of being the father, it clearly proves you engaged in sexual intercourse with a minor. In the State of Florida, that's considered Statutory Rape. I have no choice but the place you under arrest for the charges of endangering the welfare of a minor and statutory rape," Detective McCoy said getting up from his chair.

Chapter 21

Bitter Tears

All of a sudden, Richard remembered giving his mother a key to the house he was living in. It had been so long ago until he simply forgot about it. But how could he have forgotten, he remembered almost everything, and the things he couldn't remember he wrote them down. Now, he would definitely have to call her and eventually go by in order to get the key. But then again, it really wasn't a must-do-now type of thing. He would be moving soon so it wasn't like she had a key to where he would be living. Nevertheless, he would be sure and get it. Who knows, if she had stopped seeing Helen, maybe they could start calling and seeing one another again.

Helen sat on the sofa with both legs stretched out on the ottoman in front of her. She and Mason were cuddled up together watching TV. She had planned this cuddle session for one specific reason, to get more information about what went on at Richards when Mason was there. She was determined to get to the bottom of what was causing her son to lie and steal.

"Have you been thinking about going back over to Richard's?" Helen asked with her right arm gently around Mason's waste, as he laid against her with his head underneath her shoulder.

"Yes, but I know you were angry at me, and you and Richard are no longer seeing each other anymore," Mason said without taking his eyes off the television.

"Well, Richard is still very fond of you, and you like going over playing with his animal. Me and Richard no longer going out anymore don't have anything to do with you guys spending time together." Helen said, cuddling up

a little closer.

"Do that mean you're still going to allow me to go over to Richard?" Mason asked, lifting his head up from under her shoulder and looking at her in the eyes with his face full of excitement.

"Sure, as long as you share with me all the fun stuff you guys have been doing with those pets he has," Helen said.

By the time Helen and Mason had finished talking she had everything she needed to know about what was taking place at Richards. According to Mason, he had snakes, lizards, a baby crocodile, and two very intelligent monkeys he kept locked up in some kind of room he built in his basement. According to Mason, the monkeys were his pride and joy. He had even gone so far as to teach them how to use the toilet. For some reason, the monkeys actually fascinated Helen. So much that, she now needed to see them for herself.

It was at that moment Helen suddenly remembered Richard's mother telling her about having an extra key to his place. A key in which he had somehow forgotten he had given her. Helen's mind went into overdrive figuring out how she would go about getting a hold of the key without Richard finding out. That's when the idea came to her about a surprise birthday party. His birthday was less than a week away, and if she could convince his mother to let her throw him a surprise birthday party, then maybe just maybe, his mother would give her the key. It was her only chance. If it worked, after she was done snooping around, she would tell his mother she didn't think it would be a good idea to surprise him. She would say she had no idea how he would act coming home to a bunch of people in his house.

Richard signed the last of the papers that officially gave him possession of his new home. His birthday was exactly 4 days away. He had already packed all of his belongings. The only thing that was needed in order to make the move from the old house to the new house was the rental truck and someone to help him move. There were always guys standing outside the rescue mission shelter looking for work. He decided he would pick up a couple of guys to help him with his move after getting the truck. For some reason, he had not yet contacted his mother about the key or let her know he had purchased a new home. Inside, he knew it was because he believed she might still be seeing Helen. Nevertheless, he was ready to forgive her. He really wanted her to know about him getting a new home, and he needed to get his key.

Helen removed the last box of frequency resistors from the conveyor belt. Today was Richard's birthday, and both she and him were working. For her, it was just any other Wednesday. However, she couldn't imagine how Richard must be feeling. Having to work on your birthday had to suck. If she remembered correctly, the company paid time and a half or gave a day off with pay for anyone who ended up working on their birthday. None of that really mattered to her at the moment. The only thing she was concerned about was the key she had in her front pocket. Richard's mother had given her the extra key because she thought it would be a good idea to throw him a surprise birthday party. At least that's what Helen had said she was going to do. She considered it a little white lie. She thought Helen was out shopping and rounding of friends. Little did she know, Helen was at work, keeping an eye on Richard. Her plan was to leave shortly after lunch. She wanted to be sure he was at work before going to his house.

Richard was angry for several reasons. First of all, he had been mandated to work on his birthday. Secondly, his mother was still seeing Helen; and last of all, she had somehow misplaced his key. Richard had called his mother two days in a row, and she still had not found the key. It wasn't so much about the key that Richard was calling her, but it was because he wanted to tell her about his new house. It was hard for him to admit it, but he was really missing her. When he called her, she had wished him a happy birthday, and told him how much she loved and missed him. It had touched him deeply. He decided after work he would go by and surprise her. Earlier on, while gathering samples near Helen's workstation, she had called him over. She wished him happy birthday, and gave him a birthday card. Although it was nice of her, it had no effect on him whatsoever.

Helen pretended to be sick in order to be excused from work. She told her supervisor she had severe diarrhea, felt nauseous, and had a headache. He told her to take the rest of the day off, and if she felt the same way come tomorrow, be sure to stay home. After being excused, she punched out and left. Suddenly, she was feeling anxious, nervous, and excited. The thought of going inside of Richard's house without his permission had her on edge. She had never ever done anything like she was about to do, and breaking the law was something she was not comfortable doing.

Yesterday Richard's mother called her and informed her he had asked about the key. Both of them thought it was strange he would up and ask about his key after three years; two days after she'd given it to her. She had told Helen it might not be such a good idea to go ahead with the surprise birthday party. She said he wasn't at all friendly when he found out they were still seeing one another. Helen had agreed with her and told her she would be bringing the key back to her today, as soon as she finished her shift. It was one more reason why she was leaving early, she was trying to time everything perfectly. After leaving Richard's, she was would simply take the key back to his mother as though she was just getting off of work.

Helen sat in the driveway trying to restore the courage that had somehow evaporated between leaving work and reaching Richard's house. She couldn't figure out where it had gone, but it might as well had been the fumes coming from the car's exhaust as the engine burned through the gas. She needed to be brave. There were only two choices, either get up the nerve to go inside, or start the car and drive away. She went with her first choice because it was the only way to do what she had come here to do. She took a deep breath, and exhaled, before getting out of the car. When she reached the door, she couldn't help but wonder what would happen if one of his reptiles had gotten out and was now roaming around free. However, Helen realized it was just another thought to discourage her from doing what she was about to do. She unlocked the door, pushed it open, and peered in.

As soon as she stepped inside, fear rushed through her veins like a shot of adrenaline. This time, it wasn't from the thought of something attacking her, but the thought of Richard coming home. Maybe he was doing the same thing she had done. After all, today was his birthday. There was no way Helen could see him staying for the entire shift. If he had left right after she had, he would come home and find her in his house. If that happened, she didn't know what she would do. However, she did know one thing for certain, she would be in a world of trouble.

She cleared her mind of those thoughts, and shook off the fear. From what Helen could see, there were boxes stacked on top of each other everywhere. She closed the door behind her, and allowed the refrigerator and sink to tell her she was in the kitchen. As she surveyed the room, the threat of a snake slithering somewhere behind one of the boxes caused her to look down at the floor. Anything crawling on its belly always had a way of terrifying her. After dismissing the threat of danger, she could not help but wonder what all the boxes were for. Mason never mentioned anything about Richard house being full of boxes.

She slowly made her way into the living room, but noticed the door leading to the basement next to the refrigerator. However, she wanted to be sure she wasn't the only thing roaming around the house before going down there. As she looked closely, she noticed all the boxes had writing on them. The thick curtains and blinds that were on all of the windows prevented the sunshine from entering the house. Helen took her cell phone out of her purse and turned on the flashlight. She wanted to make out what was written on the boxes, and find a light switch.

After reading what was written on the boxes, it was obvious Richard was moving. Each box had its designated location written on it, living room, bedroom, kitchen, etc. Obviously, his mother had no idea he was moving. Helen was certain about this, they had gotten too close for his mother not to have mentioned it to her, especially after giving Helen his key. So far, all of Richard's pets were inside of aquarium, terrariums, and Cages. She still had not seen the baby alligator Mason had told her about. As she stood at the bottom of the stairway leading upstairs, a cloud of apprehension hovered above her. It caused her legs to feel as though they had steel rods in them, preventing her from bending her knees in order to take a step.

All of a sudden, she heard a noise coming from upstairs. Although it was faint, she was sure something up there had moved around. Whatever it was, it caused the cloud of apprehension hovering above her to thicken. She was literally paralyzed.

"You better get out of here," something inside of hers said. *"No! I have to do this. I need to see,"* she answered back to the voice inside of her.

Without thinking, she made her way up the stairs and began opening doors and looking into rooms. There were two bedrooms and a bathroom. Inside the bathtub was the baby alligator Mason had told her about. For some reason, she was no longer afraid. Richard had been very careful about keeping his animals contained.

When she was finished upstairs, Helen went back downstairs, opened the basement door, and turned on the light. As she descended the steps going into the cellar, she was now excited about seeing what she had originally come to look at. The two monkeys her son Mason was obsessed with. The question was, what would she do about knowing he had illegal animals in his house. Helen believed Richard's illegal pets might be the reason behind why he never allowed her into his house, and why he could not have an open relationship with her. Maybe if she was able to tell him she knew about the animals and didn't care, then maybe just maybe, he would let her back into his life. If so, they would be able to pick up where they had left off at. Conceivably, this might have been her real reason for coming over in the first place. Something she wasn't even aware of. Perhaps she was looking for something she could use to rekindle what they had lost. God willing, she would find it, along with the two monkeys he was hiding.

Helen stood in front of two-inch-thick steel door, and peeked through the 12" x 8" bulletproof glass window. What she saw snatched the air out of her lungs, and gripped her heart. It was almost impossible for her mind to comprehend what she was seeing. Lying across a tiny mattress at the far end of the bunker, were two little girls. They appeared to be no older than eight years old. Her eyes refused to blink from the overwhelming intensity of horror. She grabbed the handle of the door and tried to open it, but it was locked. When the two girls saw her face, they jumped up from the mattress and ran towards the door. They looked starved, their hair was matted, and she could see where the trail of tears had dried on their tiny little faces.

Richard didn't know what hit him. All he knew was that one minute he was standing up in front of one of the sanitizing station, and the next minute he was on the floor. He had been slammed to the ground with so much force his mouth was full of the metallic taste of blood. His face had been crashed into the cement floor so hard it had almost rendered him unconscious. As he teetered between consciousness and unconsciousness, he could tell his eyeglasses were broken. The feeling of glass cutting into his cheekbone told him so. As he began making sense out of what was happening, the tremendous pressure on his neck and back prevented him from moving. Someone was clearly saying something, but his brain was too scrambled to understand it. However, the feeling of his arms being pulled behind his back so hard it felt like they were coming out of their sockets, helped him to regain his consciousness. When the pain finally registered, it caused him to screamed so loud the pressure from his lungs made the veins in his forehead bulged.

He recognized several pairs of black boots directly in front of his face. Finally, his mind began clearing up enough for him to understand what was being said.

Someone was saying, "*Anything you say can and will be used against you in a court of law. You have the right to an attorney. If you cannot afford one,"*

Was the last thing he heard before a boot came slamming into his face.

CONCLUSION

The Dilemma

If you've made it this far, then more than likely, something within one of the storylines was able to hold your attention. It is my sincerest hope, it was not as a result of being a victim of one of these lifelike characters. In any event, the reality contained within these fictitious characters is something we have come to deal with in everyday society. Rape is nothing new, it has been around for ages, and is even mentioned in some of our most holy books. It is an infectious crime, like a virus riding through the evolution of time. Fortunately, we have reached a point in our evolution where we can now recognize this offense as a growing phenomenon in need of immediate attention. However, it is a crime without geographical boundaries, has no ethnic preference, and by the looks of it, doesn't seem as though it will be slowing down no time soon.

With that said, *"The Secrets That We Keep"* was written more out of necessity than for popularity. Mainly, because out of the millions who've been affected by such offenses, there is a growing need for a reference point in terms of understanding these crimes. Something we can look at, in order to see how these behaviors play out in everyday life. Especially when the list of *offenders* and *victims* both (*male and female*), now includes Mothers, Fathers, Teachers, Students, Uncles, Aunts, Sons, Daughters, Nieces, Nephews, as well as Celebrities, Athletes, Politicians, Priest, Bishops, Cardinals and even the President of the United States of America himself. Furthermore, real remorse (*when offered as an apology*) has the power to mend wounds, and heal those who may still be suffering from such offenses. Finally, Knowing the difference between predator and offender, allows individuals and society, to make better decisions when dealing with this dilemma.

Make no mistake about it, it's our Government's obligation to protect society from those who prey on individuals for the sake of sexual gratification. For they are the predators, the ones deserving of strict guidelines, incarceration, psychiatric help, and in some cases even death. Rape itself, is a crime unlike any other crime, with the exception of murder. When rape is carried out with a willful intent it exemplifies man in his lowest animal state, uncivilized, savage and uninhibited. Unfortunately, the act of rape itself strips away layers of dignity, respect, pride and trust in the person who is raped. In any event, it is usually a sickness that leaves behind a sickness. The crime itself is similar to robbery. In both cases, it involves the taking of something by force with the intent to possess it unlawfully. Unlike robbery, however, where the crime involves the taking of something tangible by force, such as money or property, rape involves the forcible violation of the body resulting in the taking of intangible things such as: Sex, Trust, Dignity, Pride, Respect etc. In place of what is taken, victims are oftentimes left with Blame, Shame, Insecurity, Distrust, Hurt and etc. in its place.

However, as the book illustrates, there are other sides to these offenses that must be considered. The example being, the 19-year-old who ends up becoming a Registered Sex Offender as a result of engaging in consensual sex with his 16-year-old girlfriend. Should the magnitude of this offense cause a lifetime of shame as well as destroy this individual's future by crippling his career, and snuffing out any chances of gainful employment? For that matter, how do you punish a 25-year-old woman who thought she was having sex with a young man who lied about his age? Not to mention the boy who took advantage of a girl after a night of drinking together, and now can no longer stand himself because of the guilt he feels.

Nevertheless, regardless of how much the 16-year-old girlfriend begs for her 19 year-old boyfriend not to be prosecuted, he will undoubtedly be charged with statutory rape, and made to register as a sex offender. This will also be the case of the 25-year-old woman who the young man lied to about his age. She will not be able to tell the court she did not make it a habit of checking the ID of every person she chose to date. She will be punished for this and made to register as a sex offender. Although this seems to be unfair, this is the reality of the laws that deal with sexual offenses.

32 years ago, I was convicted of such offenses. Today, I am a Registered Offender. Most people either know someone who's a Registered Offender, related to someone who's a Registered Offender, or live in close proximity to someone who's a Registered Offender. Registered Sex Offenders are everywhere. There's no particular age, sex, color, profession or location. They range from the average person next door to Law Enforcement itself. This dilemma has no boundaries. However, the question is, should all offenders be required to register? For that matter, are all offenses actually crimes? Sure, there are some offenders who should be required to register, and some should be required to register for life; but what about the ones who don't fall into this category? The offenders who are not predators, but the ones who have made a mistake, and are seeking forgiveness from the victim, and understanding from society and the courts.

As a society, how do we decide what the punishment should be? Especially, when each case is unique and has its own set of circumstances. God only knows how many of us have been born from relationships that could have been prosecuted as statutory rape. When your mother tells you the story of your father being 20 years old when she got pregnant at 17, do you suddenly see your father as a rapist? Surely, you wouldn't. This is because offenders and predators are different in nature. Most offenders experience remorse, regret, shame, and guilt, while predators show no remorse, regret, or shame and most likely would commit the same act again if permitted to do so. In the beginning, being required to register for life as a sex offender was a Catch-All-Law that was good for the time being. It did not take into consideration the magnitude or the effect it would have on the lives of those who did not deserve to have their entire life swept away. It gave no separation or consideration to those who were truly sorry and willing to make amends in order to be forgiven, so that both victim and the accused could move on and attempt to live a normal life, if at all possible.

It is this author's opinion that some victims may be able to go on with their lives without the guilt or blame if the, (why) could be understood. This is possible in cases where the accused has honest regret and is willing to offer this to the victim in the form of an apology and explanation.   Any system of correction that fails in allowing the acceptance of remorse, and regret, is a system that does not offer healing, and needs to be reevaluated. This in and of itself, can sometimes be the difference between, forgiveness and healing, versus, living a life of brokenness. The law needs to be fine-tuned in such a way that it becomes possible to recognize that sometimes, both the victim and offender, suffer from the same guilt, blame, and shame that this offense is capable of sickening individuals with. Any law that fails to apply these principles is a law that is outdated and no longer current. Each individual case has a unique set of circumstances. Therefore, the law must be suited to take this into inconsideration on both sides of the aisle.

This book serves as my contribution to this dilemma. It has

allowed me to bring what is considered a dirty and shameful topic to laundry. As human beings, we sometimes have a tendency to stuff shameful and hurtful things behind lies, secrets, and feelings, not to mention, doors, bars, and walls. As an individual who've carried this guilt and shame for over 32 years, I speak from experience. This book is written for everyone who has ever been raped or sexually abused in any form or fashion. It is an apology for every offender who is truly sorry but never got a chance to express this to the person who was harmed.

Before writing this book, I searched diligently, in libraries and online, to find writings by Registered Offenders which helps to clarify the difference between offenders and predators, especially in the case where remorse was the motivating factor. For some reason, I could not find a single one. It's my conclusion that once an individual is branded as a Sex Offender and made to register, the fight for understanding is torn out of them, even in the face of remorse. This is understandable because I myself have been personally plagued by emotions that have left me feeling unacceptable to myself and to society. Undoubtedly, the same feelings and emotions also haunt the victims as well. Nevertheless, it's my argument that most offenders are different in nature than predators, and that the current law fails to recognize and understand, how some offenders deserve a second chance.

A man that doesn't stand for something, is a man that will fall for anything. There is no greater insecurity than living a life of fear wondering if someone's going to find out if you are a Registered Offender. Living life on such terms is equivalent to being conscious of every breath you take, fearing your next one will be your last. It is time to bury the fear and push for understanding; for it is the only available route to progress, change, and healing. In the end, there's only one source of true forgiveness, and that is GOD, the creator of each and every one of us. So may GOD forgive us of our sins.

Made in the USA
Middletown, DE
23 November 2021

52417633R00146